The words overpower me. They bleed through my flesh like sweat, pound in my head like a thousand tiny fists beating me from the inside, churn in my gut like a hamster running amok on a wire wheel.

Too much. It's too much.

Buried alive,
buried alive,
buried alive.

OBLIVION

SASHA DAWN

OBLIVION

EGMONT
Publishing
NEW YORK

EGMONT

We bring stories to life

First published in the United States by Egmont Publishing, 2014
This paperback edition published by Egmont Publishing, 2015
443 Park Avenue South, Suite 806
New York, NY 10016

1 3 5 7 9 8 6 4 2

www.egmontusa.com
www.sashsadawn.com

THE LIBRARY OF CONGRESS HAS CATALOGED THE HARDCOVER EDITION
AS FOLLOWS: Library of Congress Cataloging-in-Publication Data
Dawn, Sasha.
Oblivion / Sasha Dawn.
pages cm
Summary: Sixteen-year-old Callie Knowles fights her compulsion to
write constantly, even on herself, as she struggles to cope with foster
care, her mother's life in a mental institution, and her belief that she
killed her father, a minister, who has been missing for a year.
ISBN 978-1-60684-476-2 (hardcover)
ISBN 978-1-60684-477-9 (ebook)
[1. Compulsive behavior—Fiction. 2. Mental illness—Fiction. 3. Recovered memory—
Fiction. 4. Missing persons—Fiction. 5. Foster home care—Fiction.
6. Dating (Social customs)—Fiction. 7. Illinois—Fiction.] I. Title.
PZ7.D32178Obl 2014   [Fic]—dc23
2013018267
Trade paperback ISBN 978-1-60684-570-7

Printed in the United States of America

For Joshua, and the two little ladies
who brighten our lives

"It was not wisdom that enabled poets to write their poetry, but a kind of instinct or inspiration, such as you find in seers and prophets who deliver all their sublime messages without knowing in the least what they mean."

—SOCRATES

OBLIVION

ONE

Lindsey and I left her portable speakers in her backyard shed last week, during the thunderstorm. The Hutches haven't yet bought us new speakers, so we're listening to some grungy funk garage band on her cranked-up iPod. The tinny sounds eking through the nano echo, as if a Pink Floyd cover band is singing in a barren, institutional hall, attempting to entertain the crazies locked in a perimeter of padded dorms.

Instantly, with the image of an antiseptic asylum materializing in my brain, I think of my mother, who belongs in one. At least that's what the county shrinks tell me. Funny. She seems so sane, so real, sometimes.

Lindsey's smoking a joint, and I'm eating a cherry Tootsie

Pop. The combination of sugar and contact high is enough for me, as my mind is too cloudy to withstand the numbing effects of inhaled marijuana. It's hard to focus on reality today, and not only because being in the shed sometimes feels uncomfortable—as if it's a reminder of something I don't want to remember. Sometimes, I think I'm losing my faculties. Like mother, like daughter.

Amputate, amputate, amputate.

This is how it begins. I fixate on a word until it consumes me. It comes out of nowhere, like a flicker of light on a distant horizon, then waxes and brightens until I see nothing, hear nothing if not the sound of the word, pushing out from the innards of my brain, begging for liberty.

Amputate.

Lindsey chokes on her smoke. "You gotta help me write something to Jon."

Amputate the cancer.

John Fogel spells his name with an *h*, but Lindsey thinks it looks cooler without it. Less is more, she says, although she's far from a minimalist. Like her parents, Lindsey Hutch doesn't do anything halfway.

"I'm talking casual, dude. But something he'll notice."

She calls everyone dude, especially when she's smoking. It annoyed the hell out of me at first, but after a while, I started feeling a little lost if I ceased to be "dude" to her. In Lindsey-speak, *dude* is synonymous with *kosher, peachy keen, groovy*, which, to be fair, are antiquated terms in

2

their own right. But none of that matters to Lindsey. If she doesn't call people dude, either she doesn't know them, or she's pissed off at them. Growing up the way I did, I don't usually care whether someone's angry with me or not, but Lindsey isn't just someone—she's all I have.

And I've seen her angry. *No one* wants to be on the receiving end of Lindsey Hutch's scorn.

The Hutch family hosts me, or at least that's the term they use. I prefer to call it like it is: they're my foster parents, which makes them saints. Not many people would take in a girl like me—a sixteen-year-old bitch who can't stop writing, can't stop hooking up with the delinquent she met at County Juvenile Hall, can't stop thinking her father is gone for one reason: because she killed him.

My name is Calliope Knowles. I'm a ward of the state of Illinois, and a clinically diagnosed graphomaniac. Unlike my pop-culture counterparts, who claim addiction to blogging on LiveJournals and watch over their Facebook pages, as if God might leave a comment there—imagine: God and seven others like Jenny Anderson's status—I'm compulsive about writing. This means that I write for the same reason most of us breathe.

While my disorder is progressive, and therefore expected to become more pronounced as I grow older, there was nothing progressive about the onset of my affliction. I used to be a normal kid. I sneaked drags off cigarettes. Skipped every other page of *Hamlet*. Crammed two weeks' worth of studying biology into the night before the test. And, sure, I'd written the occasional line of poetry, when dreaming about some boy I was likely forbidden to look at, let alone kiss; but one day, the day my father disappeared, I started writing, and I couldn't stop. The words simply would not cease.

Amputate the cancer, amputate the cancer, amputate the cancer.

The police found me that day in the apartment above the Vagabond. I hadn't lived there—no one had—in years. But I'd been hiding there, and that's where my graphomania emerged, suddenly and viciously, from somewhere deep within my subconscious soul. By the time the police came for me, I'd written on my body, on the mirror, and door. The peeling pink wallpaper had become a canvas I'd filled with tiny, red felt-tip words:

I Killed him, I Killed him, I Killed him.

The police had asked me: "Do you know where your father is?"

No.

No one had seen him in a day and a half.

And: "Do you know where Hannah Rynes is?"

No.

No one had seen her, either.

A day and a half.

Is that how long I'd been in that bathroom? How long I'd been awake? It's a long time to be writing, that's for certain. There was mud on the door, in the foyer, in the drain, which suggests I'd gone somewhere. Maybe I was out hiding evidence. I wish I could remember.

The authorities don't agree with me. They don't think I killed my father, but they think I know something about his disappearance. If I do, I can't remember. They think I'm in a perpetual state of shock, that eventually a lightbulb will illuminate the dark recesses of my brain to shed light on the disappearance. Without a body, my father's case isn't more than a missing person dossier collecting dust.

There's one problem with that, however: twelve-year-old Hannah Rynes disappeared at the same time.

In a county that boasts less than one non-family-abduction per decade, the coincidence is too great to ignore. If the police find my father, maybe they'll find Hannah.

"Nothing obvious, of course," Lindsey's saying. "Just something to get the ball rolling."

"Got it."

My fingers itch for a pen, as the impulse grows stronger, as the words reverberate in my head: *folds, folds, folds, folds. Of years.*

"Nothing too cryptic or bookish, either."

I pull the lollipop out of my mouth. "From what I can tell, he's a deep guy. He needs cryptic and bookish."

"Yeah, but he has to think I wrote it, genius."

Persistent words, begging to be committed to paper, echo in my head: *folds of years, folds of years.*

I breathe through the impulse, try to focus on Lindsey.

If history's speaking, she's going to be John's girlfriend by Halloween. I'm an integral part of this scheme, and it isn't the first time. I've hooked a couple of Lindsey's prospective boyfriends with my words, and I have to admit I've seen this one coming. He's the only guy she's consistently talked about since I met her.

Amputate cancer of the folds of years.

She's the closest thing I have to a sister. I've lived here with her and her parents for almost six months now. I'd do anything for her. Including snaring an unsuspecting soul like John Fogel.

"He's so beautiful."

She's right about that. I've caught his gaze a few times, and it's hard to look away. His eyes . . . they're a mesmerizing blue, rimmed with these thick black lashes. And his voice . . . a clear, confident tenor. Soothing. She's chosen a good one to obsess over, that's for sure.

Lindsey brings the joint, which by now is more roach than blunt, to her lips for a sharp inhale. The smoke encircles her head. Her aqua/green eyes blaze until they become gems amidst the haze. Her voice trails off, down a long corridor in my mind, overpowered by the words pounding against my brain, stretching out of their cocoons for liberty.

Amputate cancer of the folds of years. Does the scent of her linger within you? Tempt her, tempt her, tempt her.

"Callie—"

Lindsey's calling to me, but I can't focus on what she's saying. The words nearly vibrate. What's starting as a dull ache between my eyes will soon become a vise at my temples. Can't delay any longer. I need a pen. There's one in my backpack. I know there is. It's always there. For emergencies.

I'm fiddling with the zipper, but already the pressure in my head pinches, stabs, distorts my vision. Lindsey helps me to force the zipper over the lump that is my calculus text.

Where's my notebook?

Lodged under my textbooks. Can't get it out. Snagged.

Tears well in my eyes, as I frantically divert my search to the red Bic—felt-tipped, of course—swimming at the bottom of my school bag. At last, I grasp it, fumbling over simple pronunciation of even simpler words—"think, thunk, tanku"—and press the tip to my jeans:

Amputate cancer of the folds of years does the scent of her linger within you tempt her break her make her feel real devour her when she begins to bleed bleed bleed bleed her and feed.

A teardrop splats against a *bleed*, jarring the force in my head, silencing it, shaking me free, if only for the moment. I focus on the memory of Elijah. He always had an uncanny ability to bring me back to earth, and sometimes, if I think of him, the anxiety wanes and the words disappear. I breathe.

I draw in a deep inhalation, and slowly glance in Lindsey's

direction. The first time this happened in her company, I was mortifyingly embarrassed, but now, six months later, it's old hat. Not affected, she's sitting with one ankle crossed over her knee, picking at the dried mud in the sole of her grape-purple, knee-high Converse All Stars, while the roach burns dangerously close to her fuchsia-tipped fingernails. When she finally acknowledges me, it's with a steady stare, followed by a minute shake of her head.

"Sorry," I say.

"Take the meds already, will ya?"

Ah, yes. The meds. Nothing kills one's passion for living like antianxiety medication. "I flushed it."

She brings the joint to her lips and breathes in the fumes. "Cool."

I haven't seen Elijah for a few weeks, and suddenly, the need to see him overcomes me. If he's lucky, he's long gone from his new foster family by now, but I hope he'll be back to the harbor tonight. It's a Tuesday. He promised.

He's stuck with some host family, like me, bound by rules and expectations. Structure. That's what the court-appointed shrinks call it. And maybe they're right. But to people like Elijah, this cushy existence of square meals and therapy sessions is more confining than a jail cell. It's hard to cage a butterfly who's been free to flutter his entire life.

Lindsey rests her head against my shoulder. "Dude, I'm stoned."

"I know." I press a kiss to the crown of her head, directly atop a zigzag part, which divides her jet-black hair into two spiky ponytails. "Will you tell your mom I'm volunteering tonight?" Lindsey's parents don't require us to work regular jobs, but we're encouraged to do charity work.

"Don't go to the marina."

"I have to. It's Tuesday."

"Don't come home crying to me if he's not there again."

"Fine, I won't."

Her eyes roll up to engage mine. "You're better than this, you know."

Maybe she's right. Maybe I am. But I'm addicted to Elijah the way Lindsey's addicted to pot. Besides, ever since the day the cops pulled me out of that dingy apartment and stuffed me into a dorm at County Juvenile Hall, he's been there for me. He's the only person I completely trusted at County, and he's the only person, next to Lindsey, I trust now. Unlike Lindsey, he knows everything there is to know about me. He understands me like no one else can. After all, he's spent time at County, too.

"You gonna write something to Jon?"

"Yeah."

"No *h*."

"I know. I'll remember."

Her arms lazily drape over my shoulders. "I love you."

She loves everyone when she's high.

When I leave a few minutes later, I close the creaking door behind me.

Lindsey's singing off-key.

TWO

Before she went away, and for most of my childhood, my mother waited tables at the Vagabond Café. This was in the days when the establishment was more a coffeehouse than a bar, when it was populated with an artistic clientele, when it appeared fresher than it does today. But the drunken yachters didn't instill the stench of musty buoys and lake when they chased away the beatniks. The Vagabond has always smelled this way; the scent encompasses my earliest memories: three-year-old me watching in awe from the corner table as the minstrels and poets entertained one another. Breathing in the scent of the Chain of Lakes and biscotti while Mom read Tarot— which she didn't believe in, but understood to the extent that it garnered her a paycheck—on Saturday nights. Traipsing up the stairs to the apartment with heavy eyes to catch a few winks before being dragged off to the Church of the Holy Promise come sunrise.

This is the first place I remember writing, albeit I wrote for the sheer pleasure of it in those days. The tables inside are littered with poetic graffiti. Carved into tables are classic lines of Keats and Dickens, as well as witty and fresh creations of the local clientele. I wonder if my words are still visible atop table number fourteen. I see them in my mind's eye:

Travel on, yellow brick road . . . wind her past throughout her soul.

The Vagabond is nearer the more affluent towns along the Chain. It's close enough to the Hutches' neighborhood that I can walk, but it's a train ride away from Holy Promise. This minute distance—it's only about fifteen miles—stands out to me now that I'm older: Mom saw this place as an escape. Just far enough away from the ties binding her, far enough away from Palmer Prescott and his version of the word of God. Far enough to breathe.

I suppose this is why I think of my mother whenever I'm in proximity to the harbor, and tonight she won't leave my mind. I close my hand around the tiny golden ring with the marquise ruby, slung on a chain around my neck. The ring is one of the few items that still connects me to my mother. She gave it to me when I was very small. And sometimes, if I press the ring to my flesh, I can almost remember the comfort of her touch. It's been months since I've seen her, but I have the sneaking suspicion she isn't keeping track of our visits.

Much like Elijah.

It's a chilly night for the middle of September. Uncommonly cool, even for the lakeshore. I didn't bring a jacket, partly because having one would jinx my chances of warming up in Elijah's arms, partly because I look damn good in this T-shirt. It's pink, a scoop-necked, snug fit. It sports the belief that *Lennon Lives* and more cleavage than I can muster on my own, thanks to Lindsey's Victoria's Secret plunge bra.

I rub my palms up and down my arms to ward off the nip in the breeze, and gaze down the rickety piers flanked with silvery waves at the Vagabond. Its vertical siding is painted dirty white and peeling. The mauve and mint shutters, unlike most in this area, are not solely ornamental, as they open and close over mullioned, wavy glass windows, perpetually filthy with droplets of lake. The shutters are open tonight, but probably only because no one's had time to close them, as the wait staff is busy attending to the swarming crowd inside. The front porch gives the place a distinctly shanty presence—very bayou meets the Midwest—and if I gaze at it long enough, I fail to see the weathering of the old joint. Sometimes the Vagabond is just as majestic in my mind as it was in its heyday.

Mom and I lived there, above the café, on a few occasions and for only short bouts of time, but it will always be home to me. It's like that, when a place is always there for you. Whenever Mom and I left Palmer, we'd camp above the Vagabond. No matter how rank, mildewed, and stuffy, I always felt warm and comfortable there. Safe. Secure.

Sometimes, Elijah and I break into the now vacant-slash-condemned apartment and spend the night curled in each other's arms on the fuzzy, woolen pink carpeting. We eat greasy Chinese in the north dormer, and if we like, make out on the kitchen floor—a dingy depression-pink-and-green linoleum checkerboard. Life doesn't get any better than waking up there in Elijah's arms.

The trouble is that it rarely happens anymore, now that he's been placed with a foster family. I wonder if Elijah realizes he's missed the past three Tuesdays, if he knows that the three before that left me vastly dissatisfied. I'm beginning to think all he needs to feel sated and connected is a hookup, but I don't want to believe it. That can't happen to us; we've been through too much together.

I shift the weight of my backpack on my shoulder and suck hard on my eighth Tootsie Pop of the day—this one's chocolate, which tastes better than nicotine and tobacco, thank you very much—refusing to shed the tears I feel welling up inside me. Palmer ruined everything. If he hadn't committed Mom to the Meadows, I wouldn't be leaning against the rails of this pier, staring over the water at Highland Point, waiting for Godot.

Then again, everything had to happen just the way it did, or I wouldn't have gone to County in the first place; I wouldn't have met Elijah otherwise. And I can't imagine life without him.

I feel someone looking at me—it's a common occurrence these days—but when I turn around, no one's there. I wonder sometimes if it's my father's spirit hunting me down, controlling me, even from whatever heaven or hell he landed in.

Elijah's not coming—I guess I've known that for at least twenty minutes now—and he isn't answering any of my texts. But I can't go back to the Hutches'. Not yet. Lindsey won't ask too many questions one way or another, but if I saunter in around ten, she'll assume all went well with Elijah, and I won't hear all the reasons why I shouldn't come to meet him next Tuesday. Besides, if I return before dinner, the Hutches will know Lindsey lied about my volunteering tonight. They think their daughter wears a halo. I don't want to be the reason they learn otherwise.

The pier creaks beneath my feet, as I make my way to the porch. Inside, a microphone pitches, then rights. Someone's speaking poetic prose on stage. Tuesdays are open-mic nights, which is the reason Elijah and I originally chose this day as our default meeting time. Truth be told, though, we don't often enter the place anymore, or even stick around the marina to hear the artful words flowing through the atmosphere. We have other things on our minds, on the increasingly rare occasions we see each other.

If I concentrate—and lie to myself—I can see my mother whirling through the place, depositing oversized mugs of whiskey and coffee, hot cocoa and schnapps before patrons: her long, merlot-colored hair, pin-straight, bouncing against her back from beneath her paisley beret, her bangles jingling about her tattooed wrists, her subtle, oaky perfume wafting in her wake . . .

I press a hand to a window and imagine my mother placing hers against mine from the inside, connecting to me through the glass. I feel her, if only in my imagination. My skin tingles and warms with memories. When I think about things, I realize there were signs that all was not well with her, even when I was a small child. But for all her faults, she's still my mom.

"Callie." A hot breath drifts over my neck the moment before lips close over my right earlobe, and I smile. "Callie, Callie, Callie."

In a split second, my back is against the windowpanes, my bag is on the ground, and my lollipop is stuck to the dirty planks at my feet. Elijah's tongue flickers into my mouth and the taste of cinnamon pours into me.

"You're late," I say against his lips. His loose brown curls fall like silk ringlets through my fingers, and he's clean shaven, for a change.

His hands firmly travel down my sides, coming to rest

on my hips. The heat of his fingers registers against my flesh.

"I've missed you," he says.

This is evident.

He feels bulkier, broader, like more man than I remember. He's always been strong, but he's hardened in all the places that count. Is it possible for a guy to fill out and bulk up in the space of a month?

Again, he nips my lips. When my hands fall upon his, his fingers entwine with mine. He makes a move toward the pier, but I resist. Elijah prefers to break into cabin cruisers, or hook up on the upper decks if he can't pick the locks, but I want to be with him elsewhere. "Upstairs," I whisper.

Even with just a hint of a smile, his brown eyes sparkle. Without a word, he grabs my backpack. We round the building, laced together at the fingers. We brave the iron spiral staircase, the type seen in city lofts, only this one is rusting and missing a few bolts. Once we're standing on the tiny platform at the top, Elijah presses me against the siding, and nearly stops time with a deep kiss.

My heartbeat, or his, fills my ears. His tongue brushes against mine seemingly in slow motion. I feel his essence breathing me in, awakening the desire simmering in my soul, even when he breaks the kiss.

He licks his lips, flashes his grin—"One second, baby"— and turns to pick the lock.

My glance becomes an ogle as I scrutinize his six-foot

frame. He's biting his lower lip. His hair has gotten too long, but I kind of like it. He's wearing an unbuttoned, rusted-orange oxford over a beige T. The label on his jeans stuns me; I hope he scrounged the entire ensemble at a thrift store. The Elijah I know would never stoop to spending a cool hundred on pants. Of course, he wouldn't wear them, if he'd found them in the gutter, either.

Nerves spin in my gut. I want to freeze him in time. Don't change, don't change, don't change. If you change, we're done.

Reality check: he isn't the only one changing.

Burn her.

It comes on with a whisper in my mind, but soon I know the force will be raging, carving its way through gray matter, like a worm burrowing through garden dirt in search of the summer sun. Not now, I plead with the wordsmith in my head.

Burn, burn, burn her.

The door pops open.

Elijah grins over his shoulder, offering the only invitation I need.

I fling my backpack into the space and fall into his arms.

One of us kicks the door shut before he shoves his shoes off, before I kick off my flip-flops.

The fuzzy carpeting itches against my back.

My hair clings to my eyelashes like burgundy streamers, which he brushes away.

I lick his lips, trail my tongue over the ridges of the only crooked teeth in his mouth: the four front and center on the bottom.

Burn her, burn her, burn her, burn her . . .

Tears build. I whimper in both frustration and desire.

His cheek is warm and smooth against mine. "Shh," he whispers, as he wrestles out of his oxford.

But I can't let him quiet me. Quiet's no good. Quiet welcomes the words.

. . . *in an urn.*

I pull his T-shirt over his head and off his body, as he kisses a line down my neck.

"Come here." I give his hair a tug and coax him upward. "Kiss me."

His skin melts against my abdomen, and his tongue, teasing mine, ignites a fire within me. *Burn her in an urn.*

It's hot in here.

So hot.

The words are coming closer.

"Elijah. I need—"

"Let it go," he suggests. "Ignore it."

I'm trying. I can't. My fingertips tremble; I imagine closing them around a pen, putting its tip to paper. I yank my bag closer, fiddle with the zipper, and pull out a pen.

"Love you," he says. "God, I love you."

What?

The words miraculously scatter from my mind.

A sob of relief escapes me.

Slowly, my eyes open. It's just him, here, and me. Just us.

"I've got you." He smiles down at me. "I've got you."

The pen drops from my hand.

"Got a cig?" Elijah asks.

My head's resting on his bicep. I wish we could risk opening a window, but that might clue someone into where we are.

I catch my breath. "I quit."

"Since when?"

"Since the Hutches found my pack. Like a month ago."

He shrugs. He doesn't usually smoke. Not nicotine, anyway. Marijuana, though, is fair game. "Good for you, baby." He kisses me on the forehead.

"Want a lollipop instead?"

He chuckles. "No."

"So . . ." I don't want to ask what I'm about to ask, but the question has been turning cartwheels in my mind since I bid adieu to my Camel Lights. "Where've you been?"

He sighs. "Calliope."

"What?" I sit up and stare down at him. "I've been here every Tuesday."

His glance shifts away, but he quickly reengages, caressing my cheek. "You don't think I've wanted to be here? You, of all people, should know how hard it is to get away, when you live in their world. I have rules now."

19

"So do I." Not as many as I had under Palmer's reign, but rules all the same.

"You know what happens when I don't follow them?"

"They give you a gift card to the Gap?"

"Worse." He twitches a smile. "Hilfiger."

"Come on." I reach for my backpack in search of a lollipop. "I miss you. I haven't seen you in a month. You hardly return my texts anymore. We don't even talk—"

"Come here." He gives my hand a tug. "I'm kidding."

"Well, stop kidding." I open a grape-flavored Tootsie Pop and shove it in my mouth. "Last month, you were talking about running away together, and now their rules are more important than seeing me."

"Come here!"

This time my defiance is no match for his yanking on my hand. I curl into his embrace.

"Listen, if I fuck up, I lose my phone privileges, so I can't text or talk. Okay?"

"Okay."

"You know I want to talk to you every fucking day."

I nod. At least I hope he does.

"And I don't know how you're going to feel about this, but—"

"About what?" The syrupy sweetness of the lollipop is too much for me right now, but I need it to curb unhealthy yens. I look up at him. Our gazes lock.

He brushes his thumb against the dent in my chin and

chews his lip for a few seconds. "Never mind."

"Never mind what?"

"Not important. I feel stupid. Forget it."

"Stupid."

"Never mind."

"Oops-I-slept-with-someone-else-when-I-was-drunk stupid? I-cut-trig-so-many-times-I'm-failing stupid? Or . . . or is it worse? I-fell-in-love-with-someone-else-before-I-broke-up-with-you stupid?"

"Callie, don't. Don't do this."

I pull the candy from my mouth and point it at his nose. "Then don't start something you can't finish."

"It's nothing."

"Nothing. Nothing I'm going to be thinking about for the next seven days, or until you decide to show up here again."

"Hey, I come when I can."

"You know what? I come even when I can't."

He emits an overexaggerated sigh. "I made the varsity soccer team. Okay?"

"Okay." I feel like I just rode up four stories in a roller-coaster car, only to find flat land at the top of the hill. That's not so bad. Except that . . . "Since when do you play soccer?"

He shrugs. "Just started. Turns out, I'm pretty damn good at it."

"I guess so." Crossing Elijah Breshock with varsity sports

is sort of like crossing a llama with a chicken. It doesn't compute to much more than a scatterbrain who can spit, and what good is that? The guy has a juvenile record, for fuck's sake. The only sport I've known him to take interest in is running—when it's in the opposite direction.

"It started as an outlet for my"—he draws quotation marks in the air—"aggression. But the foster Ps think I might be able to get a scholarship to U of I."

"Better stop cutting classes, if that's what you want." I refrain from rolling my eyes, but there's no masking the sarcasm dripping from my words.

"Hey." He places a finger against my cheek, forcing eye contact. "Why do you think I'm doing this? For you, baby. For us."

This isn't the Elijah I know, if only because the Elijah who's been distracting me for the better part of the past year doesn't use words like *us*. But I snuggle back into his embrace for one reason: I truly want to believe him. The truth has to be far more sinister than soccer, but I deserve a break. I deserve to blindly believe . . . in something. "Congratulations."

"So now you know. If I'm not here some Tuesday, it's because we have a game, or practice, or something."

I'm so tired, and he feels so warm and inviting that I let it go.

"I've missed you," he whispers, dragging his fingers across my forehead, draping my hair aside.

Oh, those fingers. Talented. Attentive.

And he says all the right things.

But he's lying to me.

I know it.

"Baby, you wrote on your pants."

"Yeah."

I close my eyes and inhale the scent of him: musk shower gel combined with cinnamon gum. No matter how present he feels in my arms, no matter how convincing his words, I feel the distance between us. Somehow I know: he's already gone.

I concentrate on the feeling of his fingers drawing lines on my forehead and wonder if anyone's ever going to paint over my tiny, red words on the bathroom walls—the words I wrote the night my father disappeared . . . presumably with Hannah Rynes.

THREE

Burn her in an urn. Burn her in an urn. Burn her in an urn.

I'm digging in an open field. Icy rain pelts down on the back of my neck, chilling me to the bone.

Mud encrusts the soles of my shoes, making them inches thick, and the loam clings to the hems of my jeans, climbs toward my knees with every shovelful.

I don't know where I am, but I feel like I've been here before. The dense air is blowing in off the lake. It smells of fresh fish and sediment, sand, clay. I can't be too far from home.

My hair clings to my face, and my clothing is soaked through to my flesh.

Crucify.

I stifle a sob and press the blade of my shovel to the wet earth.

Crucify.

It dawns on me: I must be digging for my father's body.

This must be where he is. Must find his body. It isn't over, until I find his body.

Sobs rack my body. I drop my shovel to the mud and hide my face in my hands. *Crucify, crucify, crucify.*

Crucify, quarter, and stone her.

I can't draw a breath. I listen hard. Flinch at a wave crashing on the shore. Jolt with the distant hoot of an owl in a remote tree. I see nothing but dark bleeding into the beyond.

I spin in a circle, searching, but the night is too black. I feel my father's presence, but can't see him. His voice echoes off the lake. He could be anywhere. He could be nowhere. I'm numb, leaden, planted in the earth like an ancient oak tree. My roots intrude on my father's grave, push into his remains, curl about his bones.

Crucify, quarter, and stone her.

No way to fight it. He's part of me. I'm part of him.

The ground rumbles with the thunder in the distance. My body is shaking.

"Callie, wake up!"

Crucify, quarter, and stone her.

"Callie!"

I gasp and grab at salvation.

"Callie."

"Help me," I say.

Fingers close around my forearm, as I hold tight to whatever I'm grasping.

"Goddamn, dude. What the hell were you dreaming about?"

My eyes peel open and adjust to my dim surroundings. I'm in Lindsey's room, in her queen-sized bed, lying next to her, grasping her wrist with a white-knuckled grip. I'm wearing a tank top and Elijah's flannel boxers; she's wearing a T-shirt that reads *I'm skilled* and navy-blue tick-striped boyshort panties. For a minute, I'm confused, but then I remember: I couldn't be alone. It's always hardest to sleep on nights I've seen Elijah. It's almost as if our brief encounters only serve as reminders of how alone I am once we part ways.

When I'd shown up at her door last night, Lindsey had pulled back her covers—"Snuggle"—and I'd crawled into her bed. It's a little weird that we sleep together sometimes, but I assume it's acceptable for biological sisters, so why not for us?

Once I release my grip on her arm, she begins to move her feet back and forth beneath the covers. This is something very decidedly Lindsey. In even cadence, she brushes her feet against the Waverly sheets until she feels secure enough to sleep. She says she's been doing it since babyhood. It took some getting used to, but now it's a comfort to me, too. Sometimes, when she's asleep down the hall or if she's closed her door, I can't hear the swishing, and I feel sort of lost.

"What time is it?" I ask.

"A little after three. And after that mess, there's no fucking way I'm going back to sleep without a little medication." She crawls over me and traipses toward her closet, where she keeps her stash hidden—along with her contraband birth control pills, which she and half the girls in the junior class buy from some mysterious supplier—in the sleeve of *The Little Mermaid* DVD. "Come on, let's hit the shed."

A lime-green hoodie and a pair of pink-and-green argyle knee socks hit me in the chest when I sit up. I yawn, don the extra clothes, and concentrate on the scent of the lake in my dream. Is it a real place? Or a figment of a wild imagination?

I follow her quietly down the back staircase and to the back door, where she punches in a code on the alarm pad. Every key beeps, but the senior Hutches don't sleep as much as hibernate, thanks to regular doses of Ambien for each of them. Once Lindsey and I couldn't silence the alarm—she drunkenly pushed the wrong buttons—but neither of her parents responded to either the whir of the siren, or the follow-up phone calls from the security firm, ensuring our safety. But tonight we have our faculties about us, and we exit smoothly into the night.

My backpack, always slung over my shoulder in the likely event I need to write something, contains Lindsey's weed. I'm well aware that if we're caught on our way out to the shed, everyone and Lindsey's mother will assume the drugs are mine. Lindsey would try to set the record straight—at least I think she would—but I'd rather take the hit for my pseudo sister than watch her throw her future away.

Solar-powered lights illuminate the flagstone path with a blue-tinted glow from the orbs that pop up at evenly spaced intervals along the way. When he isn't litigating, Mr. Hutch makes a hobby of landscape design, and the sprawling two acres of their estate are meticulously manicured with gardens and water features that would put average—and some above-average—lawns to shame. Mrs. Hutch does not share his passion, but she takes advantage of it. In the six months I've lived here, Mrs. Hutch has hosted tented, catered, orchestra-music charity events on the property, most supporting the Children's Hospital, where she used to work. Lindsey says her mother is obsessed with charity, which, incidentally, works out pretty well for me, seeing as I'm relying on the kindness of strangers for survival these days.

The Hutches' back gardens remind me of my father's only semi-realized vision for the grounds of his church— mini waterfalls, a koi pond, idyllic swings surrounded by lush perennials and blooms. Yet for all the serenity here, I feel anxious walking the paths, and not because my backpack contains a nickel bag.

"I think my father's dead," I say.

"You can't know that." Lindsey doesn't know that my father's death wouldn't devastate me. She views the situation through her own lens, and because she'd be lost without her dad—or rather without that which he provides for her—she assumes everyone would be. She's too sheltered to know that some men deserve to die, and for all the hell my father put Mom and me through—and for whatever purpose he took Hannah, *if* he took Hannah—my father is one of them.

My father, Reverend Palmer Prescott, founded the Church of the Holy Promise. I spent hours of my childhood Sundays in his second-floor rectory, gazing out the window at the labyrinth below, while he stole my mother away to the room he perversely called the confessional. Some days I'd wander, if they took their time about things. It was a great pleasure to ring the bells in the tower, for their cacophony drowned the sounds of my parents having sex. I'd stand in the belfry, spying on the teenagers in the maze of hedges, watching them lock hands, lips, bodies. Forbidden energy abounded on that hallowed ground, but I didn't understand the dichotomy of such a thing back then. I simply yanked on the bellpulls so I didn't have to stand witness to the sounds coming from the confessional.

I can't pinpoint, exactly, the day I noticed that their

meetings in the confessional were less about getting off than control. But one day I noticed my mother's expression as she closed the door lingered somewhere between dread and hopelessness. It was then I'd realized Palmer had broken her spirit, but I couldn't understand why she returned to him day to day, week to week, year to year.

A man of God. A reverend. His congregation adores him still. They don't know him like I do. They don't know he abuses his position of power to manipulate, to control. They don't know, like I do, that he's capable of taking Hannah—and breaking her the way he broke my mother.

The day the police found me at the Vagabond, I provided evidence that Palmer Prescott was not what his public assumed. I think Detective Guidry believes me, even if he can't prove it.

I didn't know until Palmer sent my mother away that he was my father. She never told me, she gave me her last name, and he never treated me with any privilege, or unfair expectation, to set me apart from any other children of the congregation. In my mind, I scan the crowd amassed for one of Reverend Palmer's sermons. I search for faces like mine. I wonder if I have brothers and sisters, I wonder if he treated other women the way he'd treated Mom. And often, I'd wished I weren't an only child, when Mom would fade away for a few hours, when she'd morph from a vibrant, artistic nurturer to a sobbing mess for seemingly no reason.

I feel the stones beneath my feet, take in a deep breath of night air. Sometimes it's surreal to consider that I made it out of the chaos. Sometimes I have to remind myself that life with Palmer is over—at least for me. And sometimes, despite the concrete evidence surrounding me—Lindsey, the house behind me, the Catholic high school uniform hanging in my closet—I still can't believe it.

Lindsey unlocks the shed and flings herself into one of the vinyl beanbag chairs resting on the indoor-outdoor carpeting within. "Dude, I talked to Jon tonight."

I sink into a chair opposite her, near the leak in the roof, and toss her *The Little Mermaid*. "Really."

"Yeah. Marta and I ran into him at Caribou."

"What did he have to say?"

"Well, I mean, we didn't exactly have a meaningful conversation. Just bullshit, you know." She pulls out her bowl, a colorful contraption of iridescent greens and purples, and packs a few pinches of pot into it. "Talked about school and stuff. He says Mr. Willis must've been cracked for assigning a twelve-page essay on a novel, even if it did win a Pulitzer. Says we should revolt and crucify him. So glad I have Hayhurst for Lit."

Crucify, crucify, crucify.

"Crucify?" I shift uneasily. "That's the word he used?"

"Yeah." She shrugs, as she tests the flame on her lighter and lowers it. "He was pretty stressed out and worked up about it."

"Interesting choice of words." Considering, of course, that it's been spinning in my head all day.

"Guess you were right about the bookish thing." She brings her lighter to her bowl.

I pull this week's well-worn notebook from my backpack.

"Great idea." The crackling of leaves under flame meets my ears. She holds in her smoke. "Let's get started."

I flip to a semi-blank page. My glance trips over the nonsensical meters of words I jotted a few hours ago, and the pulsating in my brain begins.

"Print, so I don't have to rewrite it."

Soon after I landed here at *la Maison d'Hutch*, Lindsey and I discovered that our printing is virtually identical, so close in style that I can take short-answer quizzes for her in Russian history. If we can fool Ms. Hines, we can surely fool John Fogel. I nod. I want to tell her I'll print, but my tongue can't formulate the words.

"Something vague, but intriguing."

Already, Lindsey's voice echoes in the caverns of my mind, as if she's far away.

"Listening, Callie?"

"Crucify," I mutter. A flash of pain stabs me between the eyes, and a queasy feeling turns my gut. Breathe. Don't throw up.

I can't pull the cap off my pen. My fingers are too numb, or maybe my palm is too sweaty. I yank, yank, yank. The words are coming closer now. Threatening to devour my every thought. Threatening to overtake me, overpower me, engulf me like waves over a sand castle.

Crucify.

Crucify, quarter, and stone her.

Stone her, stone her, stoneherstoneherstoneher.

"You can give it to him tomorrow at chapel," Lindsey's saying.

What?

I exhale.

The ringing in my ears begins to fade.

"Hell-o?"

I wipe the tears from my eyes and offer Lindsey a glance. The grass in her bowl is smoldering. "Did you get any of that?"

"Give it to him at chapel. Got it."

She rolls her eyes—"I don't know why you don't just medicate the fuck out of yourself"—and brings the bowl to her lips for another hit.

Sometimes I wonder the same thing, but I feel so detached on the meds, so distant, so cloudy. And I can't afford any more clouds in my brain. "I got it," I say, as if proving to her that I'm functioning just fine without the Ativan. "Give it to him at chapel, right?"

I'm sure I'm leaving out a slew of Lindsey's other instructions, but she nods. "Right."

This makes sense. He sits in front of me in chapel, a

fact that recently has wrapped Lindsey in a playful sort of envy.

"And don't forget—"

My voice joins hers for the next demand: "No *h*. Got it."

I put my pen down on the bench and reread what I wrote while Lindsey was babbling.

Crucify, quarter, and stone her.

I don't know what it means.

But it scares the bejesus out of me.

We're in the same bed again, and Lindsey's asleep. But my mind is too active to allow me to rest.

Every time Lindsey sighs in her sleep, the stench of marijuana wafts from between her lips. It's a wonder her parents and our teachers don't know about her fondness of cannabis. It's woven into the threads of her being some days. Or maybe they do know, but choose to ignore it. There are plenty of parents who live in denial of their kids' extracurricular habits. My parents—the sane, as well as the insane—were never among them. They watched me constantly. Always questioned my decisions, my actions. Until I hit County, I didn't have a chance to screw up.

My fingers travel to the scar on my right shoulder. I push away the memory of how it came to be there.

Elijah did look different tonight, and he acted differently, too. Is it possible that Elijah, the supposed soccer god of Lakes High School, has found his way onto an upward-moving path? I wonder if it really is possible for someone to reform.

If so, maybe I should actually mail in some college applications.

The Hutches send Lindsey and me to Our Lady of Carmel Catholic, which means that my pre-SATs, cumulative GPA, and IQ are worthy of such a place. My eyes must've been like saucers when the Hutches told me the board had approved my application. I would've accused the Hutches of buying my admission—after all, Lindsey often proclaims they'd bought hers—but that didn't make sense. Why would complete strangers pay not only my tuition, but put up a bribe for my entry, when they could just as easily use the money to go to Hawaii . . . again?

Still, however I got in, it's no big secret that Carmel students have a leg up when it comes to securing grants and scholarships for college, and after a month into my first year there, I already see the difference. When the Hutches sprung me from County last March, they had no choice but to send me to Nippersink High to finish off my sophomore year. If Carmel is a country club compared to Nippersink, my old high school near Holy Promise is a joke, not that I'd often attended. Mom preferred to home-school me—and she used the term loosely. Most of my education comes from my own informal curiosities. I read. I wrote. I studied, but only when subjects interested me.

Things are different now. Maybe I should take Elijah's

lead and do something with the opportunity the Hutches have given me.

Burn her in an urn. Crucify, quarter, and stone her.

Images of my dream flash in my mind in conjunction with the disturbing words spinning through my brain.

Suddenly, I'm there again: knee-deep in a hole I'm digging.

Crucify, quarter, and stone her. Buried alive, buried alive, buried alive . . .

I close my eyes, and allow myself to absorb the image. I hear the clink of the shovel hitting the dirt, smell the rich soil and taste it as it grinds in my molars. Chills dart through me, as rain pelts the back of my neck.

I awaken with a start.

My right hand aches, and so does my head, to the point of nausea.

When I stretch my fingers, I feel my pen slip from my grasp.

In the darkness, I see my notebook sprawled across my belly. It's getting worse. I'd been writing. In my sleep.

Carefully, so as not to disturb Lindsey, who's still basking in her marijuana-induced slumber, I shift and hold my notebook up, so that a slant of moonlight illuminates the page.

I gasp when I read the same words I'd written on the walls of the apartment above the Vagabond: I killed him, I killed him, I killed him.

FOUR

This is all so 1960's. Writing notes by hand. Passing them in chapel. But cell phone usage isn't allowed in school, and garnering John Fogel's attention is a matter of some urgency, at least to Lindsey. So e-mailing and waiting hours for an answer is out of the question.

"John."

Either he's ignoring me, or he can't hear me, amongst the bustle of our classmates taking their seats, scrambling before Father Bernard begins his procession. If it's the former, I won't hold it against him. Morning chapel is no time to foster an acquaintance. I caught him looking in my direction on my first day at Carmel Catholic last month. He didn't look away, even when our gazes met, until our physics teacher walked the path between us. That same day, he brushed past me on his way out of the classroom, and while he offered a small smile, he didn't say much of anything.

I've heard him speak, of course—just never to me.

I've heard him laugh.

I've heard him sing.

But hearing someone and listening to him are two totally different things. Just as he's never turned more than a smoldering gaze to me, I haven't exactly paid much attention to him, either—if only because Lindsey's constantly crushing on him puts him on my off-limits list.

He's so close—sitting in the pew in front of me—that I could breathe a whisper on the back of his neck and disturb the straight, Carmel-approved cut of his sandy blond hair. I lean forward. "John."

This time he turns toward me, an expression somewhere between annoyance and surprise playing on his face. Quickly, the look mellows to indifference. He gives me a nod and strikes me with a steady navy-blue-eyed stare. I'm not used to seeing this sort of thing in high school guys, who often lack confidence, if not the political correctness and grace of holding a gaze for more than half a moment. My mother taught me at a young age always to look someone in the eye; most of my privileged peers, John Fogel obviously not included, missed this lesson. It's refreshing to see a guy who hasn't.

"From Lindsey," I say, pressing the note into his palm. My

fingers linger a moment too long against his thicker ones.

His eyes widen for a split second when our fingers touch over the back of the pew. "Thanks." Promptly, he looks away and taps the corner of the note atop his calc text, but he doesn't open it.

I settle against the back of the pew.

If John takes the bait, he'll e-mail his reply to Lindsey, or maybe he'll text it, and I'll be out of the loop. My work here was essentially done once I pressed the tightly folded square of paper into his hand.

Maybe it's because we're at church, where I'm reminded that no man can stand alone, that we're a community and must rely on one another. Maybe it's because he seems to be a genuinely nice guy. I hope it isn't because I can't stop looking at his hands, but a longing pulls at my heartstrings, filled with injustice and regret. It's crazy. What do I care if Lindsey reels in this poor soul, watches him struggle on the end of the line for a while, then bashes him on the head once he swallows the hook? It's his business if he wants to fall for a girl who won't extend him the courtesy of spelling his name correctly.

But if that's true, why do I feel like I set a trap? Maybe I won't be there when the jaws close around his body, but I laid the bait. Carefully and methodically, I designed every sentence and placed every word in the manner most certain to snare him.

I open my calculus notes and stare blankly at theorems.

We have a test first period, and after seeing Elijah, fighting off nightmares, and the late-night smoke session with Lindsey, I'm exhausted and unprepared.

Crucify, quarter, and stone her.

This is the worst, when phrases gnaw at me for days on end. I don't know how I'm going to concentrate on anything, if it continues all day long.

Signaling the beginning of chapel, a pealing of bells fills the nave, and in an instant, I'm back there: running through the labyrinth behind the Church of the Holy Promise, whilst two teenaged girls, accompanied by my father, Reverend Palmer, yank on the bellpulls in the tower. Their laughter chases me.

Get out, I want to scream to them. *You aren't safe with him. Get out of that bell tower!* They can outrun him. He'll always have the limp my mother stabbed into him just before he committed her.

I see it now in my mind's eye: the pearl-handled knife protruding from his thigh.

I hear her shriek, rising up from the confessional: "Don't you touch her! Don't you touch her! Don't . . . you . . . touch her!"

The organ music begins, jolting me from that atrocious memory.

Bodies in my periphery rise, making me feel like Alice in Wonderland shrinking in the rabbit hole.

Yasmin Hayes elbows me as she stands. "Callie," she hisses. "Come on."

I slide off the pew, stowing my textbook on the bench in my stead, but still holding tight to my pen. I rise.

Father Bernard, flanked by Ryan Waters and Gianna Watson—we're at the Ws for altar servers—walks the travertine-tiled aisle toward the stained glass Blessed Virgin and Son, which serves as a backdrop to the altar.

I clear my throat and with numb fingers reach for my hymnal.

Voices rise around me, singing the welcome hymn, but I hear the voice of only one. A crisp tenor.

John Fogel's.

"Blood of my Savior, bathe me in thy tide."

I don't sing at chapel. I can't distinguish why, really, except that Catholic Mass is extremely formal, compared to what I grew up with at Holy Promise. Singing at the latter was more like joining the crowd at a concert. Elijah calls Holy Promise the Happy Clappy Place, because our music is of the rock variety, complete with electric guitarist and amp on stage, astride which jumbo screens reach for the heavens. Singing in chapel, or at any Catholic church, feels controlled, supervised somehow. If I didn't often trust myself to unleash my voice at Holy Promise once my mother left, I don't know why anyone would expect me to sing at Carmel's morning chapel.

A soprano rises up, melding in perfect harmony with John Fogel's tone: "Wash me with waters gushing from thy side."

He turns with the onset of the powerful voice, his amused

gaze locked on mine. He raises an eyebrow and smiles between the catastrophic lines of the hymn. Only when I attempt to smile in return, which is weird enough on its own, do I realize that the soprano is belting from my lungs.

It's me. I'm *singing*.

More tragically, however, than my sharing my voice with the world of Carmel Catholic: I'm sharing a moment with Lindsey's potential boyfriend.

Instantly, I silence my tongue. This now awards me a deep frown from John Fogel, who glances at me again over his shoulder.

Need my notebook. But I have to remain standing. Can't sit before Father invites us to, can't. Once John looks away, I press the felt tip to my forearm:

Buried alive buried alive buried alive.

My mother loved to sing, loved to sing with me. And singing stirs a longing in me: I miss her.

My God, I have to see her. I've been alone too long.

"You may be seated." In a blink of time, Father Bernard is standing at the altar, with the light shining through the stained glass and illuminating him from behind, making him look like something of a saint himself. Clumsily, I take my seat, landing half on, half off my open textbook. I catch my balance and pull the book onto my lap.

Although I'm staring at *x*s and *n*s, although Father Bernard is welcoming us to his morning service, I'm a million miles away, or at least fifteen—diving into the maze of manicured bushes behind Holy Promise, hoping not to be seen, praying I've gotten away.

A twin of the note I just passed to John lands atop the pages, zipping me out of my reverie. Out of the corner of my eye, I see John's arm, clad in a Land's End light blue, long-sleeved oxford—buttoned at the cuff, slipping back over the pew.

The letter C, written in a black gel-writer and with flourish, labels the square of paper. His reply is apparently meant for me. Quickly, I clamp my hand over the note, although I'm certain Yasmin already saw it. I pray she won't tell a soul.

My heart pounds, its beat encompassing my entire body from fingertips to toes. I don't even know what John might have to say to me, but this isn't normal behavior for one of Lindsey's prospective boyfriends.

I search the chapel for Lindsey. Did she see that he wrote back?

She's sitting in her assigned row, digging in her suitcase of a Louis Vuitton purse. Completely unaware.

I shove John's note into the pocket of my navy blue pencil skirt, twenty-one inches from the waist and lacking in style, thank you very much. Whatever John Fogel has to say to me, it isn't as important as Lindsey's trust. I decide right then and there I should never read it. But my track record in this regard is less than stellar.

I do plenty of things I shouldn't.

FIVE

"I'm here to see Serena Knowles."

The droning of the air conditioner at the Meadows surrounds and encompasses me. I'd feel cold here even if I were wearing a parka in July. Through the cotton/poly blend of my skirt, I pat the square of notebook paper, which I stowed in my pocket and have yet to open. Its presence warms me, like thoughts of Elijah.

"And you are . . . ?"

"Calliope Knowles." I clear my throat. "Her daughter."

It sort of bothers me that the staff never recognizes me. Not because I'm a frequent visitor—I'm not—but because I look so much like my mother that it should be evident I'm here to see her. If they don't see the resemblance, particularly with the long, burgundy hair, I wonder how much time they spend looking at my mother, and they're supposed to be taking care of her.

Today, I'm following a twig of an African American orderly, whose name tag boasts an all-capitals SHEILA, down a maze of dim hallways, past more than two gated corridors. Her white rubber-soled shoes squeak against the gray linoleum. The Meadows always smells like an odd mixture of piss and antiseptic cleaning solution, as if cleaning bodily messes and making bodily messes to clean is an ongoing cycle within the walls.

Still, it *is* clean, which is more than I can say for some of the other state-sponsored facilities Reverend Palmer considered for her. While I appreciate the cleanliness, however, I can't imagine my mom is comfortable here. She preferred, when free choice was part of her existence, a life of clutter. I grew up amongst piles of colored tissue paper, jars of gesso and abandoned buttons, strings of beads and gems. Batiks served as curtains, pillows as chairs, and we ate off any random creation of the potter's wheel—be it ashtray or vase.

Sheila knocks on a door, which I assume must be my mother's. You'd think I'd recognize it by now. But either they always lead me down different paths, or my mother has set a record for most room changes. I don't think I could find my way here if I'd borrowed Hansel and Gretel's bag of bread crumbs for the journey. I wonder if I'll find my way back in time to report to the women's shelter, where I'm required—thanks to Mrs. Hutch—to serve dinner this evening. Time will be tight. I have to take the Pace bus back to town.

Lindsey dropped me off here after school, but she was clear on this: she can't come back to get me. She's on the homecoming committee, and they're making final arrangements for the parade float.

Final arrangements. Funny that those two words can refer to festivities, as well as funerals.

When the orderly shoves a key into the lock and turns the knob, it's clear to me that the knock was purely a courtesy. "Serena? Someone's here to see you."

A voice so familiar that it may as well be my own floats through the crack between the door and frame—in song. I close my eyes for a split second and savor the sound of the vocal vibrations: *Let my love open the door.*

The words morph to a hum by the time I cross the threshold. I wonder when and where she might've heard the song. Sometime in her childhood, maybe, although I haven't considered until this very moment that perhaps my mother had a life before Holy Promise.

But of course Mom had lived before she met my father, before he'd enveloped her into his suffocating congregation.

I join her, humming the intuitive melody.

Her glance meets mine, and her lips turn upward slightly at the corners.

When I was a child, she sang frequently; she has the voice of an angel. It seems like such a long time ago. I'd sit in awe of her at the Vagabond, or even at Sunday service, when she'd grasp the barrel of the mic and release pure symphony from her soul.

My eyes well with the resurfacing of the memory, or maybe it's the stark juxtaposition of this place and our apartment above the Vagabond that reduces me to tears. Crazy or not, my mother does not belong in these laminated quarters—clinically white walls, institutional carpeting void of nap or pad, machined furniture that reflects neither my mother's vibrancy, nor her insanity.

Her eyes are nearly black, and their fathoms impossible to navigate, especially on days like today. She's looking right through me. She knows I'm here. She knows who I am—always—but it's like any other day, if her nonchalance is any indication. I want to plow into her arms, to feel her embrace tighten, as if she'll never let me go. Instead, she leans over her snack table and resumes sketching. Continues humming, as if she's content to be locked away here, as if a life with me isn't worth a fight for her freedom.

Sheila turns to leave us alone. "Have a nice visit. Ring me when you want an escort out."

It's then I realize there's no knob on the inside. I was right. She's been moved—to a more secure wing of the building.

Buried alive, buried alive, buried alive . . .

I bring a few fingers to the pain beginning to accumulate in my temples. I can't have a graphomania attack here. I just can't. But already, I'm fixating on the image of my pen. Already, I'm envisioning the next blank page in my notebook. Please, God. Please. I feel the words engraving into my mind, actually feel the script taking form in my head. Please. Help me fight it. Just this once.

The moment the door clicks closed, the words scatter to the periphery. They're not gone—I feel them beginning to encroach again—but I'm holding them at bay.

My mother drops her project—"Calliope, listen to me"—and grasps my hands over the surface of the tray.

I startle, although I know there's no reason to be afraid of her temporarily slipping into mania. It's nothing new. This has been happening most of my life. Still, it's been a while since she's accosted me like this, and I'm taken aback.

"It's beautiful," she says, as if we're in the middle of a conversation, and I ought to know what she's talking about. "The most beautiful pendant in the world, and I want you to have it. It'll help you go home."

She's been talking about this pendant since Palmer sequestered her here, or maybe because he put her here. But no one has seen it—even, I suspect, my mother—if not in our imaginations.

"Mom . . ." I search her eyes for the here and now.

Claw at the case, claw at the case, claw at the case . . .

"Callie." She brings a hand to my cheek, her eyes softening. "Well, sit down. It ain't much, but it's home, right?"

Despite the no-way-out, it's as much of a home as any other room in this joint. I open the tabletop refrigerator and grasp a small bottle of water, the only beverage available outside the cafeteria. It's a far cry from the flavorful coffees she used to sip at the Vagabond.

"Any word on Palmer? Have you seen him?"

It's odd that she asks about him, seeing as though she's in here because of him. One Sunday evening, she knifed him in the confessional. She'd wanted to kill him, she'd told me, before he crossed another line.

"No." I drag a stool closer to her chair and sit. "No word on Palmer."

"Here. Don't forget where you came from." My mother turns her drawing toward me.

It's a sketch of a crucifix, sans Jesus's dead body. His shroud is draped over the arms of the cross, and His crown of thorns hangs from the neck.

Her thick black lashes brush against her cheeks before she meets my gaze. It's like looking in a mirror sixteen years into the future. "They have you going to church, yes? That foster family of yours?"

"Yes."

"Holy Promise?"

"Carmel Catholic."

She sighs, as if to say some-God-is-better-than-no-God.

She shakes off what I perceive as disappointment with a shudder. "How long have you lived there with them?"

"Six months now."

She rolls her eyes. "My, how time flies."

"I know it's been a while since my last visit," I say. "I'm sorry about that."

After a few moments, she replies: "Good of you to come."

"Why are you in a new room?"

She wipes charcoal from her fingers onto her jeans and pretends she hasn't heard me. She reaches for her deck of Tarot, which she keeps sheathed in a man's dress sock on her night table.

I have a deck, too, but mine is stuffed into a crocheted bag. I don't know how to use the cards, but my mother gave them to me shortly before she was sequestered here, so I carry them with me everywhere.

I try again: "Did you lose privileges, or is this a permanent change?"

If it's the latter, it means she's getting worse.

"Can you get out at all anymore?" No answer. "Mom?"

Her silence hides nothing from me. I can deduce how she got from point A to point B on my own. There was a time, in the beginning, when Palmer could sign her out for weekend visits. Now she's under lock and key. Can't leave, is my guess. Not that there's anyone left to sign her out anyway.

She shuffles the cards.

The threat of tears builds in my chest, in my lungs. Like it or not, I'm on my own from here forward. Maybe I should stop laughing off Lindsey's desire to officially adopt me, seeing as it appears the Hutches are the only family I have now.

I stare at the figure that used to be my mother. How is it that I can talk to her, touch her, feel her, smell her, yet no longer rely on her?

"I'd kill for a smoke," she says.

"I quit."

She shrugs and slaps the deck down on the snack tray between us. "Good."

We grew up together, Serena and me. I was born on her sixteenth birthday, when she was a few months younger than I am now. I can't imagine having a baby at my age, but she made it work. I indulge for a moment in distant memories of my early childhood: drawing pictures in the sand on a sunny beach, the waves tickling my toes as they washed up on the shore. Calmer days. Happier times.

It had always been the two of us against the world. Suddenly, I feel very alone without her. She probably feels the same way, especially since I haven't been here in such a long time.

I consider telling her about Elijah's lying to me, about the words perpetually consuming my brain, about the calc test I'm pretty sure I failed this morning. I even want to tell her about John Fogel, who hasn't left my mind since our hands touched at chapel that morning. But these things don't matter in Serena's world, and what would it look like, if after weeks—months, maybe—I showed up here only to complain about my life?

I take up the cards, shuffle them, cut them twice to my left. I don't believe in Tarot any more than my mother does, but lately it's the only avenue she'll travel to reach me, the only method of communication she'll explore. "I want to know," I say slowly, "where Palmer is. If I'm crazy to think he took Hannah."

Her lips harden into a thin line as she gathers the deck into a single stack again. "Crazy is relative. He's crazier than both of us."

"I'm sixteen now." I swallow hard. "I'm not the same kid you left behind when he stuffed you into this box. I deserve to know: why did you stay with him? Because he was my father?"

"You think you can date that hoodlum, Elijah, and claim to be an adult, Calliope?"

Her words throw me back on the stool a few inches, as if she physically kicked me in the chest. My heart pounds with adrenaline. "You don't even know him."

"I know enough to know what happened at that County home." Her tongue clicks against the roof of her mouth as she stares me down. "For everything I've done to protect you, I would've hoped you wouldn't jeopardize your future for the sake of a juvenile delinquent."

"I love him."

"Don't confuse love with sex." The way she talks about Elijah and me, we're nothing more than a sleazy fling, and considering my last few meetings with him, I'm starting to wonder if she's right. There's no fighting the tears now. I wipe one away.

"You think making adult decisions qualifies you?" She begins to lay out the cards in a cross formation.

I shake my head, then shrug a shoulder. "The decisions I'm entrusted to make are decidedly more adult than the ones you're making these days, now, aren't they?"

Her eyes widen, but her jaw remains set.

"But that's not the point," I say before she can respond to my rather rude observations about her circumstances here. "The point is that, like it or not, I have to be an adult now. And all these secrets . . . my whole life is a secret, Mom. I have to know. I have to know why you thought Palmer should die. What you had with him might not have been conventional, but . . . You loved him. Didn't you?"

"Calliope . . ."

She drapes a tendril of my hair behind my ear. The tenderness, the ordinary nature of this tiny gesture, evokes a sob from deep in my throat. God, I miss having a mom. The Hutches care about me—I know they do—but I don't crave the occasional hugs they give me the way I yearn for contact with my mom. And when my foster parents do embrace me, it doesn't feel like this.

"Callie, do you think I didn't know what he had in mind for you?"

Cobblestone. Cobblestone, cobblestone, cobblestone.

I shake away the word, but I hear it again, as if the pen in my mind is stamping its proverbial foot, reminding me who's boss:

cobblestone.

Shut up.

I want to know—What did Serena think Palmer had in mind for me?—but there's no use in asking. Her memory is unreliable. Most of the things she remembers about that last year never happened: we never collected shells up the coast of the lake, she never learned to play guitar, we never planted daisies on Highland Point. I'd have better luck finding Palmer to learn the answers to these questions— even if he turns up dead.

But I don't really have to ask, anyway. I think I have a pretty good idea of what Serena meant. She's one person I never have to convince that Palmer's capable of evil things. And if she'd known of the horrific possibilities ahead of me . . . that would explain the knife she stuck into his thigh.

"Do you think I could turn my back on my daughter?" She shoves her tray aside, the locking wheels of which skid on the institutional carpeting. The cross formation becomes a haphazard sea washing around an island of a card in the center: the Magician. Nothing's between us now but fifteen inches of air, pregnant with dread.

"My sweet girl." She gathers me in her embrace, holds me a bit too tight. "When it comes to you, I may as well be the damn holy trinity. Believe in me before, even, you believe in God."

SIX

The words overpower me. They bleed through my flesh like sweat, pound in my head like a thousand tiny fists beating me from the inside, churn in my gut like a hamster running amok on a wire wheel.

Too much. It's too much. I might vomit.

Buried alive, buried alive, buried alive.

Still half asleep, I throw back the covers and drop my feet to the floor, only to stumble and fall, when my numb extremities cannot sustain my weight. Carpet fuzz clings to my moist skin and accumulates under my fingernails, as I search the floor frantically for my favorite pen and this week's notebook. I see it in my mind—spiral-bound, white cardboard cover with a crease in the lower right corner, random verses recorded atop it in red felt-tip.

A wheeze sputters through my lungs, as I pinch my eyes closed, then open them again, in hopes of forcing adjustment to the dark. Elijah. A shadow of his image encompasses me.

I focus.

Elijah, Elijah, Elijah, calm me down. Silence the words.

I try to remember what it feels like the moment he kisses me, the energy consuming me the second our bodies join, but I can't grasp a single feeling beyond impending cold, damp danger. I seek the comfort of his tongue brushing along my inner wrists, but instead I meet with teeth like daggers.

Their chomping stings my skin, cuts at my flesh, like a rabid dog shredding a raw steak. It feels so real that I wonder: am I still asleep and dreaming?

At last, my fingers close around a pen. Feels like a felt-tip. That's good.

I hold the pen in my mouth and rake the carpeting in search of my notebook. The fibers itch, consume the whole of me.

As the words rise closer to the surface, the teeth dig deeper into my body.

I can't find my notebook. Can't find it. But the words won't stop.

Buried alive, claw at the case . . .

Gasping.

Can't breathe, can't breathe, can't *breathe*.

I bite off the pen cap.

Bring the tip of the pen to my left forearm.

Expunge.

Ah, sweet surrender. I feel as if my lungs are deflating, releasing excess pressure, like a tire too full with air. The pounding behind my eyes begins to wane. My skin stops crawling. The gnawing ceases.

I reach for the switch of the lamp. Even the measly forty watts of the bulb blind me, but I have to read what I've written, have to transfer it to my notebook, so I can wash it off my arm.

Fuck. It's in Sharpie. Fine-tipped. Red.

A tattoo. That's the comparison Dean Ritchie draws between the words on my arm and the rules of etiquette and conformity here at Carmel Catholic. I'm sitting in his office, yanking at my sleeve, which covers all but a few letters of what I wrote a few hours ago.

"Tattoos must be covered," Ritchie reminds me. "Therefore, those words must be covered in entirety."

Ritchie knows about my graphomania, as do most faculty members. However, I suspect many, if not most of them, assume I exaggerate the issue, use it to act out.

I can't blame them. I was a holy terror when I arrived here. Not because I wanted to be, but because I was suffocating for a while—wearing Land's End apparel, carrying a traditional Bible in my hand—and only attempting to grasp a modicum of what used to be my reality. I've gotten used to things, just as they said I would, but the lot of them has yet to forgive me for my less than desirable behavior during the adjustment. I remember when I thought attending class was too much to expect of me, as long as I got my work done to the teachers' satisfaction, and more than once I dared to tell off some teacher who dared to push me to exert my best effort, when I assumed she simply didn't understand the processes of my mind.

Now, passing notes yesterday with John Fogel aside, I'm damn near a model citizen walking these halls, but Ritchie can only remember the actions of the student I used to be.

Yesterday's note practically burns my hip through my skirt. I wish I hadn't brought it with me today. If I'm not going to read it, I ought to throw it away. There's too much anxiety involved in hiding it from Lindsey. I consider coming clean about it: *Can you imagine? He wrote me a note, instead of you. What a jerk.* But I don't think he's a jerk, and after feeling that surge of energy erupting between us, yes, I can imagine why he'd write to me.

"Miss Knowles." Ritchie rubs his rotund belly, clad in a navy sweater vest that bears the Carmel logo, as he traverses around his mahogany desk, staring all the while at the open manila file in his hand. My name is emblazoned on the tab, and like the neon lights at the Vagabond, the label suggests

Ritchie might find unfortunate things inside, if he dares to open the door. "I'd like to be sympathetic about your condition, but if I bend rules for you, everyone walking these hallways will be a graphomaniac by sundown."

I don't dare to look him in the eye. I neglect to inform him—again—of the differences between the girl who constantly updates her status because she wants to tell the world about her latest leg waxing, and the girl who writes because there's a sufferable force within her.

"You should have washed it off."

I'd tried. But Lindsey and I ran out of nail polish remover, which is far more effective in erasing Sharpie than soap. Announcing this, and explaining that the marker wasn't even mine but Lindsey's and I hadn't meant to use it, would be talking back, and I don't do that anymore. Not here, anyway.

"You're medicated," he says. The file meets his desk with a slap. He traces a few words with his thick, sausage-like fingers.

"It's my understanding the medication is supposed to curb these . . . these . . . these *urges* of yours."

I hate the way he says it, as if my uncontrollable affliction is akin to sexual desire, and therefore—especially in the context of a Catholic institution—naughty, dirty, wicked. Something I should put a cap on, for the whole of human decency.

"Forgive me for saying so, Miss Knowles, but this"—he

indicates the words on my arm—"this doesn't look like control to me."

Nausea instantly returns. Sweat beads on my forehead.

I massage my temples. Take a deep breath.

It's been a month since I've taken my pills. I wonder if I'm heading back there, to that dark place, where I don't sleep, don't eat, can't focus, can't function without a pen in my hand.

"Miss Knowles?"

What?

I pull my notebook from my backpack . . . just in case.

"Callie? Are you all right?"

The scent of lake fills my nostrils.

Rain beats on the back of my neck, my shoulders.

Sounds of the shovel, of digging, echo: *Clink, thunk. Clink, thunk.*

Everything's white. Not bright, rather dim. But white. The square of a white area rug: I know what it feels like under my bare toes. The gauzy draperies across the room: I remember how they billow, when the breeze sweeps in off the water. The linen closet down the hall holds white linens.

My fist clenches around a strand of beads so tightly that my fingers ache.

I glance down at a bejeweled, pewter crucifix—crown of thorns hanging from the neck, shroud draped over the arms.

"Callie!"

I blink away the vivid images, and Ritchie's office bleeds into sight.

I'm coughing over tears.

My red felt-tip is secure in my grip.

"Callie?"

I glance up at Dean Ritchie, then down at my notebook, where I'd scribbled over and over again:

Smile as you condone her.

Smile as you condone her.

Smile smile smile smile smile.

As you condone condone condone condone condone condone condone her.

SEVEN

Lindsey glances at me from behind the wheel of her Honda Accord. She hates the car—she wanted a convertible Camaro—but Mr. Hutch is a big believer in safety and stomped on her pleas. "Dude, that's fucked up."

I shrug and shove a Tootsie Pop into my mouth.

She isn't taken aback with my dreaming about the crucifix my mother sketched, which might be the pendant she's been babbling about for the past year or so. And I didn't dare tell her I was dreaming about a place I recognize but don't remember, although I'm certain that would give her equal pause. Simply, in Lindsey's world, it's fucked up that I blacked out in Dean Ritchie's office.

"How mortifying!" She turns up the Sirius XM station

and proceeds to scream over the Squirrel Nut Zippers.

After my graphomania attack, Dean Ritchie called the Hutches and my caseworker, who in turn called the shrink, who decided I ought to go in for a face-to-face meeting. The dean granted Lindsey and me special permission to leave school grounds, so as to fit me into the good doctor's schedule.

"In any case, thanks for giving me a free pass out of trig." She drums her fingertips against the steering wheel. "Wanna smoke a bowl?"

I chuckle. "No."

"Pack one for me."

"And you say you aren't addicted to pot."

"Physically impossible."

"I didn't say the addiction was physical." I reach into the center consul, and locate her stash.

"Hey, has Jon said anything about the note?"

My heart stumbles in my chest. "Um . . ." I pull the candy from my mouth, swallow hard, and think about the note in my pocket. I've felt its outline—and found much comfort in it—no fewer than fifteen times since I woke up on the cot in the nurse's office. "I think he said thanks."

"Thanks? That's it?"

"Yeah." I lick the sugary substance from my lips and hope my sister can't read the nervous tremble in my voice. "Why? What's he said to you since?"

"Nothing."

"Nothing?"

"Nothing. And as idiotic as that is, it only makes me want him more. Dude, we have to write to him again."

Forty-three words inscribed on my forearm in permanent ink.

Nausea.

A blackout and a school official's witnessing my graphomania firsthand.

And Dr. Warren Ewing asks me about boys.

He's youngish for a shrink, maybe thirty, with a frat-boy look about him—preppy clothes, tousled brown hair, Doc Martens. He's staring at me above his square, horn-rimmed glasses—very retro Buddy Holly.

"Elijah." He spins a pen—a fine-point black gel-writer by Papermate, comfort grip—like a miniature baton between his fingers. "When was the last time you saw him?"

I shrug. "Couple of days ago."

"And?"

"And, what?" I hate this part of therapy—the prodding, the poking, the nosiness.

Dr. Ewing raises his eyebrows, urging me to continue.

When I don't, he taps his fingers together. "Elijah has been, historically, an outlet for you. In your own words, your only trusted confidant at County, and sometimes he's a direct connection with the cessation of the impulse to write. So when I ask about him, I'm not trying to pry into your personal life, but Elijah is pertinent here."

He's right, of course. As always.

"I'm not ashamed of hooking up with him."

"In telling me that—repeatedly—you convey that you assume I think you should be ashamed."

"I know you don't think I should be with him."

"I never said that. Sex can be very healthy."

"Is it, though? I mean, between Elijah and me?" I want to shut up, but before I know it, I'm spewing details of the force I felt during the ethereal fog, which preempted the red Sharpie, and how it all emerged out of thoughts of my sometimes boyfriend. "Maybe it's a sign that I shouldn't trust him anymore."

"Maybe, but not necessarily."

"Sometimes I think . . . it's like he's afraid I'll remember what happened . . . the night Palmer and Hannah disappeared."

"You think so?"

I shrug. "Maybe he's afraid of what I might've done."

"Maybe he's detrimental to this process." Dr. Ewing tilts his head. "Maybe he's essential. We don't know. Either way, dreams can be contrary. Or representative of elements in your reality."

My reality. I wonder if mine is similar to my mother's. Shouldn't reality be stagnant? The same for everyone? "It wasn't a dream. I felt the biting, like it was real."

He nods. Gives his Papermate another spin. "Do you have marks, where you felt it? Some trauma patients self-mutilate."

"No." A sense of relief floods me. There's a lot wrong with me, but I don't do that.

"Do you think . . . did you write about the dream? On your arm?"

"Well, I don't know if it was a dream, but . . . no. Not really." I yank up my sleeve and present the scrawling to my shrink. "It's gruesome."

He's careful not to touch me, but he leans close as his eyes follow over the words. "'Pressed,'" he reads. "As in *for time*?"

"To death . . . I think."

His eyes widen, but he quickly recovers and gives me his generic response: "Hmm."

"The words were just . . . there," I offer because I can't tell him anything else, and he's probably getting as frustrated as I am with my lack of awareness and information.

I assume Ewing's goals with these sessions, while officially centered around my well-being, have something unofficially to do with a missing girl, and the fate of a missing-in-action suspect—my father. Ewing's a court-appointed shrink, after all, and if I know anything about anyone state-appointed, I know they don't act solely on behalf of their wards.

"And this blackout in the dean's office. Tell me about it."

"It was like a daydream." I shrug. "I was in a white room, holding a rosary."

"Rosary." Ewing massages his clean-shaven chin with a few fingers. "Correct me if I'm wrong . . ." His spoken thoughts trail into a misty atmosphere.

I shake my head, only to watch words disappear from the backs of my eyelids: *ashes amber her through sift.*

And just like that, they're gone—in reverse order.

"Look, I didn't mean to write it in Sharpie," I say. "I wasn't trying to be insubordinate."

"No one thinks you were."

"Then why was I sitting in the dean's office?"

"Because, Calliope, people are worried about you. Are you taking your medication?"

After a long pause, and a hard suck on my candy, I say, "Yeah."

He blinks expectantly behind his Buddy Hollys. "Callie, the meds are there for a reason."

"I'm taking them."

"No, you're not."

I break the gaze. It's no use lying to him.

"Remember," he says, "we discussed this."

I shrug. "What makes you feel alive, Warren?" His first name feels foreign on my tongue, but I let it roll around on the tip with sugary grape Tootsie Pop for a few seconds: Warren, Warren, Warren. It makes him more person and less doctor.

"My work, I suppose. Love for my kids and my wife. Skydiving. Why? What makes you feel alive?"

"Two things." I yank the nearly disintegrated lollipop from my mouth and lean forward, my elbows on my knees.

"My time with Elijah, and words. I don't care about either, about anything, really, when I'm dosed up on Ativan. I don't care about not remembering, and remembering is . . ." I shake my head. "I have to remember."

His brow creases, as if in deep thought, as if he's attempting to find a way to talk me out of believing what I said.

I twirl the lollipop stick in time with Ewing's pen. "As much as I hate the compulsion of the graphomania, I think maybe it feeds me, stirs me, motivates me to remember." Remembering is essential. Once I remember, I can be normal again. And when it's all too much for me to handle, Elijah drowns the words. "Medicate me, and you might as well have my soul."

For a while, he doesn't say anything. Simply holds my gaze with furrowed brow.

I refuse to blink.

Finally, he claps his pen down onto the coffee table and offers a hand, palm up.

Tentatively, I slide my cool fingers into the heat of his grasp. I wonder if this violates his doctor-patient ethics code, which seems silly. He's just holding my hand across the expanse of the coffee table, after all. It isn't a sexual as much as a supportive gesture. One I suspect many fathers might extend to their daughters. But not mine, even before he disappeared.

"Do you know what you just said?"

I begin to shake my head.

"You're beginning to see some good in this affliction, a means to remembering what you've forgotten."

An uncomfortable chill squirms up my spine.

"The one-year anniversary of the disappearance is coming up. There's bound to be an increase in media coverage of the case, discussions about it, what have you. I wouldn't be surprised if you started remembering more these next few weeks."

"More? More writing?" I already feel the headache of it. "I can't. I just . . . I can't."

"You can."

Tension pulls at my chest, the same sensation I get just before I start to fade away, just before the words come.

"I wish I knew what to do for you," he says.

"I know." I break the shared glance to let him off the hook—I've never expected him to find the solution to my problem—but his grip tightens when I try to pull away.

"Someday, I promise you, you'll embrace these words. Control the compulsion, even. And someday, you'll enjoy being with someone, whether it chases those words away or not. Someday, you'll seek it for its own sake."

I shift in my seat under the influence of his green-eyed stare. "Is it normal that I . . . that I like it?" It feels funny to even ask, but I have to know. I'm not like Lindsey, who's no prude, but doesn't think about it as often as I do, and because she's the standard by which I measure the norm. . . .

"Yes," Ewing says. "It's healthy to enjoy sex."

Palmer didn't think so, and he drove that point home. He assumed I'd been sleeping around long before I lost my virginity—and I didn't lose it until he was long gone.

"In the meantime, do me a favor." Ewing pinches the bridge of his nose. "Please take the medication."

A tear travels down my cheek. I wonder when I started crying. Defiantly, I refuse to wipe it away. "I want to be normal," I say. "Like Lindsey."

"I'll bet Lindsey has her own share of problems."

I ignore him. "I want the biggest concern of my day to be my French exam. I want to worry about which brand of eyeliner doesn't smudge by third period, push the limits by hemming my skirt an extra inch, and wonder if the guy in my calculus class likes me."

John Fogel's note taunts me from my pocket.

The trouble is that I don't know if I'd recognize normal, even if I were to do all those things. My life has never been mainstream.

"That's good," Ewing says, at last releasing my hand. "Deciding what you want is often the first step."

On impulse, without consciously deciding to do so, I reach into my skirt pocket and extract the note. I start to unfold it. "I think I'm starting to remember something." I glance up at Ewing, and this time don't mind when he gives me the expectant stare. "Something about digging."

He nods.

"You know there was mud in the drain that night. The night I was in the apartment above the Vagabond. The night the police found me there and were asking me about my father." I swallow hard, awaiting Ewing's reaction, which of course doesn't come. I wonder if he allows himself to react later, when I'm gone. Does he go home to his wife and say, "I have a whack-job of a patient"?

"Suppose I buried his body," I say. John Fogel's note becomes an origami worry stone in my hands.

"Suppose you did."

"I had to have had help. I mean, he's . . . was, maybe . . . a big man." I don't want to voice this next theory, but I have to: "Suppose I buried Hannah. I could've done that on my own."

"Could have. But would you have? Your comprehensive history gives us no indication that you're a violent person, or ever have been."

"Neither did my mother's," I mutter. "Until she shoved a dagger into Palmer's thigh. I mean, what if he just . . . makes us do things? What if I was following a commandment in burying Hannah's body? Honor thy father, and all."

"Callie, I want you to recognize these thoughts as possible memories, sure. But sometimes the human mind works in obscure ways. These thoughts and images could be nothing more than an avenue through which you'll remember what really happened. Like your graphomania. How many notebooks have you filled since you were here last week?"

I almost don't want to tell him. "Three and a half."

He presses his lips together. "You're already writing more as the anniversary nears."

"Not always. Sometimes I . . . sometimes I don't."

"Have you been bringing them to the detective, like they asked?"

"Sometimes. Sometimes I drop them off, but usually they call and come get them, then bring them back after they've copied them." I feel a little violated, and exposed, when I think about *anyone* reading what I've written in my notebooks, let alone a group of cops dropping doughnut crumbs over them, laughing at my insanity. Once I caught Elijah sneaking a peek, and I went ballistic. But if I want to help find Hannah, and I do . . .

The paper in my hand crinkles, draws my attention. Subconsciously, I've opened John's message. I should fold it back up.

"Do me a favor. Leave this one with me." Ewing's hand lands atop my notebook. "I want to comb through it. See if I can't find a clue."

As if he senses my hesitation, Ewing reminds me: "I've read through them before, yes?"

I nod.

"Have I ever judged you for what you've written?"

"No." I refold John's note. *God, don't read it. Don't.*

"Trust me?" Ewing asks.

Finally, I give the notebook a shove in his direction.

Ewing offers me a closed-lip smile and juts his chin toward the note I'm unfolding again. "What's that?"

"Something I shouldn't read." He's Lindsey's guy. I shouldn't care, even if he wants to offer me the world on a string. But instead . . .

His words call to me, like the beacon of a lighthouse. I meander through the foggy waters, fighting the waves of my better judgment, until the choice is no longer mine. I'm used to the feeling of coercion, in regard to my own words but not in regard to others'. This, in itself, is hypnotic, magnetic. I follow the pull.

Scan the words.

My jaw drops.

EIGHT

John wrote: *I found your rosary.*

Simple in structure. Four words, and only four words, loaded with complicated questions. Since he gave me the note last week, John and I have been locked in glances that last longer than a blink, practically daring each other to make the first move toward a conversation.

I ruminated, and avoided him, Friday and all weekend. Yesterday, I decided he needed to explain what he wrote, but I really shouldn't be talking to him about anything but Lindsey. She'd flip if she knew John had something to say to me that didn't involve her.

Now, in the moments before American Lit begins, he traipses over to me and leans a hip against a desktop.

Rubbing the palm of his left hand with his right thumb, gives me a quick smile. "Hi."

"Hi."

"You read my note?"

"Yeah, I got it. You got Lindsey's?"

He shrugs, glances away for a split second. "Did it make any sense to you? Look, this is a complicated conversation to have in the midst of *To Kill a Mockingbird*, you know? I mean, I don't even know if you own a rosary, let alone if you're missing one."

I barely get out a shake of my head, when Mr. Willis walks in and bellows, "Places, please."

John's eyes shift toward our teacher. "We should talk sometime."

"Yeah. Okay."

He rattles off his phone number. "Want me to write it down? Or do you think you can remember it?"

"I got it." Already, I'm running through excuses to give Lindsey as to why I have it, should she find out: we're working on a school project together, he wanted me to pass it along to her. . . . Or maybe she doesn't have to know I have it. It's not like I'm going to be regularly using it.

"So give a call or"—he shrugs—"I can call you."

Lindsey. She won't understand.

"Maybe we shouldn't . . ." But I allow my words to trail off. Definitely we shouldn't, but I need to know why he wrote to me about a rosary.

Ewing helped me understand that the rosary was part of the dream sequence in Ritchie's office through the power of suggestion. Because my mother had been drawing a rosary, it makes sense that it would hold a place in my subconscious.

But what does John know about it?

"Places," Willis says again.

"What's your number?" John taps the corner of my desk as he backs away.

I give it to him.

"I'll call you tonight after practice. Five thirty or so, okay?"

My heart kicks up its pace. "Actually . . ." It's a Tuesday. I'm going to be with Elijah tonight. Assuming he shows. "Actually, can you meet up at the Vagabond?"

His lips part into a wide grin. "Sure."

"I'm meeting my boyfriend there, and Lindsey'll come, too." She'll be thrilled. I'll tell her the meeting was John's idea. Which isn't exactly a lie.

"Okay." His brow knits a little, but he quickly recovers. "Five thirty?"

Elijah, if he shows, should come at six, so that's when I'll set it up with Lindsey, too. Forgive me, but . . . "Yeah. Five thirty."

Lindsey's late, and I never heard from Elijah, so I don't know if he's coming.

John's phone buzzes with a text message, which is the ninth or tenth to come through in the past half hour since he joined me here.

"Sorry." He apologizes every time he has to check his phone, and punches answers immediately, this time with a sigh and a shake of his head. "My sisters."

"Sisters? As in more than one?"

"Try four." He offers a shrug and a shy smile as a supplemental apology. "I'm the youngest of five. The girls are planning a bash for my parents' thirtieth anniversary."

"Thirtieth? Wow." I wonder what that might be like, having a big family to text with, to celebrate with.

"Do you have brothers or sisters?"

"Just Lindsey."

His frown begins to take form—"How are you and Lindsey . . ."—only to be relieved by his text alert. "In all honesty, all they have to do is tell me when and where, you know? Theoretically, my responsibility begins and ends with showing up. Not like they'd trust me to actually *do something* anyway . . . One second." He replies again. "There. That oughta do it. So." He smiles.

We're in a cozy booth at the Vagabond on the west side of the shack, overlooking the water. John's sitting across from me, sipping a coffee, black.

"Let's cut to the chase," I say. "That note. The rosary reference."

"Yeah." He looks up at me, smiles, then glances down

toward his mug. "You're going to think I'm crazy."

"Doubtful." I think of my recently refilled prescription of Ativan, which is hidden in the front pocket of my backpack, and remember my mother's commentary on the subject. "Crazy is relative, you know?"

"Interesting that you wanted to meet here." John Fogel glances again at his watch, then trips his gaze around the room, as if searching for something that used to be there. "Ever come here on Fortune Night?"

Suddenly, my throat is dry. "Yeah. They don't do it anymore."

Not in just over a year, but I don't want to talk about the reasons why their mystic is imprisoned at a mental health institution. When I glance over at the bar, I imagine my mother sitting at the end, flipping cards.

A strong sigh slips from between his lips. "You remind me of the woman who used to read cards here." He clears his throat. "Look, Callie."

I've never heard him speak my name before. It sort of stuns me for a moment, the natural intonation, as if he's spoken my name a million times before.

A nagging sensation rises from somewhere in the back of my mind, as if I've forgotten to do something, or bring something of importance somewhere. Just as I'm about to let it go, the word arises from the clutter: *Cobblestone.* *Cobblestone. Cobblestone.* I press my hand against the front pocket of my backpack, feel the small, cylindrical container stashed there. Maybe popping an antianxiety pill would be better than graphing out in front of him. Discreetly, I unzip the front pocket, open the vial, and extract a pill. I don't have to take it. But if I want to, I can. I'll bite it in half, maybe. Just take half. I rub my temples to ease the pressure building in my head. "Lindsey'll be here soon."

"I'm going to level with you," he says. "I don't care if Lindsey shows up or not. I didn't come to see her."

"Of course you did." I don't know who I'm trying to convince more, him or me. "She wrote you a note, and—"

"Did you write it? The note from Lindsey?" He squints a little, challenging me. "You spelled my name wrong."

"Well, I know how to spell your name, and I have better things to do."

Although he keeps fidgeting with his watch, his stare is unrelenting. I know he doesn't believe me. But it's not entirely a lie. I do have better things to do. Just not better enough. The Hutches are good to me. I'd write Lindsey's doctoral dissertation, if she asked, even if I had a to-do list a mile long.

"I have better things to do, too," he says.

My heart beats more intensely. *Cobblestone paths, cobblestone paths, cobblestone paths.* I feel like someone's watching me, watching us. It's a foreboding presence, one I felt on the altar moments before Palmer caught me with Andrew Drake. I scan the sparsely populated café, searching for the familiar glance of my father.

But of course he isn't here. I'm safe, I remind myself. He wouldn't come back here, and even if he did, I wouldn't have to go back to Holy Promise with him. Guidry would see to that . . . I hope. I'm just paranoid. Probably because I'm doing something I'm not sure I should be doing.

John's mug clinks against the tabletop, which is scarred with carved initials and penned witty one-liners.

Memories flash:

my mother spinning through the place, her hair flying. *Clink, clink, clink* as she serves. I'm four, maybe five, coloring pages of a Disney princess book in a booth, reading the graffiti on the wall: I'd follow half your smile for thousands of miles. *Cobblestone, cobblestone, cobblestone, cobblestone.*

This isn't going to be good. I should take the pill.

When John glances toward the door, I stick the bitter medication into my mouth and bite off half of it, which I lodge under my tongue. The other chunk I allow to fall to the floor.

I don't drink coffee, but as my water glass has been empty for an age, I reach for John's mug and take a healthy slurp to wash down the Ativan.

Cobblestone paths, cobblestone paths, cobblestone paths.

The meds will kick in. It'll just take some time. Relax.

He's staring out the window now, across the murky waters of the bay. He blinks slowly, and when he opens his eyes, he's looking directly into mine. A surge of energy zaps me—such power in his stare. It's intense. Intimate. "The mystic who used to work here . . ." His fingers graze against mine, as he takes the mug from my hands. He lowers it to the table. "She predicted I'd meet you."

I freeze.

"Not you, specifically, but you in the ethereal sense. She described things about you, things that would help me recognize you when I met you—specifically that you'd resemble her, and God, do you ever—and she told me to give you a rosary."

"It's called a cold read." I don't tell him that my mother was teaching me how to do it, too. "Vague details made to sound specific. Let me ask you something. Do you have a scar on your left knee?"

He frowns; he begins to nod.

"Okay, then," I continue. "It's simple ergonomics. Most kids, when they fall down, have landed on their left knees at some point or another. Do you know the crazy percentage of people walking around with scars on their left knees? She mentions it, and she's hooked you. She's playing the odds."

"Look, I don't usually believe in this stuff, either. But she called out the rosary. Specifically. She told me where to find it and said I should give it to you. Not *you* you, but—"

"Ethereal me. Right."

"Don't you ever want to blindly believe, Callie?" A smile

slowly spreads over his face. "In something? Anything?"

I force a swallow over the half pill lodged in my throat.

"Hey, baby."

I startle, but manage a smile by the time Elijah is nudging me farther into the booth. Sitting next to me now, he leans toward me, presses an open-lipped kiss to my mouth, and squeezes my leg. "Sorry I'm late. Missed the train."

He smells like fresh air and antibacterial soap. There's a smudge of dirt on the inside of his left elbow. I'm guessing he came directly from the soccer field, after too quick an attempt at washing up.

John offers his right hand. "John Fogel."

Elijah gives my thigh another squeeze before releasing me to shake John's hand. "Elijah Breshock."

The two of them remain locked in the gaze, hands firmly grasped, like they're involved in some sort of showdown. I wonder what Elijah overheard. Although the conversation was cryptic—anything incriminating happened only in my mind—discomfort courses through my veins like polluted water through a faucet.

I close my fist around the tiny marquise ruby ring hanging from the gold chain around my neck.

At long last, their hands part. "What are you drinking?" John asks, signaling again for the wait staff, which has effectively avoided his previous summonses.

Elijah slaps his fake ID down on the table. "I'll take a Miller."

"Omigod, I am so sorry!" Lindsey—wearing jeggings, an off-the-shoulder black sweater, and over-the-knee, five-inch-heel, black suede boots—slides into the booth.

Suddenly, I feel uncomfortable in my worn jeans, T-shirt, and hoodie. I wonder why Lindsey didn't clue me into the fact that she'd be dressed to the nines when she arrived here after the homecoming committee meeting. The ambrosia of mary jane and Vera Wang's Princess wafts in her wake, but her blue-green eyes are clear. Her black hair is twisted up in a claw clip, with a few tendrils framing her ivory face.

"Hello, Jon." Her lips curl into half a pucker, like a bow she's daring him to untie.

After a quick acknowledgment—"Hi, Lindsey"—he glances down into his mug, then back up at me, only to again look away.

Elijah gives her a nod. "What's up?"

Her eyes flash their jade brilliance. "Ooh, we're drinking." She must've seen his ID. Her yellow Fendi shoulder bag lands with a *thunk* in the center of the table, concealing a green *Musicians Do It with Rhythm* sticker. She digs into her bag and produces her own fake before nudging her way into the booth.

As John scoots in farther to make room for Lindsey, one of his feet bumps into mine. We share a glance, but I quickly look away.

Elijah's hand returns to my leg. "Want a drink?"

Cobblestone paths of her memory.

"Just more water."

Someone onstage is singing a bad cover of Eric Clapton's "Bell Bottom Blues."

It's a song I've heard a hundred times or more throughout the course of my life, a song my mother sang when I was a little kid. The memory is misty at best, but I remember her voice echoing through a long white hallway. Afternoon sun slanting through the windows and warming my cheeks. Me, stringing beads on a thread: blue, purple, pink . . . blue, purple, pink.

The image attempts to fill me with a cozy feeling, not unlike the way I feel the first moment Elijah closes his arms around me, but I can't quite grasp the warmth. I tighten my hand into a fist, but the comfort slips away. I sprint down corridors in my mind, searching for the right door, the one that will lead me back to that safe, carefree moment, but I can't feel it, can't find it.

"And the best part about it," Lindsey's saying, "is that the staff will decorate the ballroom for us. So we homecoming committee members don't have to get there early."

My ears begin to ring, drowning out the sounds of the Lindsey Show. Today's topic of conversation—All Things Homecoming according to Lindsey Hutch. Special guest of honor—Lindsey Hutch. Interviewed by your host—Lindsey Hutch.

A plate of bread and cheesy asparagus dip sits where Lindsey's purse used to be. Its aroma is a nagging lure, pulling me from the warm white hallway. Pulling me out of the memory I so desperately want to grasp.

Elijah's bouncing a quarter against the table; it clinks off the rim of a highball glass. *Chink, chink, chink.*

Another memory: cold rain, a shovel. *Chink, chink, chink.*

Elijah bounces the quarter again; this time it clangs into the glass and plops into four ounces of beer, which he'd poured from a pitcher he's sharing with Lindsey. "Niiice." He slides the drink across the table.

Lindsey takes it up, begins to drink. It's the only thing that's shut her up since she walked through the door.

John looks to Elijah and me. "So, how did you two meet?"

Elijah's hand finds its way back to my thigh again. "We had some mutual friends."

Meaning social workers at County. I'm glad he was cryptic about it. No need to go into the day I arrived there, wearing County-issue scrubs. No need to elaborate on his being there for breaking and entering . . . again.

"Been together since the day we met." Elijah's walking his fingers up and down my thigh. "Isn't that right?"

"Just about." I feel John's stare, but I don't dare to acknowledge it any more than I dare to challenge Elijah's definition of together.

Lindsey triumphantly slams the glass down on the table, and displays the quarter she's retrieved from its pool of amber ale.

Elijah refills the glass, pouring from the pitcher.

"So as I was saying, I won't have to be at the hall early." Lindsey begins to bounce the quarter, aiming for the glass. *Chink, chink, chink.*

Again, the memory of a cold night encompasses me. Digging.

Cobblestone.

I shake my head. I can't take it anymore. The medication has done nothing to help the words go away. My head pounds with the pressure. *Walk not on cobblestone paths of her memory. Walk not on cobblestone paths of her memory.*

Everything's getting blurrier by the second. It's coming. I feel it.

"You all right?" John asks.

Elijah, after a quick glance, gives my water glass a nudge toward me. "Breathe, baby." He squeezes my thigh.

I hear the *chink* of the quarter against the table.

"Pay no attention." Lindsey's voice sounds in an echo, as if she's speaking down a tunnel: "Don't make a big deal out of it."

I wonder if John's heard about my affliction, how he'll react when he sees me drowning in the words. I reach into my bag, close my fingers around my red felt-tip pen. My knuckles graze against the spiral binding of my notebook.

The Vagabond starts to spin. I focus on my notebook to ward off the dizziness. It's hot in here. Sweat breaks on the back of my neck; it feels like a pelting of icy rain.

I bite off the pen cap and press the tip to paper:

Walk not the cobblestone paths of her memory in black veiled

I need a new pen. The red has faded to pink. It's hard to make a mark.

Chink chink chink accompanies the acoustic guitar onstage, becomes the wind and the broad blade of a shovel pressing into the moist earth, shifting the dirt, disturbing a resting place.

Black halos threaten to close in on my vision.

I shove my hand back into the bag, in search of another pen. Lollipop. Hairbrush. No pen. No pen. No pen! My stash of felt-tips is in here somewhere . . . just can't find it. Too much stuff. I pile it all on the table: note cards, receipts, gum wrappers . . .

"I'll get it." Elijah's pulling the bag from my lap.

"Here," John's saying. "I've got one. . . ."

Lindsey's sigh reverberates around me. "Has to be red."

My breath comes in staccato increments. God, I'm such a freak.

Chink chink chink.

The room is spinning fast now. I focus on my notebook and blink a few tears onto the lined paper. Try again with the red felt-tip. Only a streak of light pink. I bring it to my mouth. Suck on it, in hopes my saliva will rejuvenate the tip. Just a few words. Just have to eke out a few words before I black out.

A blue ballpoint lands on a diagonal slant atop my note-book. Moments before I snatch it up—I have to, have no choice—Elijah presses a red felt-tip into my hand.

And suddenly, I feel the cool mist of lake water spray-ing off rocks at the shore. Someone's singing. Someone's laughing.

It's my mother. She's laughing.

Laughing.

Leaning back into the arms of a handsome man.

Laughing!

Chink chink chink.

I flinch, and the Vagabond bleeds back into view. I gasp.

"You okay now?" Elijah asks.

"Yeah." I wipe away a tear before it manages to escape, and release my held breath.

Elijah's lips brush against my temple a moment before I hear the quarter plop into the beer. His hand leaves my thigh, quick to snatch up the glass and pay his dues.

When I look up, John's staring at me. It's a casual expres-sion, as if he's not surprised with what's just transpired. But of course he must've heard about the girl who showed up at Carmel four weeks ago at the beginning of junior year, the girl who maybe killed her father, maybe knows what happened to Hannah Rynes, the girl who's a slave to the words in her head.

I wipe another tear.

He repeatedly clicks open and closed the blue ballpoint.

I scan the words, as familiar to me now as my own name. I've written these exact phrases before, but I can't remember when:

Walk not on the cobblestone cobblestone cobblestone cobblestone paths of her memory in black-veiled grief to relieve you. Mourn not for her mind mindmindmind, her beauty, her mouth, drawn down, so quick to believe you.

When I look up from the page, my gaze trips into John's, who was sneaking a peek at my words.

One corner of his mouth turns up.

I feel a heated blush painting my neck, my cheeks. I break eye contact.

Chink, chink, chink.

"So, Lindsey," I say. "When do homecoming tickets go on sale?"

"Tomorrow."

My phone buzzes twice in succession. I give it a glance.

"Who's that?" Lindsey asks.

Everyone who'd normally text me—Lindsey, Elijah—is here. I recognize the number. John gave it to me during Lit class. What's he thinking, texting me in front of Lindsey? In front of Elijah? "It's Yasmin Hayes," I hedge. "Question about homework for calc."

John raises an eyebrow. We're bonded now. By a lie I just told.

"Yasmin's a square," Lindsey says.

With a smile threatening to spread over his face, John engages Lindsey: "She's not so bad. Crazy smart. Going to Harvard, I hear."

"Whatever."

I click on the first of John's messages: *ur a poet.*

No, I want to say. I'm *insane.*

And the second: *slip 43. midnight.*

NINE

This is risky.

But I suppose it was risky to Facebook with him all evening, too.

Something innate is pulling at me, forcing me to put one foot in front of the other, to flee from the safe, warm confines of the Hutch house, into the black uncertainty of night, toward open, waiting arms.

I sneak out the back door, and set the alarm again before I close the door; I don't plan to be back until late. The senior Hutches won't wake up, but I left a note for Lindsey in case she does. I told her I'm going to see Elijah at my old apartment above the Vagabond.

She'll believe me. It's not like it's an unheard-of possibility.

I think about the clinking of quarters in glasses and wonder if she and Elijah now consider each other friends. If they ever compare notes about this late-night absence, I'll have some explaining to do.

As excited as I am to reach the harbor, part of me wishes I were doing exactly what I told Lindsey I'm doing. I want things to be the way they used to be. I don't like keeping things from her. I want to fall asleep in Elijah's arms, awaken to kisses and clarity, and all things that make sense.

Shutter.

Elijah's the only guy who's consistently been here for me, and he's the only one I've ever been with. I made out with Palmer's protégé a few times—on the altar at Holy Promise—but I don't think I would've taken things much further, even if Palmer hadn't caught us. God, the punishment I'd suffered for kissing Andrew Drake was brutal. I wish I'd gotten away with it, without the lash of Palmer's belt across my back, without the rebaptism in the holy water fountain in the center of the labyrinth.

I wonder if I'll get away with what I'm doing tonight.

Anxious nerves in my fingers twitch. Images of red felt-tip words dance in my brain:

Flutter shy. Shutter fly. Flutter shy. Shutter fly.

My hand is in my bag now, fumbling for a pen. I'm wheezing with every inhalation, can't draw in a breath, can't focus on anything but the words engraving themselves in my bones, stabbing my brain.

At last, my fingers close around a pen; a searing pain zaps me between the eyes simultaneously.

I bite off the cap, pull off one of my gloves, and press the felt-tip to my palm. Instantly, I'm sucked into a memory, as if a photograph has suddenly come to life and I'm in the center of it:

I'm running, looking over my shoulder. Palmer. He's coming for me. He's coming, he's coming, he's coming! I dive into the juniper bushes, the taste of Andrew Drake's kiss still lingering on my lips, but I'm too late.

Hand on my ankle.

Pulling me from the brush.

White gravel skidding over my flesh as I squirm to get away.

Thwack! Thick strap of leather biting my back. Over and over and over again.

My head submersed in holy water.

My God, he's going to kill me! Drown me!

Water rushes into my lungs, and I . . . I . . . I . . .

"Callie!"

What?

My pen falls to the pavement, jarring me from the vivid memory.

Hot tears wet my lashes, a sharp contrast to the winter-like wind whipping through my hair. I wipe them away with my multicolored scarf—one my mother crocheted for me when I was small, one of the few tangible items from my past—and acknowledge John Fogel. "Hey."

He crouches, when I do, to retrieve my pen. He grasps it first—"You okay?"—and locks me in a gaze. Slowly, he starts to smile.

"Yeah."

We stand.

"Were you writing?" His eyes, illuminated by the streetlamps, reflect a deep navy tonight. He cups my left hand in his, scrutinizing what I scrawled there. "On your hand?"

"Yeah." I attempt to coax my hand away, but he folds his fingers around mine. I'm freezing. He feels good and warm. A split second later, he withdraws.

"Hey . . . you know, you don't have to talk about it if you don't want to, but . . ." He wets his lips with his tongue. "How often would you say you . . . you know . . . write like that?"

I think about it for a few moments, and consider perhaps downplaying the affliction. *Few times a week,* I could tell him. Or maybe I could respond with *oh, rarely ever.* Although we're still blocks away, I smell the lake; the distant scent is already working its magic on my wired nerves, calming me with every inhalation. And then I blurt out the truth: "Sometimes I fight the impulse to write all day long."

"Why fight it?"

I feel my defenses rising. Adrenaline rushes through my

system, like it does when some injustice has been carried out in front of me—like when Palmer would criticize my mother for the way she was raising me.

In the back of my mind, it's happening now. I hear his boom of a voice from the other side of the confessional door: *She's a child! And you reason with her!*

"What I've read so far," John's saying, "It's beautiful. You should put it to music. You sing beautifully, you know."

I outwardly ignore the compliment, although it stirs up warmth within me. What can I say? That I don't see my graphomania as art so much as a curse? That I don't sing because it reminds me of my locked-up mother?

"You should join me in choir. Or at the very least, keep singing in chapel. Your pitch during the bridge this morning was . . ." He shrugs. "Perfect harmony."

I briefly consider engaging in the conversation, but to me, bridges are things you use to cross bodies of water. If I sing in perfect harmony, it's accidental, not a practiced skill, and I don't have the slightest idea what he's talking about. With a shake of my head, I change the subject: "So what's the emergency tonight?"

"I never said it was an emergency. I just wanted to see you."

"It wouldn't wait until homeroom tomorrow." I glance at him out of the corner of my eye.

He twitches a smile. "Well, I guess it is sort of an

emergency, then." After a few steps, he clears his throat. "So what's up with you and that guy?"

"Elijah?"

"Yeah."

"Why don't we talk about a more pertinent subject?"

"Pertinent?"

"Pertinent."

"Everything is relevant, Calliope."

I'm accustomed to the shortening of my name, as most people find it cumbersome, if not silly, to say, let alone to label a girl with. I feel mocked when people say it, or reprimanded, sometimes. But when John says it, it sounds nearly musical.

I glance at the words I've just written on my hand: Flutter shy, shutter click. Cluttered skies, scuttle quick.

He brings a warm index finger to my cheek, brushes away a few windblown strands of my hair. "Come on," he whispers, nodding toward the harbor.

I shove my hands into my pockets and follow like a lemming. Then again, why should I come to my senses now?

After a few steps, I look over my shoulder. It feels like someone's following us, but no one's there.

Flutter shy, shutter click. Flutter shy, shutter click. Cluttered skies, cluttered skies, cluttered skies scuttle quick.

My heart kicks up a few notches, along with the pace of my feet. In my mind, I'm rushing through the labyrinth behind the Church of the Holy Promise. Trying to get away, trying to disappear in the hedges. He's close . . . so close. Can't let him see me.

Flutter shy flutter shy flutter shy.

We conduct the remainder of our walk in silence, but my head is pounding with the cacophony within. As much as I want to sink into the comfort John offers, this was a mistake, coming out here tonight. Too much at stake—and Lindsey's trust is just the tip of what I might be risking. Every time I sneak out at night, I risk the Hutches sending me back to County, back to the group home to wait for another suitable foster family. Yet even when he leads me onto a pier, I comply, the soles of my boots clicking against the maze of aluminum planks, as if announcing my arrival. I climb up the ladder of a vessel at least forty feet long, bobbing in dark waters in slip 43, one of the outermost slots. *Ikal del Mar* is lettered in flowery blue script on the side.

I wrap my fingers around an ice-cold rail on deck and stare out into the darkness. In my mind's eye, I see the rocky shoreline at Highland Point. Hear the shovel. Smell the loam.

Lake Nippersink rages tonight. We could disappear in the waves, if we were aboard any lesser boat. The waves could swallow us, drown the words bobbing in my brain. I could set sail northward, fade into the forests, fade from Lindsey's memory—and Elijah's, too.

"Come on." With a hand on my elbow, John leads me

down into the cabin, where it's considerably warmer. He takes my vest, hangs it on a hook near the stairs we just descended.

I wonder if my father stole Hannah Rynes into the waterways, if I'll see either of them again, if I'll ever look at anyone in the same way after this experience. I glance at John, who is busy pulling a white duvet from a cedar-lined chest. The ambrosia of the wood, combined with the scent of apples and furniture polish, suggests the vessel is meticulously tended, despite—or perhaps because of—the end of the season at hand.

"Have a seat."

I lower my body to a built-in sofa and unlace the pom-pom strings to remove the boots from my feet. My toes are cold, and so are my legs. Jeans would've been a better choice than cable-knit leggings, but I don't have any that aren't riddled with random lines of compulsive poetry.

He tosses the duvet over my lap, then sits next to me. Close.

"May I?" He caresses the tiny ring on my necklace. "Beautiful."

"Thank you."

"Where'd you get it?"

"My mom. When I was little."

"Huh." He squints at it.

I wonder why he's so interested in it. "So now that you have me here . . ."

Shapes and bright colors tumble in the irises of his eyes, as if I'm staring down the barrel of a kaleidoscope. Squares become rectangles become lighthouses. Blinding beacons cross my line of sight at intervals.

I'm digging in the black of a rainy night.

There's a rosary in my pocket.

I hit something hard. Tap it with the blade of my shovel. Tap again just to be sure. Sounds like wood. Is this it? Is this the makeshift casket that holds my father's corpse?

The voice in my head spews clues. Must write.

It's too much, too much, too much!

I need a pen. The words echo: *flutter shy, flutter shy, flutter shy.*

John's speaking, but I can't concentrate on what he's saying.

Flutter shy, shutter click. Cluttered skies scuttle quick into the vast unknown, into the vast unknown, into the vast unknown. Flutter shy, shutter click. Into the vast unknown beyond . . . Cluttered skies scuttle quick . . . Flutter shy, flutter shy, flutter shy . . . The pressure's building. Must write it.

Tears build, encouraging me to let go, already. I flinch. Pain stabs me between the eyes. I rifle through my bag, grasp my pen. "Flutter shy, shutter click." The words come out in a whisper.

"Hmm?"

I rip my notebook from my bag. Tears blind my vision,

but I see John's blurry silhouette in the periphery. He's going to think I'm crazy, but . . .

"What did you . . . ?"

I pinch my eyes shut, closing him out of my mind.

I'm there again, at Holy Promise. I hear my mother's muffled cries, coming from beyond the closed door of the confessional, along with the slash of leather on flesh. I run through corridors, past the dark walnut carvings of Jesus and John the Baptist, to the door that leads to the bell tower. I imagine I can still hear her: *Don't you touch her! Don't you touch her!*

"Callie?"

My eyes open, only to be accosted by John's concerned, blue-eyed stare. He's holding my head in his hands, catching my tears.

Flames lick at my body from the inside out. I wonder if I'm housing a demon, if the words come from some otherworldly parasite, eating away at my chance to live a normal life.

Coming here was a mistake. Letting anyone close enough to hear the voice of the demon is a risk I shouldn't take again. Elijah and Lindsey. They understand, they accept, they love me anyway. I don't need anyone else.

I swallow some tears and attempt to sit up. "I have to—"

"You okay?"

I catch a tear on my knuckle and look to my notebook:

Flutter shy shutter click. Cluttered skies scuttle quick

into the vast unknown beyond the rain. Rumble high humble thunder. Tumbled nigh, never wondered for the fast controlled, consumed with rage.

"Flutter shy?"

God, he's reading what I wrote. I whip my notebook closed and shove it into my bag.

"There's a boat, few slips over, called the *Fluttershy*."

I'll have to remember to mention that to Ewing. Maybe these words are the product of suggestion, just like the rosary in my dream. My hand falls upon my deck of Tarot, which is almost always hidden in my bag alongside the tools of my trade. I pat it in homage to my mother. "I should go before—"

"You have talent, you know. This doesn't have to be the curse you make it."

An icy current rushes through my system, followed by warmth and comfort when I meet his glance. I'd give anything to stare into his calming gaze, a look that says I don't have to prove anything, I don't have to change. I'm good enough the way I am.

I was wrong about him. He does understand.

TEN

I'm shivering.

Nauseated.

Swaying, rolling, bobbing.

My black surroundings gradually mutate along a spectrum, softening first to a midnight blue, then raging through a cone of greens, yellows, oranges, until a screaming red speeds through my pupils, ricochets in my brain, needles me until I open my eyes.

Light blinds me, as the morning sun beats down on my body, which is wrapped in wet clothing. The scent of the lake rises around me, or rather, from me, as I'm lying in a pool of it at the bottom of a rowboat.

Sobs rack my body, but I express neither sound nor tear. I hurt, I hurt, I hurt.

My head aches with every bump of the oars against the shell of this craft. When I push myself up to a seated position, my stomach retches. I lean over the side of the boat to purge my innards, but nothing comes up. After a few dry heaves, I surrender to the misery, complacent that nothing will come from nothing, and I can't remember the last time I ate. I breathe through the queasiness and try to relax. But it's hard to ease tense muscles while trembling.

A thin, pale yellow cotton sundress clings to my skin. The pearlescent buttons threaten to split open like the Red Sea, but I'm certain if Moses were here, he wouldn't be parting waters to carry me home. A prophet wouldn't help a sinner like me.

And a sinner I am.

Palmer is sure to remind me of that. Every second he gets.

My teeth chatter as a breeze whips around me. I gauge my surroundings, which include nothing but water. Silvery water, twinkling with diamondlike reflections of the early morning sun. In the distance, I see it: a white cottage. So far away.

How long have I been out here?

Too long.

I'm so cold, so weak. But I take up the oars and row. With every pull, the muscles in my arms, in my back, in my neck, strain with lethargy and stiffness. Something shiny entertains me from its position on the boat floor near the aft of the vessel. To thwart my discomfort, I focus on it, as I draw the oars through the water. It's a beaded string. A necklace, maybe. The pendant clangs against the inside of the hull.

Laughter echoes in my mind, the giggly cadence of girls playing yard games. Red rover, red rover . . .

Static washes through my system, and my eyes glass over. Girls' black patent leather Mary Janes—straps crossed over white ruffle-cuffed socks—crunch against pink quartzite stones. Their hands brush against juniper, shedding tiny blue buds from the branches; the berrylike things bounce to the ground and roll to the dirt beneath.

I pinch my eyes closed, and in time with the *whoosh* and *squeak* of the paddles, I count my heartbeats. Push the oars forward, pull them back again. Listen to the little girls in my mind. Pocketful of posies, pocketful of posies.

The scrape of land against the keel is music to my ears.

On shaking legs, I climb out of the boat into ankle-deep water, sink into sandy muck and reeds, and yank the vessel ashore in a small alcove between boulders. I'm at the foot of the cottage. Exhausted. Wet. Cold. The sunlight is the deceiving sort—bright and luminous, yet not warming.

I rest on a boulder and wait, as I can't possibly climb up the rocky terrain after that voyage.

I curl into a shivering ball, tucking my dirty, bare feet beneath the soaked cotton sundress.

The shiny necklace in the boat draws my attention. Small

beads of pink topaz, larger of peridot. My fingers ache to hold it, to curl it around my palm, to pray.

Fingers snap in front of my face.

I startle.

"Dude."

I flinch again. I'm in Lindsey's car. We're parked at Carmel High. I'm wearing my uniform. My hair is a tangled mess of damp strands, and my stomach threatens to turn out onto the floor mat.

"Dude, maybe you should go home," Lindsey says.

My fingers tremble, still holding the red felt-tip I pulled from my bag at the onset of this trip.

I glance down at my notebook:

crimson crimson.

"You look like hell."

"I have a French test today." My backpack rests at my feet. I grasp a strap and open the car door.

"You okay?"

No.

"Yeah."

She's rifling through her suitcase of a purse and finally produces a lip gloss. "Hungover?"

"No!" Lindsey knows my vices; she knows alcohol isn't one of them. I open the car door, and my feet find purchase on the blacktop. The ring slung on a chain around my neck bounces against my chest. I caress the precious metal, feather a finger over the marquise ruby.

"Must've been a late night with Elijah for you to be worn out like this." Lindsey turns the rearview mirror toward her and touches up her lipstick.

I couldn't explain, even if I wanted to, even if I thought Lindsey might understand the growing connection between the most recent object of her infatuation and me. Because I don't quite understand it myself. It was a good night, but not the kind of night I usually spend with Elijah. It was intellectual and intense. Stimulating. Contemplative.

Lindsey casually slings her purse over her shoulder and glides out of the car, as if she's on some sort of pulley system for how smoothly she moves. I wonder why John doesn't want to get to know her better. She's got it all together— looks, money, family. Compared to her, I'm an unraveled sweater.

And these daydream/nightmare sequences are almost pushing me over the edge.

I can't be sure the events in my memory are snippets of my life, but they don't seem to be solely figments of my imagination. The business with the little girls running through the labyrinth . . . that was real. I was watching the younger children of the congregation from my post in the bell tower the morning Palmer committed my mother to the asylum.

But the rowboat? The yellow sundress with faux pearl buttons? I wouldn't be caught dead wearing such a prissy thing, particularly if I'm rowing a boat. Is it possible to meld memories with daydreams? I feel as if I've physically experienced the occurrences spinning in my mind, as if I'm an actress who has played these scenes on screen. I've experienced them vividly, but they have no correlation to my reality.

I do know this: I haven't slept. My eyes threaten to close, and my limbs are still heavy and aching, as if I really did row miles across Lake Nippersink.

Crimson. Crimson. Crimson.

"Are you coming?"

I cap my pen, hike my bag higher on my shoulder, and follow Lindsey into the building. At the first fork, I turn right when she turns left. I stow my navy blue peacoat in locker number 1307. There's a box of red felt-tip pens on the top shelf. I take another one from the box—can't hurt to have a spare—walk a few hundred paces to homeroom, collapse into my assigned chair, and rest my head on my folded arms against my desk. The pounding in my brain pumps through my fingers, my toes, my eardrums.

"Hey, beautiful."

I momentarily lift my gaze to acknowledge John Fogel, who isn't sitting where he ought to be, but my head is too heavy. I can't hold it up.

"Listen."

At his insistence, I reengage. He's wearing a vintage leather bomber over his Land's End apparel. The dark umber of the jacket makes his eyes look bluer.

He licks his lips. "Wanna get out of here?"

I shun the Jiminy Cricket in my head—the voice telling me not to cut class, not to go anywhere alone with John Fogel—and nod. While Jiminy might be right to warn me, he's neglected to realize I'm in no condition to learn right now, certainly no condition to pass a French test.

"Grab your coat on the way to chapel, and meet me in the parking lot." He drums his hands against the desktop for the few moments it takes for me to nod my head again. He offers a quiet smile—"Great"—then saunters across the room to occupy the desk at which Mrs. Kenilworth expects to see him seated.

Crimson.

I'm stunned that he brought me here.

"We don't have to stay long." John walks beside me at a lazy pace, his hands stuffed into his pockets. "It's cold."

I spread my arms wide and float in my tired delirium toward the winding paths of the labyrinth behind Holy

Promise. The wind cuts through me like a razor blade, a blunt reminder of all that's happened here over the years, yet also proof that those days are nearly three hundred sixty-five behind me. Ewing would call me a survivor, and every day that passes is another victory over Palmer Prescott.

I close my eyes, if only to test myself. I can traverse this trail in the pitch-black of night. How many times had I traveled these paths on my mother's hand? Countless. Too many. And on my father's?

"You've been here before," John observes.

"My father insisted walking the labyrinth was an exercise in spiritual centering," I say. "If you concentrate on a question as you walk, you gain direction by the time you reach the center."

"Direction might be good in a place like this. What do you do if you get lost?"

"You can't get lost."

His fingers hook around my hand. "Because you know the way."

"Because there's only one way. No dead ends, no tricks. That's the point. The complications of life are mostly human-handed. Cleansing the spirit ought to be as simple as meditation, reflection, and prayer."

"This is a place of new beginnings." He slows his pace—and therefore mine, too—until we're standing face-to-face between two seven-foot-high walls of juniper. "Did your father tell you that, too?"

We're hidden here, but someone's watching us. I feel it.

Crimson crimson crimson.

"Do you know what happened here?" he asks.

I sweep my glance over my shoulder, over the white stone path behind us, the last known location of Hannah Rynes.

I see no one, nothing out of the ordinary.

Much like the day she vanished.

What was I missing that day? What am I missing now?

"This is the church, the last place anyone's seen Hannah Rynes."

My heart kicks up its pace. My name's been kept out of the newspapers for most of the past year, but I'm not naïve enough to think people can't put two and two together. Anyone who was paying attention to the case would remember that the original report included two missing girls—and I was one of them.

I can tell by the way he's looking at me—narrowed gaze, brows slightly slanting downward in a minute frown—John knows who I am, knows how I landed at Carmel Catholic. He knows about the girl whose memory Hannah Rynes's family rests their hopes on. The girl who can't remember what she saw, or if, in fact, she saw anything at all.

A fiery blush crawls up my neck. I don't know how I can't remember what happened that day. I fear it's written all over my face—guilt, frustration. Humiliation. And his stare is so relentless that I can't hold it, can't bear its weight.

"Your father had lots to say about this labyrinth, and this is Palmer Prescott's church. Is Reverend Prescott your father?"

I consider ignoring the question. If I could find a way to answer cryptically, without lying, I'd do so in a second. But I know it's futile. "Yes," I say. "He was."

"Was?"

I shrug. "Is, maybe."

"I know he's supposed to be some great man, but . . ."

I involuntarily shudder with the assumption.

"Do you think he took Hannah Rynes?"

"I can't prove it."

"But do you?"

"Yeah. Yeah, I do."

"So do I."

The threat of a memory stretches at my brain. The truth of what happened is here . . . in the center of the labyrinth. Just out of reach. At the fountain.

The groundskeepers have already drained the water in preparation for the upcoming winter, but I imagine it in all its glory, spouting the essence of rebirth. When I was four years old, Palmer baptized me here for the first time, yet despite the purity this location represents, memories of its evil haunt me. He had me in this fountain several times, attempting to show me a better way, trying to force me down a purer path. Even the thought of my mother—a softer, kinder, saner version—can't soothe the prickles of dread taunting me now.

The marble ledge surrounding the fountain at the center of the labyrinth is cold against my back; it chills me to the bone. The stone always feels cold, even at the height of summertime, because the sun rarely shines down upon it. I think that's why Palmer chose this place to release his wrath on me.

I try to drown the bad memories with better ones. But shadows flash. I wonder if I'll ever forget.

No one climbed up to the bell tower without Palmer's permission, and the bell tower is the only vantage point from which one can view the paths of the labyrinth. He knew when no one would be looking. He knew when it would be safe to strike.

Distant memories course through my mind; dreamlike apparitions dance in the dark recesses of recollections, so vague they must be part of a collective subconscious. I wonder if I'll ever trust my memories again, or if I'll live in a perpetual fog, recalling things I couldn't possibly have witnessed.

My head pounds with the words and spins with every breath I take until I feel as if I'm spiraling in midair.

I can't, I can't, I can't. Notebook, notebook, notebook, notebook.

The zipper on my bag. It's stuck. Won't open.

I struggle to inhale.

Watch John's nimble fingers work on the zipper.

I need my pen need my pen need my pen needmypen!

Kissing Andrew Drake on the altar; Palmer drags me out the door. The juniper branches scratch my skin as I brush past them.

Slash! My father's leather belt bites across my back, the scent of holy water swims in my nostrils.

Slash!

Blood—my blood—drips into the fountain, a curdling red ribbon quickly dissipating into the pool—red to pale pink to nothing. Fading.

My vision goes fuzzy.

I'm in the garden house beyond the labyrinth, where the gardeners keep their tools. There's a cot in here, too, although I've never understood why. I'm lying on the cot, and I can hardly breathe in the musty, cool air.

He'd dunked me in the fountain to cleanse my soul. I'm drenched and shivering.

Stone-cold eyes like coal penetrate my gaze when he leans over me.

A stale breath puffs in my face. I tense on the spot. Sweaty palms crush me.

John's voice gives me a jolt. "Callie?" A bright light blinds me.

I tumble back through the tunnel, toward the light.

Tears trickle down my cheeks as the feeling of cold marble permeating through the backs of my thighs slowly pulls me back to reality. The brisk breeze washes over me, sends a chill through my veins. I'm sitting on the ledge surrounding the fountain. My hand aches with the grip on my pen.

"Callie, breathe."

My eyes open. I wheeze a "sorry" before I know what I might have to apologize for.

He's squatting before me, and he's cupping my face.

I hook my hands over his wrists, caress his watch. "John."

His concerned stare settles on me. "Breathe." A smile twitches at the corner of his mouth. "I've got you. You're okay."

I am.

I draw in a slow breath, breathe in the scent of him.

My fingertips are tingling.

He gives his head a shake. "You're kind of amazing, you know that? Don't fight this. Let it come to you."

"I feel like a carnival sideshow."

"It's just something you do, all right? It isn't who you are. It's like . . . football. I play it. But it doesn't define me. This isn't any different."

"There's a point to football."

"Yeah, I guess." He bites his lip for a second. "But there's purpose to these words, too."

I swallow over the lump in my throat and brave a glance at my notebook:

Close close close close close the crimson door crimson crimson crimson crimson door crimson door door door close the crimson door in your mind . . . close . . . shattered shattered shattered tattered tattered tattered. Shattered in tattered sheets sheets sheets sheets shattered in tattered sheets torn torn torn torn torn from the will of salvation.

Shattered in tattered sheets torn from the will of salvation.

Close the crimson door in your mind.

ELEVEN

I'm turning through my deck of Tarot, musing that every time Elijah crosses my mind, I flip over the Magician. Maybe he's smoke and mirrors. "I'm becoming my mother."

"Fight it tooth and nail." In the damp confines of the shed, Lindsey brings a lit joint to her lips and breathes in a lungful of cannabis.

Blue October blasts through the new iPod speakers Mr. Hutch delivered to us last night. We knew he'd give in eventually, if only so he didn't have to listen to us complain about how empty our lives had become without music to share. Lindsey's head bobs in time with the beat—lackadaisical, carefree.

I guarantee her tune would change if she knew I hadn't

cut class alone yesterday, if she knew that John and I shared a moment, if she knew he held my head in his hands.

And, God, I can't stop thinking about it. It wasn't an overt move . . . not really. I mean, sure, there was energy there, but . . . but it was probably because of the words, because he knows things about me, about my past.

He doesn't mean anything by it. I don't think, anyway.

"One thing I'll never be," Lindsey says, "is my mother."

"I don't mean I'm becoming Serena in the way most chicks fear in their late thirties." I shove a lollipop—yum, cream soda—into the hollow of my cheek. "I mean I'm going crazy."

Lindsey's ponytail whips around when she shakes her head. "Impossible."

But the words in my head won't stop. This alone I can handle, but combined with the slide show in my mind, with the memories popping up out of nowhere, with the hints of images I can't explain, I'm scared.

Confused.

A hazard to myself.

My phone buzzes with a text message. It's from John. It's the third one inside ten minutes. I turn over another card: a Knight.

"Give my love to the soccer stud," Lindsey chokes out because she thinks I'm messaging with Elijah.

John: *c me 2nite?*

Me: *time? place?*

"Dude, I'm definitely gonna ask Jon to homecoming. Maybe double-date again. That was fun."

I don't think it's a good idea for the four of us to be together. I fear John's stare will linger. I fear I'll respond.

Lindsey kicks her feet, clad in red-and-green plaid Keds—which are new, but came out of the box faded and ripped, to look old—against the wall of the shed in rhythm with the music.

"Elijah's not the school dance kind of guy," I say.

"The old Elijah isn't, but he's a kick-it boy now." Lindsey nods toward my phone, still cradled in my hand and presently buzzing with John's reply. "Go ahead. Ask him."

John: *pick u up at harbor, 11ish.*

Me: *will b there. ask L to HC.*

John: *?????*

"Jon hasn't asked anyone else, has he?" Lindsey asks.

I shrug. "How would I know?"

Buzz.

John: *would rather ask u.*

A warm sensation floods my heart, and my cheeks are probably flushing with something between satisfaction and flattery. A second later, however, I'm nervous. He can't mean that. We can't go there. He's Lindsey's. *Lindsey's.*

"What'd he say?" Lindsey obviously assumes I asked my pseudo boyfriend to homecoming via text message.

I don't like lying to her, but the whole truth will never suffice. "He says we'll talk about it later."

"Figure it out. I'm asking Jon tomorrow."

"I'm going to meet him tonight." My voice is hushed, as if I'm far away from myself, although I know such a thing is impossible. "We'll figure it out by morning."

"Cool," Lindsey says, bringing the joint to her lips and again assuming I'm talking about Elijah.

I close my eyes and lean against the slats of the shed wall. It's raining again. A slow trickle of water beads down the wall, beneath the place where a few shingles have failed above. The scent of autumn encompasses me: crisp wind and wet leaves.

The shed is fading, regardless of my holding fast to the wall.

A barrage of raindrops pelts the back of my neck like bullets from an automatic weapon.

Dig. Chink. Sift.

Dig. Chink. Sift.

Classic rock—some song about a Christian girl about to lose her virginity—filters out of the speakers of John's enormous SUV, when I slide onto the heated leather seat at the harbor.

My skin and clothing are damp with rain, despite my bringing an umbrella, which I'm shaking beyond the door so as not to drench the floor mat. The ink on my jeans blurs with rainwater.

"Hi." He turns down the radio.

"This is crazy." I slam the car door.

"Yeah, really coming down out there."

"No, I mean this." I wave my hand back and forth between us. "You and me. Sneaking away."

His warm right hand closes around mine, after he puts the vehicle in gear. "So what do you say? Homecoming?"

"Yes," I say before I have time to stop myself.

He grins, tightens his grip on my hand.

"But," I continue, "there are two people who wouldn't be too happy with that."

"Two people on your side of the fence." He clears his throat. "What's with you and that guy, anyway? He's hardly around—and trust me, if I had a girl like you, I'd be hard-pressed to leave you—and when he is, he barely looks at you."

"That's not true. You don't know Elijah at all."

"Sorry." John's thumb roves over my knuckles. "But it's true enough. Is he taking you to homecoming?"

"Mine or his?"

"Either. Both. Just figured you'd be going with him, since you want me to ask someone else."

A canyon depresses into my soul, leaving me feeling empty. I suspect Elijah and I aren't going to either of our schools' dances. Last year, we wouldn't have even known when homecoming was taking place, but things are different now. "I think he's seeing someone else at Lakes." Suddenly, I feel as if I've missed out on a lot of things, sort of like a patient emerging from a coma. "But you should ask Lindsey."

"I like Lindsey," he says, shrugging a shoulder.

"Good."

"But we don't have anything in common. There's just . . . nothing there."

A dash of heaven erupts deep inside me.

I pull out my last card: "If you take Lindsey, you'll at least be able to spend the evening with me, too."

"What if I want to spend the evening with just you?"

"John . . ." I sigh and stare out the window. "We can't."

He turns onto a gravel path, twisting and turning through a wooded knoll. "You can't tell me you don't feel this connection."

I wouldn't dare. I feel it everywhere.

The SUV comes to a bumping stop beneath a massive maple tree. He puts the car in park and shifts in his seat to engage me.

Although I meet and hold his glance, I'm acutely aware of our surroundings. Maple leaves slap against the windshield in my periphery. Toward the rear of the vehicle, illuminated by the red glow of the taillights, an expanse of prairie grass bends to the whims of the wind. "Where are we?"

"Near Highland Point." His tongue momentarily touches his lower lip.

I'm powerless to look away.

His lips part into a brief smile. "Feel like walking in the rain?"

With a swift yank, hooking me under the arms, he art-fully pulls me across the consul to his lap. The maneuver is so smooth that I imagine he's done it before—probably countless times, but I'd guess with only a choice handful of other girls. I'm sitting sidesaddle, with my back against his door. When he gives me another hike to readjust, my foot hits a Red Bull nestled in a cup holder. The crown of my head bumps against the roof of the car. Maybe he isn't as practiced as I assumed.

"Sorry," he whispers. "But I can't stop thinking about you. Can't stop thinking about your voice, the words you write . . ."

For a few moments we sit in silence, our mouths linger-ing dangerously close to each other. His breath carries a faint hint of chocolate mint, which always reminds me of the Vagabond, of the scents of sweet coffees wafting from the kitchen.

"I can't do this," I say. "Lindsey's way into you."

"Lindsey and I don't make sense."

"You might. If you tried."

His hand burns against my leg, atop a meter of vengeful poetry: pay no dues to the years in kind, tear and quash, rip the ties that bind. "Can I trust you?"

I wonder how most girls my age would react to this inquiry, whether I'm a freak for answering: "I don't know. Can anyone really trust anyone?"

"Good question." His fingers knead my leg, as if

massaging the words like lotion into my flesh. His breath wafts over my lips.

For a few seconds, nothing is wrong in the world. I'm safe and cozy in his arms.

Half a breath later, however, I'm tumbling out the door when it gives way behind me.

John's hand grips my wrist; his arm folds around my waist to catch me.

But it's too late.

Suddenly, we land—laughing—in a heap on the soft, wet terrain of the Point. The cold, wet earth bleeds up through my jeans, through my sweater. His body acts as an umbrella, shielding me from the heavenly pelting, but soon, he's drenched. I'm completely wet, too.

His laughter rings out in a hearty chuckle, which reverberates against me, inside me. "Sorry," he whispers.

When he sits back on his haunches, and pulls me up with him, I realize I'm still laughing. Straddling his lap now, I'm surrounded by his strong frame. He gathers me against his chest and encloses me into his now sopping fleece-lined flannel coat.

He draws a wet curl over my cheek and tucks it behind my ear, then he trades glances between my mouth and my eyes. Licks rainwater from his lips. "I want to show you something."

"That sounds dangerous."

The beam of light filtering over us from the open car

door slants over his eyes and casts the rest of him in shadows. He peels one of my hands free from its position on his shoulder and presses something cold and metal to my palm.

My thumb travels over the object, deciphers its shape. It's a cross, attached to a string of beads.

Memories flash. I remember worrying the beads, reciting a prayer I never learned at Holy Promise. A prayer to the holy mother. "The infamous rosary," I say on a breath. "You think it's mine." It's too dark to see its details, but I feel the shape with the pads of my fingers. Draped with a shroud. Crown of thorns hanging from the neck. Just like Mom drew.

"Come on," John says. "Let me show you where it was buried."

In a heartbeat, I'm on my feet, grasping the rosary with one hand, while holding him tightly with the other. Together, we're running through the wet and darkness, leaving the open vehicle behind, as if ignoring a homing beacon.

I stumble when he stops short.

"Careful." He catches me a hairsbreadth before I slide to the earth, my feet slipping on the mud.

The scent of the lake carries in on a gust of wind.

A flash of lightning illuminates the view before me, but its impermanence leaves me uncertain about what I think I just saw.

"John?" We're standing on the high land, overlooking a rocky shore.

His arms envelop me; my back rests snuggly against his chest. He presses his moist cheek to my temple. "The Vagabond mystic . . . she told me I'd find a rosary buried up here. Twenty-five paces southwest of the old lighthouse foundation. Was *that* a cold read?"

I tighten my grip on the rosary.

"She also said I'd find the body of an angel here."

"She said that?" Once again, the yellow sundress protrudes into my senses. I feel it clinging to my skin. My mother was sent away months before Hannah disappeared. I wonder what she was talking about, if she was giving bogus information, or if she knew something. Did she know Palmer had been planning to take Hannah?

"I'm thinking she must've meant it metaphorically. Like maybe I'd find you here."

Lightning again splits the midnight sky, awarding me another glance at what's down below. Amidst the rough terrain sits an old, overturned rowboat.

"My God," I manage to say, although my head spins and my tongue suddenly feels too large for my mouth. "It's *real*!" If the rowboat's real, maybe I'm writing more than words. More than vague memories. They *mean* something. I'm trying to remember something.

And the rosary exists, which means my mother's trying to remember, too.

Words begin to emerge, as if from mist, in my mind: *Close the crimson door. Close the crimson door. Close the crimson door.*

I'm already brushing my lips against John's.

Crimson door, crimson door, crimson door.

My fingers feather over the rosary. It's a piece of the puzzle. And somehow, John is, too.

"I wish I could remember," I say.

Close the crimson door in your mind.

"Well, maybe you will someday." Cradling my head in one hand, he brushes his lips over mine.

I smooth a hand over his chest.

His lips part, and he deepens the kiss. Our tongues meet.

But the words still echo in my mind, morphing to kaleidoscopes, blooming and bursting with color. The words become part of me, dancing in my veins, instead of beating at me from the inside of my brain.

I tighten my grip.

On him.

On the words.

On distant memories.

The wind hisses, chiming with the words within me: *remember.*

TWELVE

Dr. Ewing dangles the rosary from his hand and studies the sketch on the table before him. "Your mother drew this?"

"She gave it to me last time I saw her." I've foregone my posture in order to accommodate a raging headache, and I'm lying across the worn leather sofa in Dr. Ewing's office—elbow propped on the armrest, cheek resting in my palm.

"And John Fogel gave you this." He jingles the rosary, as if it's a strand of sleigh bells instead of semiprecious stones.

"Uh-huh."

There's a concave roundel at the cross's intersection, where my mother drew a stone. When I close my eyes, the stone is red, but if ever it was there, it's gone now.

"Uncanny." He looks at me above his Buddy Hollys. Blinks. "I don't think it's yours. There's a name etched on the back, see?"

I lean forward to see it. In tiny, hand-scratched block letters on the horizontal arm: *Lorraine Oh*. It looks like subsequent letters have worn away. "I didn't notice that."

"Interesting that John Fogel would give you a rosary that very obviously belongs to someone else." He glances up at me. "Hmm."

"So let's cut to the chase," I say. "We know the song and dance: you prompt me, you lead me around the block, and eventually I arrive at the right hitching post. The heavens open up and shine down on me, and I say what you want me to say."

He cracks a smile. "Is that what you think happens here?"

"I know that's what happens here. So in the interest of saving time, tell me what you want me to say."

"Why do you think I want you to say anything?"

"John Fogel met my mom at the Vagabond on Fortune Night. He told me."

"They talked about this rosary?"

"A rosary. Maybe that one." I shrug. "He said she told him he'd find a body up there."

"A body?"

"A body of an angel, to be exact. And he knows a lot about me." I gauge Dr. Ewing's expression; he looks genuinely interested. "You'll think I'm crazy—*crazier*, I mean."

His fingers become a steeple under his chin. "I don't think you're crazy."

How can he not? It's my turn to challenge him with a steady stare.

He shrugs and actually smiles a little. "I don't, and I have the degree to prove my discerning is worthy."

"John found the rosary, right?" I take a deep breath. I feel silly even thinking the words, let alone saying them. "He knows something, something I don't know."

"Hmm."

"I mean, I have these memories, almost bordering on visions. The other day, I wrote the words *flutter shy*, and John pointed out that there's a boat called *Fluttershy* docked at the Vagabond Harbor."

"So John Fogel's filling in the blanks?"

"Well . . . maybe." My stomach tumbles a little. I can't believe I'm about to be this honest. With a frigging shrink. Telling him about my string of sexual escapades with Elijah was one thing; telling him my deepest hopes and fears is another. "I feel like there's something living inside me, and John taps it, whatever it is. When I'm with him, I write. Almost constantly. Here. Look." I shove my current journal, which is sitting on the table, closer to him.

"So on one hand, we have Elijah, who's been known to impede the process. On the other, we have John, who seems to encourage the words. Do you find yourself gravitating closer to John because of it?"

"No, but I guess I don't really know why I keep sleeping with Elijah." I swallow hard, unsure I want to admit the next thought. "I think he's seeing someone else."

"Hmm."

"Recently, I guess, I've seen a glimpse of how things are supposed to be."

"Via John Fogel."

"Yeah, I guess so."

"Have things gotten, you know, physical"—his nose crinkles a little when he says the word—"with John?"

I should tell Dr. Ewing about what happened last night in the rain. I should tell him that John Fogel and I hooked up, that making out with him was the stupidest, yet most natural, most incredible and dangerous thing I'd ever done.

Unless, of course, I killed my father.

Did I?

Do I believe in murder?

I ought to, if I committed it.

"Callie?"

"I remember things. About the past."

My shrink lifts his chin. "What kind of things?"

"Well, that's just it. Not the kind of past you and Lake County PD are hoping for. I don't remember anything about Palmer and those hours I spent writing on the bathroom walls.

"I remember things I don't exactly remember doing."

One of his eyebrows contorts, bends downward toward the bridge of his nose.

"I'm crazy," I say.

"No, no, go on."

"It's like a vivid dream, only it feels more real. I taste things, smell things . . ." I shift on the sofa, sprawl on my back. This is real psychoanalysis now—me, lying on a sofa, under the watchful stare of a man in glasses. "It's like when your mom starts telling you a story about something you did when you were little, and slowly, bit by bit, the picture emerges until suddenly, it isn't a story anymore. You remember."

"Have you had any more blackouts since that last one at school?"

I can't look him in the eye, but I feel his stare beating down on me. If his pupils shot lasers, I'd be charred right now. A chill jolts through me. I shiver and briskly rub my arms from elbow to shoulder. "Yeah." In the periphery, I see him nodding. The pressure of his stare is too much to ignore. I offer him a glance.

"How long are the blackouts lasting?"

"Nothing like that first one, not like at the Vagabond."

"Not thirty-six hours?" He cracks a smile.

I know he's trying to relax me, but I shake my head.

"How long, then, would you say?"

"A few minutes, tops. Sometimes not more than a few seconds."

I'm still cold. My head pounds. Words close in on me. *Close the crimson door in your mind.*

"Callie."

"Close the . . ." I pinch my eyes shut, force my tongue to stop moving. Tears build behind my eyelids. Don't give into the impulse. Don't say the words. *Crimson door.*

"Callie." His voice garbles, like when cell reception starts to fail. "Callie, focus."

"On what?"

Close the crimson door in your mind.

I'm trembling now. Shaking. Chilled. I think of nothing, if not my pen, my paper. Putting pen to paper. I nearly taste the words; they're that powerful. I close my fingers into a tight fist. Sweat. Shiver. I can't take it. Can't take it anymore. I reach for my pen.

Everything blurs.

I'm in the garden house at Holy Promise. Soaking wet. There's a pair of panties on the floor. Yellow floral pattern, cotton.

God, what are they doing here?

How did I get here?

If I could muster the strength, I'd stand, but what's the use? The door is locked. From the outside.

From the outside! And I'm in, I'm in, I'm in.

A blanket descends over me, comforts me.

My eyes open to see Dr. Ewing taking his seat again.

The blanket is a blue-and-orange plaid fleece, the type

football fans bring to Soldier Field. Tears blur my vision. I glance down at my notebook:

Sift through as the hours pass.

"How much time do we have?"

"Don't worry about the clock. Talk."

"I don't know what you expect me to say."

"I don't expect you to say anything. Want to tell me about what you wrote?"

I read it to him.

"Any images materialize along with that line?" he asks.

"Ashes. Buckets of them. In the garden house. But I don't know why."

"Was this indicative of what usually happens?"

"Yeah, that's about it." I think of the day in the labyrinth with John, and my breath catches. The terrible things I felt . . . horrific images I remembered . . .

"And what happens with the words, when you're blacked out?"

"See for yourself." I shudder with an inhalation. The tears intensify. They're pouring out of my eyes, as if someone turned on a spigot in my head. "One word, written over and over again sometimes. It feels like a violation. Like something's invading me. Like rape."

"Rape?" Dr. Ewing shoves a box of tissues across the table toward me.

But I can't reach for it. I'm frozen beneath the blanket. The pain at my temples is nearly unbearable. "I feel it sometimes. Vividly." The nausea. The pain. The shame.

"Tell me what you think you remember."

"The labyrinth behind Holy Promise." A violent sob escapes me. I've never cried like this before, not even on the day Palmer sent my mother away. I hear movement across the table, but I can't open my eyes to see what Dr. Ewing's doing. I'm afraid, I realize. I'm afraid of the words—those I'm about to say, and the ones racing through my brain. Afraid of why I think them, afraid of what they might mean. Afraid of what Dr. Ewing will think of me, once I blurt them out.

The world spins before my eyes. I'm dizzy, so dizzy. I feel heels of hands against my inner thighs, spreading me wide.

I can't breathe.

Can't fight the hands.

Can't block out the stabbing pain.

"Warren?"

"I'm right here." His comforting hand lands on my shoulder.

He's standing over me. Staring down at me.

My cheeks flush with humiliation. What a mess I must be. I wipe at my face, but the tears are coming too quickly. I can't dry them. The little bit of eye makeup I'm allowed to wear at Carmel hangs on my lashes in midnight black gobs. I see it, glowing in the iridescence of my tears.

He gives my arm a pat. "Let it out, Callie. It's okay." He moves to withdraw.

I grasp tightly to his wrist.

Alarm registers in his wide eyes in the split second it takes for him to realize I'm admitting I need him.

I hold tight. Manage to sit up.

He lowers himself to the coffee table.

Our knees graze.

I hiccup over a sob. "Warren . . ."

"I'm here for you."

"What do you think of me?"

His shoulders dip. He tilts his head slightly to the left, but refuses to break eye contact. "I think you're strong."

All evidence to the contrary, I'm unraveling before his eyes.

"And, Calliope, you're special. These words . . . your ability to write them . . . it's a gift. Not everyone can do what you've been doing."

I resist the urge to roll my eyes at his attempt to bring me down off the ledge. "Am I a bad person?"

"Sometimes good people make bad decisions. Whether or not you've made a few of those . . . well, we're getting there, aren't we?"

I remember the feel of John Fogel's body in my arms.

I nod. "Yeah."

THIRTEEN

Elijah kisses my temple, while I snuggle in close to his warm body.

It's Tuesday, and we're in the apartment above the Vagabond. Elijah was late, nearly half an hour late, and I think maybe he shouldn't have come today.

My head is pounding relentlessly, poisoned with the mysterious crimson door in my mind. I'm resting my head somewhere between Elijah's bicep and shoulder. His arm curls up, framing my head; he brushes hair from my face.

Today, a single word haunts me: *strangled*. So far, it's just a nagging sensation, but I know it's only a matter of time before I'll have to write it.

The music of a flutist and a timpani drummer filters

up from below. Yet despite this easygoing, beatnik atmosphere, I feel dirty inside.

Strangled.

We've hooked up tons of times, and usually, it's an experience I crave. Tonight, however, I did it out of obligation, so he wouldn't be able to sense the impending end of us, so he wouldn't know that I noticed the faint scent of girl in his clothing. Even while lying in Elijah's arms, I feel the distance between us.

The distance has been growing, if only in minuscule increments, but suddenly, the small steps we're taking to create the gap between us are lengthening.

Elijah and other girls is nothing new. But John's changing everything.

I wonder if Elijah tastes John Fogel when he kisses me.

I wonder if Lindsey can smell him on my body.

It's only a matter of time before my world erupts, and I feel powerless to stop it.

John doesn't—or perhaps can't—understand what Lindsey means to me, and Lindsey, despite John's blatant disinterest, won't give up on him. She's used to getting what she wants, and I don't want to be the reason she fails this time. Thus, I've talked John into doing what Lindsey says she wants—the four of us together at homecoming.

Strangled by cords.

"Promise me you'll show up," I say.

Elijah tenses, then he touches a thumb to the dent in

my cheek, where a blue topaz stud used to be. "Yeah, I promise."

"Come to the door."

"Wearing a sport coat." He tickles my ribs. "On time and everything."

His fingertips lazily graze over my flesh.

"God . . ." He pulls me up, so I'm straddling him and he's staring into my eyes. Yet still, he's holding me close, pressing my body to his. "I love you, you know that?"

My lips brush against his as I speak: "I know."

He fingers the scar on my right shoulder, lightly at first, then applying some pressure. "I wish I'd always been there to protect you." His gaze won't relent; he wants me to talk, to admit I relive the moment the mark came to be there.

I break the stare when I feel heat climbing up my neck, flushing my cheeks. I don't know why the reference to the scar embarrasses me; if I've learned anything from Warren Ewing, it's that it's Palmer's shame, not mine. "I'm okay."

His tongue ripples against mine.

Scenes flash in my mind—partial recollections, anyway, as it happened so fast—of the altar, of Palmer pulling Andrew Drake away from me, punching him square across the jaw. Recollections of the labyrinth, of the fountain. Of the belt across my back.

As Elijah's fingers now caress the spot my father connected with, my tongue dips to feel my sometimes boyfriend's four crooked teeth.

Holy water stings when it meets with raw wounds.

My eyes well with tears when I remember the pain.

Elijah rubs away a tear, while his other hand worries my scar. "I wish I could have stopped him from hurting you."

Finally, his fingers trail away from the mark on my shoulder.

"Elijah?"

He laces his hands into my hair.

"Hannah Rynes was in the fountain that day, the day he took her."

He brushes his cheek against mine, and his fingers tense against my scalp. "You don't know that, baby."

"Right now it's more of a feeling than testimony, but I *do* know. I'm remembering things. Flashes." The pair of yellow floral-print cotton underwear—wet—darts through my mind. On the floor of the garden house.

I withdraw from his embrace, grab my notebook and pen. Stand.

"Callie?" He follows me toward the dark hallway.

The police tape still quarantines the area, although I know it's only because no one's come to take it down. The department has everything they need from this area—the four pens I'd used over the course of those thirty-six hours, as well as photographs of every inch of the walls on which I wrote. They have the little bit of clothing I was wearing, which is probably still caked with inches of lakeside mud. The only thing they found in this room and don't have sealed in an airtight evidence bag is me.

I dip under the yellow tape and cross the threshold into the bathroom. Harbor lights shine through the lone window, illuminating the walls.

I'd written the same thing over and over:

I killed him I killed him I killed him.

Some other nonsensical poetry is interspersed, but Ewing says I wrote it—*I killed him*—a total of one thousand two hundred forty-six times.

Elijah spins me around, props me on the old-fashioned, pink porcelain sink, which stands on two thick porcelain legs and is skirted in a faded blue gingham print. It's been there as long as my earliest memory and is just as tattered.

The words on the walls race around me, becoming red blurs.

My hand begins to ache. A dull pain registers in my shoulders. I yank off the pen cap.

Dig. Sift. Chink.

Someone's digging in the labyrinth behind the garden house.

I can't see her, but I hear her sobbing, hear the sift of dirt in the pan of her shovel.

I can just barely see over the brick ledge of the open-air bell tower, but I can't see past the garden house. Too many tall shrubs.

I press my hands to my ears to block out the sound of her wailing, as my eyes well up with tears of my own. They dampen my cheeks, blur my vision, stuff my nose.

It's pure torture to hear your mother cry . . . and not know how to soothe her.

"Shush, Callie."

I recoil, back away from the hands attempting to calm me.

"Callie! Callie, come on, baby. Relax."

Elijah.

I release a held breath and blink away hot tears.

The red words racing around me come to a screeching halt the moment he stops me from spinning.

I shake out my throbbing hand, sore from gripping tightly to a red felt-tip, and stare down at what I'd just written:

Strangled by the cords of daisies. Close the crimson door in your mind. Escape from the world of the crazies. Tear off the ties that bind.

Elijah lowers his mouth to mine.

An image materializes in my mind, but threatens to fade.

I knot my fingers in Elijah's hair to keep him right where he is. I'm safe and secure while he's kissing me, despite the vile thoughts entering my mind.

Focus.

Highland Point.

Near the steep, rocky shoreline, where John Fogel and I crossed the line.

That's where it happened.

Long ago.

A body.

When I get home, Lindsey's light is on, and a Said the Whale ballad pumps from beyond her door. Still, I'm careful to be quiet as I pass her room, in case she fell asleep while reading—or whatever it is people like Lindsey do before going to bed.

"Dude, get in here."

I'm exhausted, but I can't help smiling at Lindsey's desperate-sounding demand as I push her door open.

She's lying with her back on the floor, one ankle resting on the opposite knee. She's wearing rainbow, over-the-knee socks—the type with individual toe spaces—hot-pink boyshorts, and a white tank top scrawled with a fuchsia *I Kissed a Farm Boy*. Her ebony hair fans on the carpet like a peacock's tail, and her MacBook is open on the floor to her left.

Without awarding me so much as a glance, she shifts the laptop toward me. "Help."

I toss my backpack to the floor and kneel on the plush carpeting next to her. "Oh. Wow."

On the screen before me is a poor attempt at communication with John Fogel, who apparently sent her an e-mail this evening.

I temper the jealous gremlin kicking up dust in my gut, demanding that I stake a claim to John. It's evident by the words on the screen—*I'm totally excited for homecoming. I should switch with Brittany, so I can ride in the same car as you in the parade*—that my pseudo sister's connection with him is more superficial than shallow. A soft spot churns inside me. The night on the Point with him was a spiritual experience; mistake or not, it was more than a cheap encounter. And he's writing to another girl because I told him to.

I want to be angry. But angry with whom, if not myself?

"Why can't I just say what I want to say?" Lindsey taps her fingers against her thighs in time with the music.

"What do you want to say?"

For the first time, she glances up at me. "Whoa."

"What?" I peek at my reflection in the full-length mirror on the back of her door. I don't need to hear her reply. I look as spent and flushed as I feel.

She's up now, legs in butterfly position, pressing the back of her hand to my cheek. "You look like shit."

"I'm okay. Just a headache. Long walk from the marina."

"Dude, tell the soccer stud to drive you home. You don't have to worry about the serial wine taster and the workaholic golfer hearing the car pull up."

But Elijah's foster parents will hear him roll out of their driveway, if he drives. Elijah's on a tighter leash than Lindsey and me, so he always crawls out his window, travels on foot to the depot, and hops the train that runs along the shoreline.

I type:

John,

Backspace and retype:

Jon,

"What do you want to say to him?" I ask.
"That I'm totally excited."
I type:

I'm inspired by the possibilities, all the places we may go, all the things we might see, everything we may someday be to one another.

Hugs,
Lindsey

"You're a genius," she says.
I hit send.
Kiss Lindsey on the forehead.
"Love you, dude."
Head down the hall to bed.

These days, sleep doesn't come easily. I toss and turn over scenarios in my mind—some things in my past, some things in my future, some things in my imagination.

I'm not the only girl Elijah's into. I wonder if I ever was.

What kind of a girl am I if I sleep with him anyway?

What would John think if he knew what I'd done with Elijah tonight?

Palmer said I was a nymph, a servant of the devil, put on God's earth to lure good men to the dark side.

He put me to work on the altar the Saturday night I'd turned fifteen. He said hard work serving the Lord would help purge me of unclean desires. I scrubbed and polished every chalice, every square tile of every mosaic, every plank of that altar table, whilst he ordered my mother to the confessional.

I'll never forget the way her black eyes settled on me the moment before she turned to follow him—as if she knew things would never be the same again.

Their cries of sex filtered down from the balcony and echoed in the nave.

No amount of volume on my iPod, which Palmer had loaded with a selection of preapproved Christian-based music, could drown out the sounds.

"Don't you touch her!"

I startled, dropped a brass chalice when I heard my mother scream that.

"Don't . . . you . . . touch her!"

Unable to listen to another syllable, I'd run out of the sanctuary and directly into the arms of Andrew Drake, whom my father had been grooming to take up the word of Holy Promise.

And then I kissed him for the first time.

I still don't know why I did it, why I kept doing it for weeks after.

A dollop of regret sinks to the pit of my stomach when I think of that night. Here I am—life in shambles—and Drake's now twenty-three and studying to be a minister, taking my father's place in the pulpit.

He regretted it, he said, because I was too young. But he didn't regret it enough. We hooked up a few times after that, too—a few heated kisses in holy places, nothing as major as the trouble I get into with Elijah, but to a man like my father, even kissing is a sin—especially with a man seven years my senior, bound to another and bound to God.

I wonder if Palmer was right, if I'm here only for the pleasure of others.

My phone buzzes with a text from John: *u write beautifully.*

I return: *???*

John: *the note from L. u wrote it.*

Me: *have other things 2 do.*

John: *c me?*

Me: *when?*

John: *look out ur window.*

I traipse across the room, toward the bluish glow illuminating my window. Mr. Hutch's koi pond is lit with blue bulbs, and he always forgets to turn them off at night. I pull back the draperies, sit on the windowsill, and stare down at the pond, where John Fogel is concentrating over his iPhone.

My phone buzzes again: *must c u.*

When I return my attention to the yard below, my gaze trips into John's.

A smile spreads over his face.

I return: *answer first, y u were digging the nite u found rosary. Y listen 2 a mystic?*

He looks up at me, shrugs.

I text again: *y?*

He replies: *what if Hannah Rynes is the body of an angel?*

FOURTEEN

"Dude, just wear it."

Lindsey's decked out in a jade velvet strapless gown with a trumpeting bottom that flares from her knees to her strappy Claiborne shoes. It's one of four new formals in her wardrobe, and if it doesn't accentuate the unusual color of her eyes, I don't know what might. She looks like a mystical mermaid, complete with sparkling, glittered skin.

Two of the other dresses—one red, one smoke gray— are hanging in her closet. The fourth, however, hugs my body like a second skin. It's a dusty rose halter of satin and crepe, and it boasts a slit from my right ankle to mid-thigh.

"I feel funny in it."

"Well, you can't wear Land's End to homecoming."

"I feel funny in Land's End, too."

"Fine. Fucking wear leggings if you want." She reapplies her lip gloss and bats her lashes at me. "You look hot, all right?"

The guys are already here. They're downstairs, likely lifting Mr. Hutch's decanter of scotch, as Lindsey's parents left for a charity dinner at the Whitehall Hotel hours ago. There's a limousine parked in the driveway, alongside Elijah's borrowed Jeep Wrangler, suggesting this is a normal, anticipated high school event, but I'm much too nervous to enjoy it.

How do I conduct myself with Elijah under John's watch? And how do I interact with John? How will John interact with Elijah? God, I hope they don't compare notes about their experiences with me. I hope they get along. This night could be mighty stressful, if they glare at each other all evening.

To assure John I'm thinking of him—and that I haven't forgotten his admission about Hannah Rynes—I'm wearing my rosary like a double-strung necklace. It'll have to be enough for him, as I can't imagine looking at him tonight, let alone touching him, without being utterly transparent. My fingers gravitate to the crucifix pendant, then to the small ruby ring perpetually rubbing my skin, hidden amongst the peridot and topaz of the rosary.

I follow Lindsey down the stairs and into the den, where Elijah instantly wraps me in an embrace. I breathe in the scent of him—all asphalt and manliness today; no rose-scented perfume remnants of the girl about to take my place.

One of his hands lands on my rear, the other, on the back of my neck. "Oh, baby," he whispers into my ear.

"You look great," John's saying, leaning into Lindsey, politely kissing her on the cheek. They look like the ideal, new high school couple, and having ridden side by side perched on the back of a convertible wearing Carmel brown and gold in this morning's parade, they've been acting like one, too.

"Nice." Although Elijah backs off, he tightens his grip on my body and flicks the crucifix. "Where did you get this?"

"It's vintage," I tell him.

This is my first school dance. It's a far cry from the homecomings of Elijah's high school, which are held at the school gym and are no big deal, he'd said, which is the excuse he gives for why we aren't going to attend. Carmel Catholic's homecoming dance, on the other hand, takes place at a resort in Lincolnshire in a small ball-room. Ducks waddle astride the flagstone path down which we're traipsing through a courtyard on our way to the entrance. It's the end of a season, but the gardening staff has replaced the summer blooms with multitudes of autumn foliage. Mums, vines, hay bales, and pumpkins populate the stone planters that rise from the earth at meticulously planned geometric intervals.

Lindsey and I are holding hands and leading the way, which leaves the guys a few steps behind us on the path. This is one of Lindsey's techniques. On the long walk from the curb, where the limo dropped us, she knows John will be staring at her ass. A glance over my shoulder, however, tells me he's taking in other sights, lackadaisically strolling with his hands in his pockets. Elijah's doing the same, with my backpack slung casually over his right shoulder. He winks at me when he catches my gaze.

The breeze is cool, and I don't have a shawl. The crucifix at my throat bounces like an ice cube against my skin. I'm nervous . . . and a little excited.

Quickly, once we enter the building, however, I decide I haven't been missing much. I don't know what I expected, but I didn't think there'd be breathalyzers at the entrance and flasks smuggled into the girls' room, tucked into lacy garters at inner thighs, where rent-a-cops aren't allowed to pat, not that anyone at Carmel Catholic—or the Marriott Lincolnshire—garners a frisking. I didn't get the memo, apparently, because nearly everyone brought something to sip on—even Lindsey.

She takes a sharp sip off the vessel bedazzled in faux purple gems—"Just to calm the nerves"—and passes it to me.

I don't want it, but I take a nip, too. It can't hurt to mellow, considering the night I have ahead of me. The peppermint-flavored liquor burns going down my throat. "John seems really into you."

"He does, doesn't he?" Her eyes sparkle. She takes the proffered flask and tucks it into her purse. "You know, I thought for a while he was seeing someone else. Yasmin Hayes, maybe."

The green-eyed monster within me rises in my throat like bile. I hadn't considered I'd have competition outside my own household. "Yasmin?"

"Yeah, last week in chapel, he kept looking over his shoulder, ogling her. And remember, he defended her that day at the Vagabond."

The snippet of relief I feel quickly turns to nervousness. My heart races; the beats bombard my eardrums. He wasn't staring at Yasmin; he was looking at the girl who sits next to her—me. Maybe Lindsey knows this, maybe she's testing me. "Have you asked him?"

"Doesn't really matter." She shakes her head as she checks her reflection, fluffs her hair, gives her breasts a lift by tugging on her strapless bra. "I think I've got him now. I mean, think about it. He's on the football team. Yasmin's into academic clubs. He needs someone more social, you know? Just in case, though, I started a nasty rumor that she got crabs from some public school scum."

Our glances meet in the mirror.

"What?" She smooths her lipstick with her ring finger. "Oh, don't tell me you feel sorry for her. Served her right, trying to horn in on my territory. If it isn't true, the truth will come out—it always does—but that doesn't mean she shouldn't sweat a bit in the meantime."

Poor Yasmin. "I don't think she's ever been into him."

"Well, just in case. He won't give her the time of day now that she has crabs. Besides, he was holding my hand all through the parade."

I force a smile—and hope it doesn't look forced.

"And it's all thanks to you." She throws her arms over my shoulders, plants a kiss square on my lips.

When we meet the guys in the ballroom, John's explaining to a senior on the yearbook staff that although the sign in the parade read *Jon Fogel*, he does, in fact, spell his name with an *h*.

"Anyone up for a smoke?" Lindsey tosses one arm around me, and another around Elijah. "We have a long, dull two hours here before the party starts."

I'm confused. Lindsey's been looking forward to this night for months, and she's already bored? I shake my head in refusal. But Elijah, after only a mere glance in my direction, shrugs. "I'll hit it with you."

She brushes a kiss over John's lips. "Be right back."

Elijah nibbles my shoulder and flashes a smile, as he drops my backpack at my feet. He makes his way toward whichever courtyard my pseudo sister has secured for her appointment with her bowl.

Seconds later, my glance collides with John's. His eyes soften upon contact. "You're killing me, you know that?

Did you have to look this good for him?"

"It's Lindsey's dress."

"Your body's inside it."

Passion surges from parts deep inside me, radiating out like a halo. "You're one to talk." My voice remains at a whisper, but my nerves are so inflamed—angry, turned on, edgy—that I can't imagine how I'm going to keep it cool. "Do you have to be so good at playing the role? I mean, in the rain at Highland Point, we . . . you know . . . and now you're—"

"God, that was great." His shoulders slouch; he leans against the wall, kicks at an imaginary stone on the floor. "It was like spontaneous combustion."

"Now you're holding her hand, acting like—"

His glance darts up, fiery. "Hey, you told me—"

"I know what I told you! I asked you to take her to homecoming, not fall in love with her!"

"Fall in love with her? Is that what you think is happening tonight?"

I want to hold my tongue. I sound so desperate, so jealous, so . . . girly. I'd never dreamt of putting myself in this position with Elijah, yet here I am: a couple of late-night conversations and a few forbidden moments into things with John, and I'm losing my head. "No. I mean, maybe. Lindsey's amazing. Why wouldn't you fall for her?"

He pushes away from the wall. Without a word, he sweeps up my backpack and gestures for me to follow.

Three minutes later, my back is against the wall in an

empty coat check closet, and John's lips are on mine.

I melt over him, around him.

My eyes fall closed. I smell the lake, but we're too far from the shore for it to be anything more than my imagination—or a memory. I hear the shovel. Feel the cold rain. I tighten my hold on John's body.

"We should stop," I whisper.

"Mmm hmm." He draws out another languid kiss.

I don't want to stop. We're good together. But—

Voices rise outside the door: "Well, they have to be here somewhere!" It's Lindsey and Elijah!

He breaks our connection, backs away, and readjusts his clothing, while I straighten my dress.

I smoothe away a trace of my lipstick from his lower lip. *Strangled.*

We make a clean exit and are standing about four feet apart by the time Lindsey and Elijah round the corner, wafting an overpowering Vera Wang scent in their wake. I cough when the strong aroma enters my lungs. At least it masks the pot. John's leaning against the wall, his arms crossed. The words start spinning in my head. Suddenly, I can't breathe. It's as if someone's sitting on my chest, covering my mouth. I shove a hand into my ever-present backpack, which Lindsey beseeched me to leave at home. With my refusal, she decorated it with an obnoxious pink satin bow.

"Baby?"

Elijah.

But speaking is impossible. I answer only with a wheeze. Shove my notebook at him, when he comes at me. Keep digging for a pen. Lollipops, Tarot, gum, folded square of paper . . . God, that's John's note!

The notebook claps against the marble tiled floor when Elijah drops it.

In surprise, I glance up at him.

"Callie, are you—" Lindsey's voice dissipates, as the words in my head drown out whatever my sister is about to say.

My sometimes boyfriend lifts my chin, crushes my lips with a kiss. He tastes like cannabis and cinnamon gum.

But the words don't fade this time. In fact, they start to scream, reaching an unprecedented decibel, rattling my brain. I'm struggling to draw in a breath.

I pat Elijah's cheek and push away. Retrieve my notebook, take the red felt-tip pen from an outstretched hand. Bite off the cap. Purge. Breathe. And once the words have escaped the confines of my mind, I allow the notebook to slip from my grasp.

Strong, warm hands cup my cheeks. Thick fingers wipe tears from my eyes. "Are you okay?"

No. "Yeah." I flutter a gaze upward and gasp when I see John Fogel's face before me.

Elijah's fingers tighten at my elbow. I gravitate toward him and nestle against him.

"Sorry," John mutters. His glance passes over me, returns

for a split second, then rises, I suppose to meet Elijah's.

Elijah's jaw is set.

Lindsey glides between them, so that her back is to John. She pulls her date's arms around her, leans against his chest, and addresses Elijah: "He was only trying to help."

"Yeah," Elijah says. "He had a fucking pen! The kind she uses!"

"Coincidence," Lindsey says.

I glance down at the pen I'm still holding. There's contempt in Elijah's voice, and I can't blame him. I assume it's as obvious to Elijah as it is to me that John's well versed in touching my face. I'm pretty sure Elijah suspects this isn't the first time John's looked into my eyes.

"You can't blame him for his reaction. Do you remember the first few times you saw her write like that?" Lindsey's speaking to Elijah as if I'm not in the vicinity. And part of me has yet to return. Lindsey's words carry an echo, as if she's still a few halls away, but I know I'm the one not totally present. "Kinda freaky, right?"

"I didn't mean . . ." John's voice trails off. It's the first time I've ever seen him stumbling over words. He clears his throat. "I didn't mean to intrude. Just wanted to be sure she was all right."

"I'm fine." I push away from Elijah, clear my face of tears, and crouch to pick up my notebook. "I'm fine."

When I'm standing again, John's extending his hand in Elijah's direction. Hesitantly, Elijah takes it. John grins. "I can imagine that looked pretty bad, huh?"

Elijah chuckles. "A year ago, I would've kicked your ass."

And I don't doubt it. The Elijah of old has the arrest record to prove it.

I discreetly offer the pen back to John as the four of us head toward the ballroom.

"Pretty lucky you had a pen," Lindsey says.

"Yeah," John says. "Lucky."

But I know he carries it with him now, whenever he's in my company. He carries it for me.

If I'd known our after-dance plans included hanging out on the *Ikal del Mar*, I might not have agreed to attend the homecoming dance at all.

The boat is packed with athletes violating their training rules, and drunken, giggly girls making out with one another—Lindsey among them—slowly shedding pieces of their expensive dresses. At present, Lindsey's walking around in her bra, underwear, and lace-top thigh-highs covered only with John's button-down shirt, which she demanded with a seductive whisper and a lick from his collar to his earlobe.

I'm sitting at the banquette with a group of guys, rolling dice and controlling my intake of bittersweet pink wine from a box. I haven't seen Elijah since he went on deck to smoke up about ten minutes ago, but I hope he'll be back soon. John's sitting immediately to my left, his leg pressed

159

against mine. He's wearing a white, short-sleeved Hanes T-shirt, which I assume he wore under his more formal attire. The cotton hugs his chest and biceps.

"Promise me." He leans in closer and whispers, "Don't sleep with him tonight."

I accidentally-on-purpose elbow him in the ribs. After a split-second meeting of our glances, I redirect my attention to the dice game and apologize for jabbing him. "Sorry."

Without a flinch, he speaks again. "You're going to, aren't you?"

Shame rises, contracting like hands around my heart, slowly squeezing the life out of me. The truth is, I don't want to sleep with Elijah solely out of habit. But I don't know how I can avoid it, or even if I should. I have a history with him, and John knew that before he laid his lips on me. While not all of Elijah belongs to me, we'll always belong to each other, in a sense.

Tiny patch of red.

Not again.

Tiny patch of red red red red red red red.

I pinch my eyes closed when the pain needles my brain.

I feel John's breath against my neck. I know he's still talking, but I can't hear him over the words in my head.

Have to go.

Excuse me.

Need to get out.

But I can't speak. Instead, I stumble over John's lap, for a split second straddle him, and make a beeline for the stairs leading to the deck.

Elijah?

No answer.

Elijah?

He has my bag, my notebook and pens.

Elijah!

Then I see him: kissing some girl on the far side of the deck, his hand fondling a breast through her clothing.

Omigod. Slowly, I back away.

Tiny patch of red. My feet are bare, but I don't care. I pass through the boat's gate and climb onto the pier, then run the maze toward shore, where the Vagabond greets me.

Someone's following me, but I can't hear his footsteps over my own heartbeat clanging in my ears.

Gaining on me.

I'm bawling now, sparring with the demon within me, the devil that won't shut the fuck up. I dart up the iron spiral staircase, toward home. My hand lands on the knob, but it won't surrender. It's locked, and my locksmith is currently massaging a stranger's left tit.

I'm cornered. Trapped.

Elijah's feeling up some other girl.

I'm alone.

Cold.

Scared.

Tiny patch of red.

I spin around to confront whoever is on my heels, but I meet only a navy horizon and silver stars winking from their distant skies. I sink to the grate at my feet and drop my head into my numb hands. I don't have my backpack. Nothing to write on, nothing to write with.

A vicious sob escapes me, but I don't hear it as much as feel it.

Tiny patch tiny patch tiny patch. Of red red red red.

My heartbeat pounds in my ears, deafening me to the outside world, and my head feels as if something is squeezing around it.

Then I feel it again: the overbearing presence, the feeling of someone watching me.

The grate is vibrating; someone's climbing the stairs.

FIFTEEN

A silhouette appears before me. All shadows and bulk. Just as I'm about to scream, moonlight glints off his blond hair.

My backpack lands next to me. My notebook lands in my lap. John Fogel plops down on the grate and encircles me with an arm. He's so warm, despite the fact that he isn't wearing more than a T-shirt on a brisk night. I inhale the scent of him—leathery musk, clean-scented hair gel—and dampen his shirt with my tears.

Tiny patch of red.

I see the words racing over the insides of my eyelids, feel them etching into the soft tissue of my brain, as if the demon within me is embossing the inside of my head with an artist's carving knife.

"Shh." I feel the consolation more than hear it. "Write." I don't know if it's John's voice, or another unexplainable force echoing in my brain.

But I take the pen John offers me, and although it's too dark on the stairs to see what I'm writing, I press the tip to the paper and let the words flow. *Tiny patch of red bleeding up from the heart.*

With every word I record, I regain a modicum of my senses in return. By the time I scribble the last words— *unearth her*—I realize John's fingertips are massaging my head in all the places it hurts.

I appreciate the comfort, let him support my weight.

He caps the pen and stows my notebook.

The ringing, buzzing, beating in my ears wanes, and after a few deep breaths, my sobs emerge from the white noise, match the trembling of my shoulders, and consume me.

"I'm sorry." John attempts to wrangle my hair into some semblance of order, but as it's a burgundy cloud of chaos right now, his attempts are futile. "I shouldn't have talked to you like that. I have sisters. I know better. You *deserve* better."

I don't know when it happened, but I must've placed a hand over his heart because now I feel it pumping under my fingertips. I focus on the beat.

"It just makes me crazy to think of you with him." His chin grazes my temple. "He doesn't deserve you, anyway. I . . . uh . . . I saw what was happening on deck. When you left so fast, I figured you'd need your backpack, your notebook, so I went to get it from him. I saw what he was doing."

I pinch my eyes shut and shake my head, as if I can shake away the image of Elijah's hands on that girl's body.

"And if you were my girlfriend—"

With a sniffling attempt to get my tears under control, I grasp him on the back of the neck and raise my lips to his, but stop myself before I kiss him. I open my eyes; he's staring down into them.

"Give me a chance," he whispers.

"I wish things were different. I wish Lindsey had never set her sights on you. But it's too late, Johnny."

"It doesn't have to be. She'll forget about me sooner or later, and—"

"Even so." I touch his lips to silence him. "Even if she forgets, you'll still be the one who wasn't interested, the one who got away. You're off-limits to me. Perpetually."

"Don't I get a vote?" His arms tighten around me. "I mean, why would I be interested? She's on my boat, in her underwear, kissing Marta Atwood."

"Probably for your benefit. You should be watching."

He shrugs. "Doesn't do much for me."

"Well, she's a little drunk."

"Yeah, her and everyone else. Except us, apparently. And Lindsey drunk is . . ." He shakes his head, as if weighing adjectives. "Just disastrous."

Silence hangs in the air like smoke after gunfire.

His hands frisk up and down my bare arms to warm me. I shiver with the contact.

"I used to live here." I swallow the last of my tears. I want to further explain why I ran up here, but I can't formulate words enough to describe the insanity my life's become.

"Let's go in," he suggests. "Show me."

"Can't. It's locked. There used to be a key hidden out here, but the police took it that night . . . the night after Hannah disappeared, when they found me here."

"They found you here?"

"Yeah. I'd been here for about a day and a half. Writing all over the walls."

"What did you write?"

"Mostly 'I killed him.' And some other things. Same things I write about in my notebook."

A gradual smile appears on his face. "Just like that. You killed him."

"I don't know what it means. I don't know why I wrote it . . . or why I write anything I write."

"Are you hungry?" He brushes a kiss over my temple. "Let's go downstairs for a bite."

I shake my head. "The kitchen's closed."

"Come on. I want to be alone with you for a while."

We're sitting across from each other in what used to be my booth at the Vagabond. Sounds of classic rock pipe in through speakers hanging from the walls on rudimentary hooks. Billiard balls crack into one another, and although the place is fairly populated, a somber hum of general silence depicts the quiet discontent of the patrons. Tonight I identify with the crowd and take comfort in blending in, despite my satin attire and dirty, bare feet.

John's drinking coffee—black—to my hot cocoa. My feet are perched on the bench on which he's sitting, and his warm hand presses against my cold toes.

I sip from my mug, feel the warmth of the cocoa spreading through my insides. It's all the encouragement I need to broach a difficult subject. "You think Hannah Rynes is dead."

His eyes widen, and he coughs over his coffee.

Maybe I shouldn't have asked so bluntly, but the lack of sleep, Elijah's public infidelity, and, well, everything else is wearing on me. Besides, I don't know when we'll have another chance to discuss Hannah. We're never alone if we aren't sneaking out at all hours of the night. And we can't keep doing that. I continue:

"I don't know why you'd be digging for her, if you thought she was alive."

He shrugs, but isn't looking me in the eye. He turns his mug on the tabletop, as if screwing it into invisible threads.

"Do you think she's alive?"

"I don't know. I mean, I hope she is, but after a year without a trace of her . . ."

He nods. "Yeah."

"So why does a seventeen-year-old guy go digging for a body, when no one knows if that's all that's left of her?"

He shrugs again. "Can I trust you?"

This time I tell him what he wants to hear: "Yes."

"I did a Google search on you," he says.

My gaze involuntarily snaps to meet his. "Why?"

"Too many coincidences. The mystic . . . the rosary . . . I wanted to know how you fit into this mess."

"What, are you a detective or something?"

He shrugs a shoulder. "Let's just say I'm interested."

"Why?"

"Look, I know it sounds crazy, but I'm sort of obsessed with missing kids. Hannah in particular, obviously, because it happened so close to home, but given everything the mystic said . . . I searched your name."

"What did you find?"

"Not much."

Good. I start to breathe.

"Found a missing persons file with your name on it."

I freeze.

"It took some digging. Your name's been removed from just about every article I read. The early ones, in the first twenty-four hours . . . you're mentioned in those, but later articles recant, say an anonymous girl—you—had been found, listed as a runaway, unsure of your relation to the case."

My heart is beating like crazy. My fingertips tingle like mad.

"Did you run away that day? Is that why you were gone?"

I had run away before, when Palmer had taken to flogging me daily for my preoccupation with Andrew Drake, but . . . "No."

"But the fact remains. You were missing the same time as Hannah. Were you with her that day?"

I shake my head, fight the images pouring into my brain. Something about the fountain situated at the center of the labyrinth . . . I feel the cold marble edge against my back, feel the rush of holy water against my face. "Look, I don't know what happened to her. I wish to God I did, but I don't know anything but what I write—"

"Is *that* why you write the way you do?"

"—and none of it makes any damn sense to me." I glare at him in frustration. "It doesn't make sense to me, and it doesn't make sense to the cops. I can't possibly explain it to you, simply because you're *interested*."

"It's okay," he says. "Whatever you went through that night, or even before that night, you came out of it with a voice."

"It's a voice I can't use," I say. "I don't remember what happened."

"You're using it, Callie. Every time you write. Every time those poetic words flow from your fingers."

Maybe it's just poetry to him; I'm glad, as I wouldn't

wish this hell on anyone. But I'm starting to think that every word, however confusing, is about the day Hannah disappeared, which means every word could potentially save Hannah Rynes's life. It could also be good for nothing. "I don't remember. No matter how much I write, I just can't remember."

"Maybe you will one day." A hint of a smile appears in his lips.

"Maybe I won't. Will you still be interested, even if I never remember?" I raise a brow.

"I have a cousin—my godfather, my dad's brother's son—who went missing fourteen years ago. No one's seen or heard from him since. No trace of him. No leads to follow. Which isn't the case with Hannah. They've got a lead with your father. They've got one with you, and—"

"But I don't remember anything."

"—and they have one with this mystic."

At this, my eyes widen.

"I . . . I know it sounds crazy," he says, "but the mystic . . . she draws a line between Hannah's case and my cousin's. She told me it was going to happen."

"She knew Hannah'd go missing?"

"Well, not Hannah, exactly. But . . . okay . . . she was reading my aura."

I feel a smile coming on. It's a mystic's parlor trick. Hook potential readings by describing the target's aura. "What color was it?"

"I don't know, blue? Bluish purple? To be honest, I wasn't paying much attention, until she told me she'd seen my watch a hundred years ago. Of course, I hadn't been wearing it that day, because we'd been on the lake, but she described it to me down to the inscription on the back."

I trade glances between his watch and his navy eyes. "Wait."

"She knew it was a family heirloom, she knew—"

"Wait." Pictures of the watch around another man's wrist flash with intensity in my memory bank. I close my eyes and massage a temple. "I remember this."

"How—"

"Shh."

He shuts up.

It's coming to me. I focus on the memory of his watch. Smell the lake. I concentrate until I feel the watch in my grasp, trail my fingers over the words.

"Only you," I whisper. "Only you." I open my eyes.

John's lower lip descends a fraction.

I press my lips together and shrug.

"How'd you do that?" he asks.

"I just saw it."

"How?"

I shake my head. "I . . . I don't know. I mean, it's possible I might've overheard your reading."

"No."

"Actually, yes. It is possible. I used to spend a lot of time here."

He adamantly refuses to consider my theory with a persistent shaking of his head. "No, no, no. A: if you were here, I would've seen you."

"Not necessarily."

"Yes, necessarily. A girl like you . . . I would've noticed you like I did on your first day at school. And B: if you overheard, you wouldn't have had so many questions about the rosary. You would've known that I first thought it belonged to you because of your voice—you were singing that day in chapel, remember—and if you'd overheard, you'd have known long before I gave it to you that you have the missing stone."

"What?"

"The missing stone. The one that belongs in the cross."

It's my turn for refusal. "I don't know what you're talking about."

"Exactly. You still don't know, and I'm not one hundred percent sure about this, either. But that tiny ring you wear on your necklace . . . the ruby . . . doesn't it look like it's supposed to fit into the center part of the cross?"

My fingers rake under the string of topaz and peridot until I find the ring.

"That ring." He nods toward my chest. "The ruby in that ring . . ."

Frantically, I pull the rosary from my neck, unclasp the

chain I've been wearing since about birth. I fumble it and the ring spins on the table until John stills it with his palm.

With trembling fingers, I take it from his hand. I trace the concave in the crucifix, then touch the marquise ruby, like I've done a thousand times before. Feels like a fit. Maybe I would've caught on sooner, had I paid more attention. But it's been fastened around my neck for as long as I can remember. I haven't given it more than a quick acknowledgment, let alone a intense scrutiny, since my mother gave it to me.

When I look up at John, his eyes look bluer than ever.

"And the mystic told you I had this?"

"Yeah."

I wonder why she never told me.

"She didn't tell me it was you, as in 'Calliope Knowles has the missing stone.' She said I'd know you by your voice, that you'd sing, and I'd know."

That sounds like something she'd say, all right. Cryptic, yet intriguing. Incredibly vague.

"She also said I'd have to keep you safe, that you were gone, and I had to help you come home. That the rosary should be placed with you, to protect you, to lead you home. She didn't call you out by name—she was very careful about that—but . . ." His voice is soothing, calm. "If you ever wondered why I couldn't stop looking at you at school, it's because you look a lot like the mystic, just like she said you would. I'd been expecting a girl named

Lorraine . . . you know, because it's carved on the back of the rosary. I'd done a few searches online for a *Lorraine Oh*, and even Lorraines with last names that begin with *O H*—it looks like maybe other letters were worn off—but I couldn't find anything but Facebook pages, and not one of those girls replied when I wrote about the rosary. I searched missing girls named Lorraine, and I didn't find anything there, either. It was a frustrating search. And then . . . then I heard you sing. That afternoon, I searched your name, found out you were missing once, and I stopped looking."

"Given the chance"—I sip my cocoa—"would you want to talk to this mystic again?"

"Well, obviously, but she isn't here anymore. And they don't know where she went. I asked."

"I know where to find her. She's not always reliable, you know, but, John . . ." I engage him in a stare, as I look into his eyes. He knows a lot. My mother invited him into this mess long before I met him. I take a gamble: "She's my mother."

He shrugs a shoulder. "I might have guessed that."

I wonder how he'll react when I reveal what's next:

that my mother isn't a mystic at all. She's just a burnt-out soul with a lot of unexplained information, a deck of Tarot cards, and one hell of an imagination. The fact that she led him anywhere but on a wild goose chase is the only amazing element of his history with her.

"And how is it she drew a line between Hannah's case and your cousin's?"

"Well . . ." He unbuckles his watch and places it in my hand. I turn it over, see for myself the engraving I somehow knew I'd find on the back of it. "That watch," he says. "It used to be my cousin's."

SIXTEEN

I pull a pink feather boa from a tangle of arms and legs. Lindsey's passed out, entwined on a bed on the *Ikal del Mar* with Marta and two other girls. "What a mess."

"Always, after a night like this." John's heavy sigh is the only clue to his exhaustion. He sweeps beer can after beer can from the built-in bureaus and into the trash.

"I'll help clean up tomorrow."

"Tomorrow." He lets go of the waste can and glances around the room before meeting my gaze. "Tomorrow will be an interesting day, won't it?"

He's right. Tomorrow, everything will be different.

The soft sounds of Marta's iPod emanate from the next room, where the last two guests of the evening—John's teammates, the dates of the girls in bed with my sister—chew on unlit cigars and sip on Mr. Fogel's bourbon.

Elijah's gone. Probably left with that girl when the crowd started to thin out. The thought of it both debilitates me and relieves me. If he's doing what I think he's doing, the time I spent with John tonight is more than forgivable.

"Well"—John smiles—"let's get you home."

While I gather Lindsey's dress, her shoes and mine, and her bowl and stash, John lifts her from the mattress and carries her out to his SUV.

I join him in the harbor parking lot and slide onto the front seat because Lindsey's sprawled in the back.

He glances back at his date, then turns the key in the ignition and reaches over the center consul and places his hand on my thigh.

As much as I'm addicted to his touch, I'm uneasy. Any moment, Lindsey might open her eyes and witness the intimacy between us. As much as I want her to sleep until morning, if only to give myself an extra stay of execution, she has to wake up some time. I can't carry her into the house on my own.

A few minutes later, in the Hutches' driveway, which is barren of Elijah's borrowed car, she won't budge. John determines he'll have to toss her over his shoulder to get her to bed. It's late, but Lindsey's parents aren't yet home. This isn't good news. They're less of a threat whilst Ambiened to the gills.

But maybe it's just early enough to deposit Lindsey into her bed and sneak John back out of the house before they return home from their night out.

I lead him up the back staircase, down the long hallway to Lindsey's room. I kick aside the pair of DKNY jeans rumpled on the floor, and turn down her covers. He spills her onto the designer sheets and pecks me on the cheek, on his way toward the door, while I tuck her in.

But the sound of the garage door stills him before he sets foot in the hallway.

I nudge him, but he's frozen, bolted to the floor. I finally yank him by the arm, and push him into my room.

"Wha—"

"Shh. Stay." I close the door and dart across the hallway to Lindsey's room, where I stick her iPod into the docking station, turn it on, and jump onto the bed. I'm lying with my back to the door, hopefully blocking any view of their drunken daughter, should the Hutches peek in.

Footsteps slow outside the door for a few measures, but then continue.

Just as I'm about to breathe a sigh of relief, the door creaks open. A stream of dim light filters into the room.

"Whose car is that?"

Fuck. Didn't think of that.

I look over my shoulder at Mr. Hutch, who is backlit by the dim hallway light, and hope he can't see more than the shadows of our bodies. "Um, it's John's. Lindsey's date's."

"Where's he?" His gaze sweeps the room, I assume in search of an extra body.

I swallow hard. I'm going to have to lie. I'm not good at lying, due to lack of practice. Lying, particularly to the Hutches, is new territory for me. Usually, I let Lindsey handle questions from her parents, since she's been getting away with murder for sixteen years. But seeing as she's indisposed . . . I try out a few replies in my head—I borrowed the car to get us home on time, he left it here when the limo came—but eventually blurt out mostly the truth: "He'll be back tomorrow to get it. Early."

Mr. Hutch's creased brow knits a degree further before his head bobs in acceptance. "Okay."

Wow. Vague, but no further questions.

"Everything all right?" my foster father asks.

I rake through Lindsey's hair and hope it appears as if I'm comforting her. "Just some . . . boy stuff." I'm not just saying this only because I know Mr. Hutch is afraid of the topic, although that's certainly a bonus, but because it's true. Lindsey might not know it yet, but we have a huge boy conundrum ahead of us. And I don't know if we'll make it through.

"Oh." Mr. Hutch takes a step back.

I hold his gaze.

"Well, get some rest."

I nod. "We will."

He closes the door.

I rest my head on a pillow and study Lindsey's face—still made up and flawless. John Fogel is no more than a passing interest for her. If he'd responded the way he should've, the way she'd expected him to, they'd already be living the last chapters of their couplehood, and she'd be on to the next big thing. Homecoming would've been the pinnacle, and she would've been over him. But because her life has been so easy, she doesn't know or understand this. In her mind, there's always a chance at Happily Ever After—why wouldn't there be?—and there's always a prince ready to kiss her feet.

It isn't Lindsey's fault her scope of the world is so narrow. It's enviable, actually. Charming. She lives under the illusion that life is like a cupcake—sweet, delicious, uncomplicated, and not a bite more than she can handle—because hers is anything but inconvenient, let alone difficult.

She certainly doesn't deserve what's coming—no one would—and I'll receive the brunt of her anger, when the illusion begins to crumble.

We've never let a guy come between us before, primarily because I've always had Elijah, and I've never needed someone she wants. If this were solely about a guy, I'd send him packing. But this is bigger than John Fogel's gorgeous blue eyes, his strong arms, his uncanny ability to kiss me into oblivion. This is beyond my control.

I sweep a few strands of hair from Lindsey's forehead, kiss her cheek, and wish her sweet dreams. Tonight may be the last night she falls asleep happy for a while. Tonight may be the last time I feel this close to her. I want to fall asleep with her breathing next to me, to hold on to this moment. She'll always be my sister, but I don't know if I'll always be hers.

Can I live without Lindsey?

No. My heart aches with the thought of it.

But I can't live the way I've been living, either.

This isn't a matter of choosing between my best friend and a guy, between my head and my heart; this is about choosing between clarity and clouds. If I want to live in a cave for the rest of my life, with those thirty-six hours a blackout and the possibility of my father's blood on my hands, or Hannah's, I can turn my back on John Fogel, push him into Lindsey's arms. But that cave might be the death of me.

John's the key. My mother chose him to protect me, and I remember things when I'm with him. One day, these clues might finally put an end to my suffering. In exploring these mysteries with him, I might someday write the last of the words consuming my soul. What's more, I might learn what happened to my father—and to Hannah.

After a while, when I'm certain my foster parents are asleep, I return to my room, where John Fogel is seated under the window, reading last week's notebook by moonlight.

"Hi," I whisper.

He looks up. "Everything okay?"

Tears rise, fruit of the battle raging inside my head. "I can't believe we're going to hurt her like this."

"Do we have a choice?" He's on his feet now and I lean into his embrace. "She could decide," he says. "She doesn't have to pursue me."

"In her mind, she does."

"But why? I gave her no indication—"

"That was before you turned into super-boyfriend at the parade." I shake my head, rumpling my hair against his chest. "She was wearing your jersey, holding your hand! God, what kind of a sister am I?"

"I wouldn't have taken her to homecoming, if it weren't for you. Some might say you're doing everything you can to make her happy."

"Was. Now I'm hooking up with you in coat closets. Even though I have a boyfriend."

"Had. You had a boyfriend, right? He was . . ." He trails off. I know he doesn't want to say the words any more than I want to hear them.

I don't have the energy to explain to John that Elijah's indiscretions on the boat weren't his first, and that his infidelity doesn't make me love him any less. I don't quite understand it myself. I voice the mantra repeating in my head: "Elijah might deserve this. Lindsey doesn't."

"Calliope, listen. We aren't doing this to her. She's taking part, too."

"We set her up."

"No. Well, sort of."

"I wrote the notes that got you together! You know that!"

"From a certain point of view, I guess we did set her up. But look, I didn't say this wasn't complicated." He lifts my chin with two fingers.

"I'm tired of complicated. I want a clear head." I want things to be the way they used to be—Elijah here to catch me when I fall, my mother reading Tarot at the Vagabond, Hannah Rynes skipping through the labyrinth.

"Your life is too big for you," he says.

"Lately, yes."

"You must be exhausted."

I climb into bed, still in my dress.

I know I have to get John out of the house. I'll have to walk him down and reset the alarm. But just for a moment . . .

I hear the click of the doorknob lock, then feel the length of John's body sliding in next to me. "You really are a poet, Callie, you know that? If these words didn't torment you, I'd beg you to foster this talent, turn your poems into song."

"Perfect harmony," I whisper.

He's still wearing his clothes, and he isn't touching more than my cheek. But I need more. I reach for him.

Our mouths meet.

He shifts, and I find myself atop him. My tears rain down over him.

"Shh." He holds me close. "We can make it better."

The sounds of seagulls reach my ears. Waves crash in the distance. The scent of hyacinth wafts in through a sunny window.

I know I'm not really there, in that white room on the rocky shore—and maybe I never was—but it feels real, and so right.

His hands hold me tight to his body. "Callie," he says on a breath. "Don't ever run away again."

Judgment.

When I awaken, the word relentlessly ricochets in my brain.

Judgment.

It's hard to focus on anything other than the word, but I train my eyes on my alarm clock. Neon green geo-cubes glare at me: 4:37 in the morning.

Judgment, judgment, judgment.

Have to write it before it gets out of hand.

I move to slide out of bed, but I'm trapped. Shackled.

I gasp, fighting for liberty, attempting to wiggle my way free.

Judgment like the moon.

Something long and hard presses against my back. Something unmistakably male. Masculine arms surround me.

"Elijah," I whisper.

My hand travels up a warm arm, past a shoulder to a neck to a cheek. I flinch.

Not Elijah.

In a rush, the events of the night scream through my mind:

John's asleep next to me.

In the Hutches' house.

"Wake up," I whisper, giving him a shake.

He murmurs a bit, but doesn't budge.

Judgment.

I jump out of bed, yank on a dresser drawer, look for something to wear. I dart into a Carmel Catholic sweatshirt and a pair of old sweats cut off at the calves. "Johnny!"

This time, he jolts. Gauges his surroundings. "Callie."

"We fell asleep." Finding his clothes proves more difficult. A sock here, his shirt there, his boxers bunched in a twisted ball of sheets . . .

"Sorry." He shoves his arms through sleeves and pulls the shirt over his disheveled, blond head. "Just felt good to hold you." He rubs an eye and gives me a tired, boyish smile.

I sink into the glory of the moment for a split second before my nerves kick in. *Judgment like the moon.* "You have to go." I step over the puddle of mauve satin that is last night's dress and hope the wrinkles will pull out if I hang it in a steamy bathroom.

My heart is racing as I stand at the doorway. Hair pricks on the back of my neck, as if someone's watching me, as if someone knows I've sinned. It's the same feeling I get when I'm walking the labyrinth, the same feeling that disturbs me whenever I sneak out late at night to meet Elijah. But this time, it doesn't make sense. I'm—we're—surrounded by four walls. There's no way Palmer could be watching me. I mentally give him the finger and place my hand on the doorknob. Here goes. I take a deep breath and listen hard.

Hold no judgment like the moon.

No sounds stir in the hallway, so I slowly open the door.

Stealthily, we creep down the hall, to the back staircase. The third step creaks when my foot lands on it, but after a brief pause, I decide that none of the Hutches heard. We continue.

I key in the alarm code and open the door.

John gives me a hurried kiss on the lips. "Holy Promise," he whispers. "Ten."

"I'll be there." I close the door, reset the alarm, and let out a long breath of relief.

I watch as he unlocks his car door, opens it, and gets in. He starts the car. Gives me a wink and a smile. Puts the car in gear. Looks over his shoulder as he backs down the driveway.

Warmth spreads in my gut like butter on fresh-from-the-oven bread.

This is a new feeling for me, a new emotion, and while it's confusing, it feels good. Fulfilling.

I begin to climb the stairs and rub sleep from my eyes. Must write. Must sleep.

Hold no judgment like the moon.

Must hold John Fogel again. Must do lots of things with John Fogel again.

"What the fuck was that?"

"Oh, God!" I put my hand over my heart. Grasp the railing to steady myself. Stare into Lindsey's eyes.

Mascara is caked on her lower lashes. She wipes at it with the cuff of the oversized shirt she's been wearing since she demanded John remove it on the *Ikal del Mar.* "What. The. Fuck."

SEVENTEEN

I shove a grape Tootsie Pop into my mouth. I spread the wrapper flat atop my notebook, and peruse the waxy, purple paper for the warrior shooting the star. When I was small, I used to think finding him on my wrapper meant good luck was about to come my way, and let's face it; I need all the help I can get.

No such luck. No warrior today. I shove the wrapper into my backpack, which is propped against my hip.

We're sitting in the shed, Lindsey and me, but while I'm seldom at ease here, never before has this place felt more like a courtroom. There's a red felt-tip pen clipped to the collar of my sweatshirt, but seeing my sister at the top of the stairs scared the words off the tip of my tongue, so I've yet to use it. But I know the words will come back eventually.

She didn't bring her iPod, so the place is deathly quiet, save the far-off sounds of Canadian geese squabbling. They're probably in a V formation, on their way to some southern paradise.

I'd like to be a goose right now, and not just because I can't seem to get warm. If I could, I'd fly away—far from here, far from Elijah Breshock and John Fogel, far from the Hutches. However good they've been to me, I know it's all about to change.

The crackle of burning leaves accompanies the hiss of Lindsey's inhale. What I wouldn't give to be able to numb my mind with mary jane, to be able to mask the truth of my thoughts. But I'll need a clear head later.

I scribble words onto the cover of my notebook:

Hold no judgment like the moon.

"You wanna tell me what the hell happened last night?" Lindsey's irises practically glow, and her lashes are still matted with old mascara. The blue-green shines from the center of the raccoon rings like jewels among coal.

I pull the candy from my mouth—"You were making out with Marta"—and shove it back into the hollow of my cheek.

"I know." She shrugs. "Was he mad?"

My brows come together. "I don't think so."

"But he didn't like it."

"I don't think he did. No."

"Okay." She brings her bowl to her lips and lights the grass again, holds her smoke.

The suspense is killing me. I can't sit here and wait for her to ask for meticulous details until something trips me up. "Elijah cheated on me last night."

At this, her glance darts to mine.

"Publicly," I add.

A puff of smoke escapes her lips, followed by a full-blown cloud. "Asshole."

"Yeah."

"With who?"

"I don't think she goes to our school."

"He sleep with her?"

"I didn't stick around to see." I bite into the sucker, crack it in half with my molars. "I um . . . I ran." Crunch, crunch, crunch. "To the Vagabond."

"Why didn't you come get me? Dude, I would've . . ." Her eyes soften. "Are you okay?"

"I don't think it's hit me yet."

"Is that why . . ." She licks her lips and refuses to break eye contact. "Is that why you spent the night with Jon? You needed someone to talk to, and I was out of it?"

Her eyes are pleading with me to give her an explanation she can buy.

I don't want to lie to her. I know a lie is only going to delay the inevitable, and when the truth eventually comes out, the consequence will be far worse if I lie now. But I can't heap more onto my already overflowing plate. Double, delayed insult is better at the moment than being tossed out of the Hutches' home. I'll deal with the fallout of a half-truth later.

"I didn't spend the night with him," I say. "I spent the night with you. In your bed. Ask your dad. He came in, saw us there." I tell her about John's carrying her inside, about her parents coming home in the middle of it. I explain that I was trying to protect her. She was drunk, I remind her, and half clothed. There was a boy in her room, and his car was in the driveway. What choice did I have?

"So when you and Jon came out of your room this morning, it was only because you just woke him up to get him out of the house."

"Yes." But flashes of hooking up with him play like a movie in my mind.

"Did you kiss him?"

"I'm in love with Elijah."

"He cheated on you."

"Wasn't the first time, won't be the last." I lift a shoulder and let it drop. "Doesn't matter. I love him."

"Do you?" I see it in her eyes: she wants to believe me. Still, she baits me: "You like sex, you said so yourself. Maybe you like it too much."

"Maybe I'm comfortable with it, but that doesn't mean I've—"

"Maybe you're a whore."

My heart bottoms out in my stomach. Maybe I am. Last night, I slept with John, and earlier this week, I slept with Elijah. Tears well in my eyes. What kind of a girl am I?

"Yasmin got crabs." Lindsey shrugs. "Maybe you get to be a whore. Don't fucking cross me. Not with Jon."

My jaw descends a fraction of an inch before I pull myself together. "I wouldn't."

"Correction: you shouldn't. There's nothing wrong with a retaliatory fuck, I suppose. The rat's ass deserves it. But there's a matter of choice involved. Don't do this with Jon."

All is silent for a few dreadful moments.

I focus on Lindsey's bowl, which is resting easily in her grasp.

"I saw the way he looked at you, you know." She clears her throat. "At the dance, when you were writing."

"He was worried about me."

"I worry about you, too."

"You don't have to."

"And he had a pen. The kind of pen you use! He knew what you were looking for."

"Coincidence," I hedge. "You said so yourself."

"No one believes that was a coincidence." She slithers off her beanbag chair and crawls a few paces to mine. She rests her head on my lap. "Dude, I'm so stoned."

I rake through her hair. "I know."

"I love you," she says.

"I love you, too."

"Snuggle." She tightens her arms around my waist.

I brush hair from her face.

"Don't let him come between us." If she weren't high, she wouldn't be this honest with me. She wouldn't be this needy. This vulnerable.

I want to assure her nothing is more important to me than our sisterhood, to wrap her in strength and security, to tell her I'd never hurt her. So I do the only thing I can do. I lie: "I won't."

My phone, stashed in my backpack, buzzes. Someone sent me a text message.

Lindsey digs into my bag and hands me the phone.

The message glares at me: *we need 2 talk*.

Yes, Elijah. We do.

EIGHTEEN

It's a little after nine in the morning, and while service doesn't begin for nearly an hour, the nave below me is already filling with members of the congregation. It's the one-year anniversary of Hannah Rynes's disappearance. There's a poster-sized print of her, looking much like I remember, resting on an easel near the meditation nook. Candles blaze in her memory. There is no reference to the man who might've kidnapped her, probably out of courtesy to Hannah's family, although some of the parishioners were so snowed by Palmer's word that they assume my father is as much a victim of foul play as Hannah, that he followed whoever took her to save her.

They wouldn't feel that way, if they'd stood witness to the man beneath the alb.

I walk the length of the balcony, toward the reverend's quarters, and find the door slightly ajar. I sneak inside the rectory, and tiptoe to the far side of the room, toward the room my father called the confessional.

Now that I've been to confession at Carmel—reconciliation is a requirement in religion class—I know that Palmer's confessional was anything but a safe place to reconcile sins with God. His calling this small room of terror a confessional is further proof of his twisted mind, if you ask me. I very nearly hear my mother's screams as I approach.

My gut churns. My fingertips buzz with warning, although logically, I know I won't find my father behind that door, but his replacement, preparing for this morning's sermon. I draw in a long breath, searching for any hint of Palmer's aftershave—piney, like something reminiscent of an evergreen forest.

When I don't catch the scent, I trudge on.

I meet with subtle differences instantly. The draperies are no longer a navy-and-forest stripe, tied back with gold ropes; rather, they're airier, beige corduroy tab tops. Evidence that the world has continued to turn without Palmer's pushing it. Evidence that all the things around me have progressed, and my life can't continue in the past. Hopefully, all that will change soon, if not today.

A quick peek into the confessional, the door to which is propped open with a wedge of wood, confirms my assumptions: Andrew Drake is bent over the writing desk. I enter and close the confessional door behind me with a loud clap.

Andrew Drake looks up from whatever's busying him on my father's—now his—tabletop. His mouth forms a small o. He's an attractive man, but I'm not attracted to him. Never have been. My history with him embarrasses me, and judging by the flush crawling up his neck, he's none too proud, either. The girl I am today would never have done what I did with him, but the girl I used to be didn't care about right and wrong as much as she craved security and understanding. At least that's what Dr. Ewing says.

"Morning," I say.

His mouth clamps shut, and he watches as I steadily approach.

It's a closet of a room, about nine by nine, but it feels larger, due to a stunning leaded glass window directly behind the desk—the desk over which Palmer once bent me to whip my rear raw, over which Palmer bent my mother for purposes much more demeaning than corporal punishment.

Drake scoots back on his chair to gain some breathing room.

"I'm not here to start any trouble," I tell him.

He opens his mouth, as if to speak, but no words come out.

Antique choir stalls line the left wall perpendicular to the window, but barring them and the desk, no furniture occupies the floor space. I take a seat in the stall closest to Drake. "I want the keys to the garden house."

"Why?"

"Does it matter why? I just do."

He persists: "It matters."

"You know what else matters? The statute of limitations on contact of a sexual nature with a minor child."

Trumped, Drake slides open the wide center drawer of the desk, produces a single key on an oversized ring.

While I desperately want to grasp the key and bolt out of here to meet John, I force myself to stay seated. My gaze wanders to the leaded glass. The morning sun filters through the divided shapes and casts shadows on the walls around us.

He drums his fingers against the desktop. "What do you want, Callie, in the garden? What do you expect to find out there?"

Nothing tangible. I'm certain everything there is to have and to hold in that outbuilding was whisked away a year ago . . . along with Hannah's twelve-year-old body.

I shrug. "Just a safe place to be alone with a certain someone."

His eyes narrow, even as he slides the key toward me.

I eye the key, which is still held against the tabletop with the power of his index and middle fingers.

"You can't expect me to believe you have nowhere else to go."

"Well, I don't think you want me on the altar right about now, do you?" Despite my weariness, I smile. "Or maybe you do."

Slowly, he presses his lips into a thin line.

I challenge him with a raised brow. "You were here that day, the day he sent my mother away."

"Yes."

"You were here the day Hannah disappeared."

"Earlier that day, yes."

"Knowing what you know now . . . about my father, about the likelihood he kidnapped Hannah . . . do you think my mother is crazy?"

"First of all, no one knows for sure what happened to your father and Hannah, and second—"

"Do you honestly believe it's coincidence that—"

"Second . . . yes. Your mother needs help. Severe psychological disorders."

"Is that what my father told you?"

"She's still there, isn't she? Regardless of what Palmer said, regardless of whether he is what we thought he was, she's not well enough to be discharged. Look, haven't you been through enough? Leave well enough alone."

"Not until it's done, and I need to comb over everything—including that garden house—to put it all to rest."

"Your best interest—"

"Give me the key, or I'll talk. Maybe we didn't do the deed, Drake, but that doesn't mean you didn't want to."

If I decide to tell the world about my brief connection with Drake, life as he knows it is over. He was twenty-two. A consenting adult—and engaged to Nini. I was too young to be doing what I did with him.

"The Lord's forgiven me," he says. "It would be nice if you did, too."

"You didn't do it alone."

"What I did with you was wrong," he says.

"It's all right." I rise from the choir stall and reach for the key, which he reluctantly releases. "My best to Nini and the baby bump," I say. "How far along is she?"

"Six . . ." He wets his lips. "Six months."

"Boy or girl?"

He raises his chin. "Girl."

"Congratulations."

"Thank you."

"In fifteen years, some altar-boy-cum-reverend-in-training is going to love the hell out of her."

He winces.

I offer a wave.

"Callie?"

"Yeah."

"Be sure to bring that key back. It's the only one I have."

I nod. "Okay."

The Holy Promise choir, armed with tambourines, begins their set of welcome hymns, accompanied by an electric guitar and timpani. "Holy, holy, holy!" rises up from the apse below.

The song moves in my nerves. When I close my eyes, I see my mother's smile, hear her voice. I grasp the ruby ring on my chain and concentrate on the energy it holds.

"The Bible estimates the age of Mary of Galilee around

fourteen when she conceived Jesus," Drake says. "Maybe younger, but not older than sixteen. By present-day standards, you were a child, but when paralleled . . ."

When he trails off, I look over my shoulder at him, if only to encourage him to finish speaking.

"I blamed you for luring me." He shakes his head. "Your father was incensed with your wanting me, you know that?"

Yes, I know. The scar on my shoulder burns to prove it.

"I was wrong, Callie."

Through tears, I regard the man who'd sinned with me. "I have to go."

"What I did with you was wrong."

His admission sends a ripple of relief through my system. Maybe I'm not crazy after all. I wipe away a tear—"I agree"—and retrace my footsteps.

By the time I reach the nave, I'm singing along with the choir, if only to distract myself from the tears.

It's funny how a place can hold such horrific memories, yet still feel like home. The words belt out from deep in my lungs: "Bring me home, bring me home to holy, holy, holy."

I feel a hand on my shoulder.

John's.

"Your mother was right. You sing like a seraph."

Thankful for his support, I lean into his embrace.

"Did you get it?" he whispers.

I place the key in his hand.

Someone's following us into the labyrinth. I'm certain.

More than once, I glance over my shoulder, yet everyone's inside the church. This isn't your average Christian institution, and it holds meetings nothing like the Catholic Masses I attend at Carmel. This is more like a Sunday matinee performance than the simple relaying of God's message. Attendees are passionate about the word spoken inside. There's no need to excuse someone to quiet a child outside because children don't act up at Holy Promise. They're too busy dancing in the aisles, sitting on the altar, or exploring crafts in the children's chapel, which means that while service is in session, John and I are alone in the labyrinth. My gaze lifts to the heavens and settles on the belfry.

Someone was ringing the bells that day. She kept ringing them, long after Palmer tossed me into the fountain. It had to have been Hannah; no one else has come forward to testify about what she saw that day, and the police have done the due diligence to know for sure.

Tears blur my vision.

"Callie?" John's voice sounds far away.

"Pen." I feel him slipping away, as a black halo closes in on my peripheral vision. "I need a pen!"

I'm worn thin, and suddenly I feel very alone. The labyrinth morphs in my mind to a barren and cold place, covered with a dusting of leaves. I hear the shovel, feel the ache in my back and shoulders, shiver with the onset of cold rain.

Honor thy father.

Honor thy father.

Honor thy father.

My tears meld with the raindrops on my cheeks. I hurt. Everywhere. My muscles strain, as if walking might be impossible. My head pounds. My extremities feel numb, as if at the onset of a flu bug.

I want my mother, want to feel her arms close around me, want to fall asleep to the jingle of her bangles or the serenity of one of her lullabies.

I let out a sob, mourning what is lost. I keep digging.

"Callie."

Suddenly my fingers begin to warm. I concentrate on the feeling; it slowly brings me back to the here and now. Slowly, the labyrinth bleeds into view. I focus on John's hands wrapped around mine. The red felt-tip pen rests at my feet.

"What happened in here?" John persists. He's crouched before me, presumably to retrieve my pen, holding both my hands, capturing my gaze with his own concerned stare. "You can tell me."

I shake my head.

"I won't judge you. You can trust me."

I glance down at the back of his hand, on which I had written:

Hold no judgment like the moon. The witnesses are speaking soon.

"I . . . I can't." My fists close into tight balls.

"Callie—"

The tiniest of stones at my feet scatter with my frustrated stomp. "I can't tell you what I don't remember!"

"Okay."

I shake my head and I walk farther into the labyrinth at a clipped pace. John follows closely behind.

When I arrive at the center of the maze, I climb into the fountain, and brush my fingers against the border of sparkling glass mosaic tiles lining the sides as I walk the circumference.

Memories flash in my mind—water entering my lungs, my hair knotting in Palmer's fist as he pulls me up for a quick breath, only to shove me back under the surface. The rush of water fills my ears, marble braises my knuckles as I fight for purchase, church bells peal out as if in lost hope.

I survived it all, but . . . at what cost?

I glance up at John. "I might've killed my father."

"I've read up on that, too. There's no evidence that says Palmer Prescott's dead, let alone that you're responsible."

Except that I confessed to his murder on the bathroom wall.

My gaze trails to where the path disappears into a wall of juniper. I know from the days I'd spent wasting time in this maze that beyond the hedge, off the path, is an iron gate. This is the route, I'm convinced, I took to escape that day. I would have needed the key to the gate, of course, or someone would have had to open it for me. But if I'd traversed the same, laborious path out as I had on the way in that day, someone would've eventually seen me. Stories are consistent: no one saw me leave, and no one mentioned seeing my father or Hannah again, which suggests Palmer and I left the grounds together—likely through that gate.

Why can't I remember?

Maybe the answers lay behind that gate, where a structure is hidden amongst the brush—the garden house—a one-room building used for garden supply storage. I used to play in that place when I was small, but never do I remember accessing it from the center of the labyrinth. Elijah and I made out behind it once, but only after traipsing around the perimeter of the gardens.

I reach for John's hand and climb over the white stone, out of the fountain.

He grasps my fingers. With trepidation, I lead him to the hidden gate. The juniper branches scratch me as I duck between them. My heartbeat kicks up again, as if I've been running, and chill bumps rise on my flesh. "Someone's watching us," I whisper.

On pure reflex, he flinches, looks over his shoulder, but soon, he's shaking his head. "No. No, we're all right."

"Just open the gate before someone catches on."

"Who's going to—"

"Please!"

His tongue touches his lower lip, and his brow creases in concern. I must sound crazy. But he diverts his glance and inserts the key with ease. "I thought it opened a garden house."

It does. It should.

The key won't turn the lock. John's fingers tense with another attempt. "Doesn't work."

It has to. "Let me."

Our bodies are so close, imprisoned between juniper and iron, that I feel his breath ruffle my hair.

"It's a finicky lock." But I don't know how I know this. With trembling fingers, I pull the key toward me a millimeter, turn it to the left. The lock gives way half a second before the gate swings out. I stumble through the opening and meet with a cobblestone walk, which surrounds the garden building.

"Cobblestone," John says. "You wrote about cobblestone."

I remember a few references. John would know, as he spent a good hour reading my musings last night.

"The first time I saw you write, it was about cobblestone. At the Vagabond that day. With Lindsey and Elijah." He approaches the door to the outbuilding. This time, the key turns effortlessly in the lock. The door clicks open.

My footsteps clap against the floorboards of the confining space, silencing only when I cease walking.

I'm staring down at army green canvas stretched over chrome rails—a cot. *Honor thy father.*

"Calliope." John's voice rises behind me.

But too entranced with the cot, and the fuzzy recollections that come with it, I can't turn around to answer him. Not yet.

"You've been here before," John says.

Honor thy father.

A few times, when I was little. I remember wandering down here occasionally when my parents were busy in the confessional. I played in here while the gardeners were trimming the hedges. I think I fell asleep here once.

"You've been here recently."

"How can you be s—" I turn around. Gasp.

He's right. Handwriting roves over a slat of wood near the cot:

As the hours pass.

Gardening tools hang on a pegboard wall opposite the cot. There's a dry sink situated under a minuscule window, which allows in almost no light. Under it are bins of soil and seed, and nested stacks of clay flowerpots, which, come summertime, will flourish with petunias and impatiens. All appears mundane, if not for my graffiti and the suggestion of a sinister memory.

The walls seem to close in on me. I'm suffocating. Shivering. I'm looking for something. Something I can't find. What am I looking for?

I hear remnants of voices, but I'm not sure if they're mine and John's or someone's in the past. Flashes of yellow cotton pass through my memory in intervals, like the beam from a lighthouse beacon. The scent of loam fills my nostrils. I feel the rain, the fatigue, the desperation.

Yellow cotton.

Wet wind.

Worn wood.

I can't breathe, can't move.

Strong hands grip my biceps.

"Callie!"

I open my eyes and gasp a breath. Ground myself in John Fogel's blue eyes. "What am I looking for?" I blink away the tears accumulating on my lower lashes.

John shakes his head and releases his grip on my arms. "I don't know."

"We have to . . ." I bolt out of the garden building and travel the cobblestones around the outside of the labyrinth, toward the Gothic sanctuary.

I'm out of breath, and so is John, by the time we burst through the door.

The entire congregation is standing, singing, clapping in time with the music or raising hands to heaven in worship:

"Rock her in the arms, rock her in the arms, rock her in the arms, the arms of the Lord!" At the front of the main aisle, Drake leads the song and dance. He's so into his role that he pays no mind to us latecomers.

I feel the music inside me, like it's emanating from my soul. I can't help singing; an uncontrollable force within me belts out the words. But I don't fight it. I'll blend into the crowd if I'm doing everything everyone else is doing.

John takes my hand, an expression somewhere between fear and wonder plastered to his face.

As we walk a side aisle, I search the crowd for familiar faces, scan over Drake's pregnant wife, and finally settle on the portrait of Hannah, which is illuminated by candlelight.

What am I missing?

I stare into the eyes of the oversized photograph, as if its subject will somehow answer my questions.

John and I begin to draw stares, as we near the altar. I slow my pace and before long, when my feet have come to a stop, the song within me wanes.

We're a few paces from Hannah's shrine when it hits me: yellow cotton.

My fingers tighten around John's; I pull him back the way we came.

Soon, we're running again. Sprinting toward the heavy doors that open every Sunday like loving arms, providing a false sense of security. I can't get out of there fast enough.

Although the day is gray and overcast, the daylight blinds me for a few seconds upon exit, a contrast to the dim interior of the church.

I throw my backpack to the ground. Tear open the zipper. Yank out my pen and notebook. "Yellow cotton," I wheeze.

The moment the tip of the pen hits the paper, words begin to flow:

Row the boat. Row the boat. Row the boat.

Yellow cotton sundress in a box under the stairs.

In a box in a box in a box in a box under the stairs.

"Callie, sit down."

"No." I shake my head. "What was she wearing in the portrait? What color?"

"Yellow."

The material stretches and pulls over my chest.

But it isn't my dress, and I never wore it, if not in my mind.

I see it. In a box under the stairs.

Don't you touch her don't you touch her don't you touch her.

NINETEEN

"Dr. Ewing? Calliope Knowles needs an appointment."
John's on my phone. "Now . . . it's an emergency."

I'm sobbing so violently that I'm hardly making a sound.

"Yes." John's speeding east, toward Ewing's office, but
he doesn't know where it is exactly, and I can't stop weep-
ing long enough tell him. "She can't stop writing."

Pressed like a rose in a book from a lover from a lover
from a lover from a lover from a lover.

Sift through sift sift sift sift sift through. Sift
through as the hours pass pass pass passpasspass.

Claw at the case claw at the case claw at the case.

"I don't know," John says. "Callie, did you take your
Ativan?"

I shake my head. Tears splat onto my words.

"No, she says she didn't. We were at Holy Promise. Yeah. Hannah's memorial . . . Yeah, she has it now. She's writing . . . I don't know . . . How much have you written? Four pages? I'd say four or five pages. In six minutes, maybe? Not more than ten. Where? Okay."

A tiny pickax chisels away at my skull from the inside. My stomach flip-flops. My vision blurs as the world slants forty-five degrees to my left.

God, I'm going to be sick. My hand cramps, my head throbs, my teeth hurt from gritting together.

"Stop," I manage to say.

"Huh?" John's still on the phone, but he glances at me long enough to see what's about to happen, and careens to the shoulder of the road.

I allow my journal to slip from my lap as I open the door and tumble onto the gravel, landing on all fours. Dry heaves jolt me, but nothing comes up. Everything spins, blurs until the scent of piney cologne wafts through my memory. Palmer's voice echoes in my mind: *It's because of you. You're the reason.*

Mom's voice now: *You think I can't stop you? Don't you touch her, you son of a bitch!*

Blood everywhere.

Her bloody hand grazes against the walnut statue of John the Baptist.

Pearl-handled knife protruding from his inner thigh, just inches from his privates.

Palmer's limping from the confessional, trailing blood

behind him: *No, no charges. She needs help. I'm a man of God. I'll help her.*

"Callie."

I flinch when I hear John's voice. His hand is warm against my back.

When I look up at him, stars like silver glitter wink around his face.

The hum of the motor, the heat of the engine, and the stink of roadside exhaust register, pushing away the memory of Palmer's cologne, and the images of screams and blood.

Under the influence of John's hand, I rise, pick up my journal from the gravel, and resume my seat in the SUV. I lean back, close my eyes, concentrate on breathing.

A few minutes later, when my nausea begins to subside, I take in my surroundings. "This isn't the way. We need to head back toward the lake."

"He wants to meet at the county police station."

"Why?"

"Do you know a Detective Guidry? He said we should ask for Guidry, if he's not there yet."

Guidry's the one who found me in the apartment above the Vagabond. He's the one who combs through all my journals.

My mouth dries instantly, and something akin to panic settles in my nerves. I wonder if this will be the day they ask questions I can actually answer. I wonder if this is the time they find enough evidence to send me away.

I allow John to hold my numb hand as we drive, then walk up to the door at the Lake County PD. He gives it a squeeze when I pass through the door.

My gaze locks on the table, where one of my journals sits. It's the one I left with my shrink after my last session. I then trail my glance to Ewing, who occupies one of four beat-up, uncomfortable-looking chairs with cushions the color of bruised apple flesh. He's sitting with his forearms resting on his knees, typing a text. He's wearing jeans and a Chicago Bears sweatshirt—the pullover type with a hood and a front pocket. I've never seen him looking so casual. It occurs to me that I've pulled him away from a Sunday at home with his family.

When he greets me, glancing over his Buddy Hollys, with a smile and a "hey, kiddo," tears well anew in my eyes.

The moment he stands, I plow into his arms. "I'm sorry, I'm sorry, I'm sorry, I'm—"

"It's all right, Callie. It's all right."

He's still comforting me when Guidry walks in, slurping on a coffee. I wipe away my tears and take a few steps back.

John, who has slung my backpack over his shoulder, extends a hand first to the detective—"John Fogel"—and then to my shrink. "Want me to . . ." He thumbs toward the lobby.

"Actually, can he stay?" I rub at a black smear of mascara on my index finger.

"Have a seat," the detective says. "So . . . how you doing, kid? What happened at Holy Promise?"

As Ewing records my testimony on his tiny digital recorder, and as Guidry jots notes on a yellow legal pad, I fill them in on everything I can remember. John interjects a few things I forget, and draws a few lines between Hannah's case and that of his missing cousin. When my purging comes to a close, I slide my journal across the table for Guidry's perusal.

"Here. Even trade." He slides a stack of three back toward me—three he's already skimmed and copied for Hannah's file—and deposits the one I just gave him atop the one Ewing brought. His chair creaks when he leans back in it. His arms stretch over his head and come to settle, pretzel-like, as a sort of headrest. "Okay, first of all, this business with yellow cotton. Can you describe in better detail what you remember about it?"

I feel it again, see it again, in my mind. "It's too small. Wet. Thin material. Three buttons . . . fake pearls . . . down the front. Ruffled sleeves . . . like a pinafore."

"And you think it's Hannah's?"

"I don't know, but it isn't mine."

"Sometimes," Ewing interjects, "when witness to great trauma, the survivors mentally switch places with the victims. There are cases of posttraumatic stress disorder in survivors of battle, who swear they know what a bullet feels like when it enters bone, yet they've never been shot."

"Huh." Guidry chews on his bottom lip for a moment. "Here's what doesn't add up about that. Hannah was wearing blue leggings and a pink cardigan sweater when she disappeared."

"And yellow floral underwear," I add.

The detective darts me a glance. "Her parents don't know what pair she was wearing that day."

I shrug. "That's what I remember seeing on the floor. And I might be wrong, I might be remembering some other instance, or some other damn millennium in another lifetime, for all the sense this makes to me, but that's what I remember."

"And it's good that you're remembering. But the trouble is, Callie, that too many leads, too many theories come out of these notebooks of yours. I can write it down, maybe we can have discussion about it in a meeting, but without more tangible evidence, I can't do anything about it. So don't be discouraged when you have these breakthroughs, and it seems like nothing's happening on my end."

"So I go through all this"—today's been brutal—"and it isn't going to make a difference."

"It'll make a difference," Guidry says. "In time. And hey."

I look up, meet his gaze.

"With the one-year anniversary, there's going to be a lot of media coverage the next few days. There's bound to be more speculation on whether Prescott's capable of doing this, whether he ought to be my chief suspect." He gives

215

his head a minute shake. "Don't listen to the doubt, the bullshit about him being a man of God. I remember your mother's testimony at the Meadows, things she said he did to her."

I nod. He's referencing the confessional.

"And I remember the proof you gave me, kid."

Tears—of embarrassment, of frustration—rise again. He's talking about the slashes on my back, the scar on my shoulder. He photographed me the night he found me at the Vagabond, just before he ordered, much to my resistance, a rape kit. I don't blame him for ordering it, in hindsight. He couldn't locate my jeans; I couldn't remember the past thirty-six hours. We were both relieved when the kit turned up no evidence of trauma.

"A lot of perpetrators return to the scene on anniversaries of the crimes. They go to vigils, to funerals. They go for the same reason you went to Holy Promise today—to remember. Do you realize that if you'd gone alone, you might've put yourself at risk, had Palmer shown up?"

I think of the feeling I get . . . the feeling that someone is watching me, following me. A chill races up my spine.

Guidry's lips press into a thin line. "I know what kind of guy he is, and so do you. Pay no attention to those who don't. Anyone tries to contact you . . . what do you say?"

"No comment."

"Atta girl."

All is silent for a few moments. The *tick, tick, tick* of

the second hand on John's watch consumes the space until Ewing speaks up:

"Tell me more about this memory."

I take a deep breath. "I wake up on the floor in the garden house, and I'm wet with holy water. Hannah's on the cot. I see a pair of underwear on the floor, and I think they're Hannah's." I shake my head. Another wave of nausea churns through my gut.

"Let's talk about the garden house, too," Guidry says. "You saw a line of your writing on the wall."

I nod.

"Here." John leans in, flipping through options on his phone. "I have a picture."

"You took a picture?" I ask.

"Yeah." He hands the phone across the table to the detective, who studies it. "I can forward it to you, if you want."

"Thanks." Guidry gives a curt nod. "That'll help until our guys have a chance to circulate in the area."

"Can I see that?" Ewing asks.

Guidry hands over the phone and then leans forward. "Callie, when was the last time you were in the garden house before today?"

"If my memory is correct, I was there the day Hannah disappeared, but I haven't always known it . . . if I was there at all. Before that . . . I don't know."

"We scoured that garden house after Hannah went missing," the detective says. "Scoured it. But we didn't find anything. No yellow underwear, and nothing written on the walls. Which tells me, Callie, that if you wrote on the wall there, you did it recently."

"That's not possible," I say.

"I can bring in the photographs. There's nothing written on the walls of that garden house the night after Hannah disappeared. You've been in there since we did our investigation."

"I can't just walk in there whenever I feel like it," I say. "I need a key. It's locked all the time."

"Who has the key?"

John tosses it to the table. "We got it from the new reverend there . . . what was his name?"

"Andrew Drake."

"I'll call him in. See if he's lent the key to you or anyone else recently."

"He did say he had only one key," I say. "I think Palmer used to have a couple."

Guidry meets my gaze. "Do you think the keys are missing? Or misplaced?"

"I don't know. I didn't ask."

"Did you take the key, Callie?" Guidry taps his pen against his legal pad. "On some other occasion, and maybe you don't remember it?"

"I haven't been there!" I reach for and squeeze John's hand. "I mean, I can't have just gone there one day and not remembered it!"

"Hmmm," Ewing says.

I glance at him, but soon direct my attention to Guidry. "Okay, I know I black out when I'm writing, but I've never come to somewhere else—not since that first time at the Vagabond. I'm getting better. I've never blacked out long enough to take a train to Holy Promise and back again without noticing, and I've *never*—"

"What if she didn't write it?" Ewing says.

My head spins. "What?"

"I don't think you wrote this." He licks his lips. "Callie always writes in red felt-tip. This looks like black ball-point."

Guidry reaches for the phone, gives it another gander. "Yeah, it does."

Someone else has been in that garden house. Someone who's been writing the same things I write.

TWENTY

John kisses the crown of my head—"See you tomorrow"—and does as I ask: he drives home, and lets me walk from the harbor to the Hutches' house. He doesn't want to hide anymore, but I've convinced him to hang on a bit longer. Furthermore, I've talked him into calling Lindsey in half an hour, if only to thank her for the night.

He's part of me now, as if he, like the ring on my necklace, has been with me since long before I can remember.

Lindsey's going to smell him on me, read him in my face, hear him in the catch of my breath, if she doesn't first notice that I'm wearing his watch, which he lent me, so I could show my mother the next time I see her. This secret John and I keep from Lindsey puts more pressure on me, and makes my situation even more unmanageable than it was before John reached over that pew to collect the note I wrote on my sister's behalf. I can't keep up with this charade. I have to come clean.

When I approach the foot of the driveway, a weird sort of energy hits me. I already know something's wrong. For the thirtieth time, I sniff my hands, my shirt, the handles of my backpack, searching for any trace of John Fogel. I know I'm immune. I can't smell him on me if I smell like him, too.

As I near, I realize Lindsey's parents aren't home. When they are, their bedroom light is on—always—but now, their window is dark. I glance toward the garage and see one of the two double doors is open. Only Lindsey's car is inside, but neither her mother's nor her father's is parked there.

"Hey."

I practically jump out of my skin.

Lindsey's seated on the steps leading up to the front door, tapping her Keds against the asphalt. She's bundled in green cargo pants snapped at the shins, white cable-knit leg warmers, a white waffle-knit T, and a blue-and-yellow tie-dyed hoodie with *Ask Alice* scrawled across the top of the hood. While her fingernails looked flawless for last night's dance, she's now gnawed them to nubs, and her eyes are rimmed red, suggesting she's been crying.

Rivet.

"Hi." I brace myself for the shellacking that's undoubtedly about to come my way. But nothing happens, save the two of us staring at one another.

Rivet, rivet, rivet.

Finally, she breaks the ice: "Let's take a walk." She pushes herself up from the steps and yanks on my arm as she passes me.

I fall in step beside her. As much as I want to keep my mouth shut, I can't handle the suspense by the time we round the corner to exit the neighborhood. "Where are we going?"

"7-Eleven."

"You want a Big Gulp?"

An exasperated laugh—something between a snort and a sigh—escapes her. "I want a cigarette."

"Oh. Why?"

"Gotta smoke something."

While I don't understand why she suddenly wants to acquaint herself with nicotine, I do know that she didn't have to wait for me if she wanted to buy a pack of smokes. Not only does she have countless connections to supply her with whatever contraband she wants, be it grass or Seasonique, her fake ID is a near perfect match. She can buy a pack on her own.

"Linds?"

She hooks her arm through mine, and shivers a little as she rests her head against me. I'm far too tired to walk another half mile, let alone hold up her weight while I do it, but because I know this may be the last time she leans on me, I endure the burden.

She pets my arm.

I wonder if she can feel the outline of John's watch.

When our destination is in sight, Lindsey straightens. "Elijah's been looking for you."

"I know."

"Do you? Because it used to be you'd jump when the phone rang."

"I'm mad, that's all." And distracted. And confused. And busy with the guy she thinks she's in love with.

"I talked to him about eighteen times today."

"Elijah called you?"

"Yeah."

"And you talked to him?"

"Well, no one else was calling."

She pushes the door open, and gives me a shove toward the counter.

I look over my shoulder at her.

Her eyes widen and her jaw clenches.

All right. I suppose I owe her twenty cancer sticks. One for every time her pseudo boyfriend breathed my name.

"Camel Lights," I say. It feels funny to ask for cigarettes after nearly sixty days without them. In anticipation, I drum my fingers against the laminate surface. "Box."

The clerk slaps them onto the counter without asking for

223

my ID, which is good, as I no longer have the one Elijah gave me at County. The Hutches confiscated it when they took away my last pack of smokes.

In some Pavlovian response, my fingertips tingle when I grasp the pack, just like they do the moment I inhale. This is when I know: I'm going to smoke one. At least one. Not more than two. Or three.

As we exit, I slap the box against my inner wrist to pack the nicotine. I don't know why I do it. I suppose a cigarette would burn just as well without the extra effort. But it's something I've seen my mother do since my infancy, so I do it, too.

I hope I won't always blindly mimic her actions.

"Light one for me." Lindsey produces a fuchsia-and-orange lighter.

I slip two sticks from the pack and bring them to my lips. Flip my thumb over the flint ball to make fire. Savor the sound of crackling paper and tobacco leaves. Breathe the poison into my lungs.

Rivet the shore.

I hand a cig to Lindsey, who brings it to her lips and puffs on it, as if she's sending smoke signals.

"I think I fucked up with Jon."

Speaking of John, he really should've called her by now. "Why?"

"The lesbian shit," Lindsey continues. "Obviously, it doesn't work for every guy."

"Probably works for most." I shrug. "Elijah seems to really like it."

"You ever . . . you know . . . ménage with him?"

"No."

"Come on, you can tell me."

"I haven't."

"Not what he says."

I dart a glare at Lindsey, who's holding the cigarette like she would a sparkler on the Fourth of July. I think she's writing J-O-N in the air. "I may not remember everything I've done, but know I've never been part of a threesome."

"*C'est la vie.*"

"Whatever he told you wasn't true. If he had a threesome, it wasn't with me."

"I drank too much last night," she says. "Been hurling all day. I should just stick to pot."

"Maybe you should quit it all."

"Maybe you're a whore who can't keep her legs together."

Her words knock the wind out of me. I drop my cigarette and pick up my pace. Tears sprout like twin waterfalls.

Rivet the shore.

She's a few paces behind me when I hear her phone ring. Her hello is an echo.

I'm running now. The town fades to nothingness, to a day last autumn, and I'm running, running, running through back roads of gravel and muck at night.

My hands sear with cuts and abrasions.

My legs are bruised, my back burns with slashes.

Rivet the shore with celebration of the dead.

I'm wet with sweat, tears, rain, holy water.

Blood.

Footfalls threaten behind me.

I can't run fast enough.

The gravel path becomes asphalt becomes iron.

I don't know how long I've been running, but the spiral motion of the staircase dizzies me, and I have to sit.

My breaths come in short hiccups.

The earth spins before my eyes.

The staircase jounces, as if someone's climbing up.

Coming for me.

Wants to tear at my clothing, my trust, my sanity.

I hook my fingers into the iron grid on which I'm sitting.

Steady.

I'm going to faint.

He's going to have his way with me.

I don't have breath enough to scream.

"Baby."

Through a curtain of my hair, I spy Elijah crouching in front of me. My surroundings bleed into view. We're at the door to the apartment above the Vagabond. I'm freezing. It's getting dark. How long have I been out here?

I wonder if this is the longest blackout I've had since the night Palmer took Hannah. Maybe it is possible that I don't remember an entire trip to Holy Promise, and maybe

I did write on the garden house wall.

The fingers on my left hand hurt from interlacing with the iron-grid platform, while the fingers on my right are closed tightly around a red felt-tip pen. Heaving, attempting to catch my breath, I release my grip on the platform, finger by finger.

My journal is open on my lap:

Rivet rivet rivet rivet rivet.

Rivet the shore with celebration of the dead.

Celebration of the dead dead dead dead dead dead dead.

I killed him I killed him I killed him I killed him I killed him I killed him I killed him I killed him I killed him I killed him I killed him I killed him I killed him I killed him I killed him I killed him I killed him I killed him. IKILLEDHIM.

Rivet rivet rivet.

Celebrate him. Celebrate Him celebrate celebrate celebrate the dead.

He brushes aside my hair. "You okay?"

I shake my head, and through my sobbing, manage one word: "Lindsey."

"Yeah, I know." He chucks me under the chin. "She's pissed." He stands and goes to work on the lock.

I pinch my eyes shut to gather a few thoughts, and promptly shove my notebook back into my bag. The moment I've pulled myself together, I punch Elijah in the thigh.

"Ouch!"

"Well, what did you expect?" I'm on my feet now, honing in on his space, as if I can physically squeeze an apology out of him. We're practically nose-to-nose.

"Give me some fucking room."

"You want space? Room to feel up some other girl right in front of me? You got it, Elijah. You can have the whole fucking planet."

The lock gives way. I shoulder my way into the apartment, dig for a lollipop, but turn up only my new pack of Lights. I wander into the kitchen. Maybe the stove still works, maybe I can burn through the rest of this pack instead of eating tonight.

"Look, I took things too far last night." He takes the pack from me, helps himself to a cigarette, which he lights with a purple lighter produced from his pocket.

I lock my gaze on it. Purple. Probably belongs to a girl.

"How'd you know to come here?" I turn the knob on the 1982 stove, the newest thing in the place. It hums. I smell the gas; the utilities are on the same meter as the café below. But no flame is produced. Old appliances. Out of use for too long.

"I've been checking back here all day, waiting for you." He offers the purple lighter, which I refuse on principle. "Saw you and Mr. Tight End cleaning up last night after the bash, counted every second of the seventeen minutes he took to service you—"

"Shut up." I want to correct him, to explain that nothing

happened on that boat, but I bite my tongue. Explaining would imply that I think he has a right to know the details. And as of last night, I don't think he does.

A smile plays on his lips. "Callie, I get it. I understand why it happened. It's what you do when I run around on you, and I deserve it, yeah. But you chose the wrong guy this time. This is Lindsey we're talking about."

"That's what you think this is? Revenge? You think I'd sacrifice Lindsey to get you back from Ms. D Cup?"

"Did you enjoy it? Was he good?" He offers me the smoke.

"Yes." I steal the cigarette from his grasp and look him in the eye. "God, yes."

"All seventeen minutes of it, huh?"

"That was round one. You didn't stick around for the finale."

He presses his lips together and looks away. I see the twitch in his jaw muscle. It's the same tension I see when he's about to wallop some poor soul in a fistfight.

I retort with a sniff and: "Did you enjoy her D cups?"

"No." He glances at me.

"Right."

"This doesn't have to be over between us, you know." The muscles in Elijah's forearms tense when he pulls himself up onto the countertop. "We both fucked up. It happens."

I exhale a long stream of smoke. "I guess."

"Love you, baby."

I roll my eyes, wipe away tears.

He kicks his heels against the white, aluminum cabinets. *Dink, ding, ding.*

"You have a connection with this guy?"

Dink, ding, ding.

My glance hardens. "None of your business."

"You still love me?"

I weigh responses in my mind and settle on "Yeah." I don't know what I'm going to do about that love, but I know he'll always be in my heart.

"Then, yeah, it is my business. Think about it, Callie. Does it make sense? Does it make sense that suddenly he's into you, just when you happen to be into him?"

"Not sure it made sense that you were suddenly into me, either. I mean, how does it happen for anyone? Paths cross, flames ignite, right?"

"God, Callie. Don't make him out to be more than he is."

Is that what I'm doing?

He takes the smoke. Drags. "So, what're you gonna do? Go back to Lindsey's?"

"I don't know. Probably not. Not tonight."

He returns the cigarette, which I don't really want anymore. But I bring it to my lips, anticipating it might carry a trace of him. His lips were wrapped around it, after all. But there's no remnant of his kiss, which I suddenly, fiercely miss.

Elijah is slipping out of my grasp, like fine-grained sand. Slipping away.

"Well, if you're going to stay here for a while," he says, "lock the door when you're in. If you accidentally lock it on your way out, call me, and I'll come let you in again. You need anything else? Cash? Food?" Before I can reply, he says, "Think you can sneak back home for some clothes? You'll need a blanket. I'll see what I can do."

"Thanks." I flick some ashes into the sink.

I stare at the cinders of tobacco against the faded pink porcelain receptacle, and my peripheral vision begins to darken.

Something's familiar.

Visions dance in my head: cold water raining down on me. Muddy water circling the drain in a pink tub.

I showered when I came here the night Hannah disappeared. What evidence did I wash down the drain?

TWENTY-ONE

'm almost late to school. While everyone was preoccupied last night—Lindsey in the shed, Mr. and Mrs. Hutch still gone, doing whatever it is they were doing yesterday—I sneaked home to gather as much as I could carry back to the Vagabond.

Our old apartment is only a temporary hideout. I know I can't stay there indefinitely. Someone's going to catch on if I keep coming and going, for one thing. But until Lindsey cools off, there's nowhere left for me to go.

And make no mistake: she's pissed. So pissed, in fact, that she hoarded every last one of my uniform skirts. I managed to scrounge an oxford and a sweater, but I couldn't turn up a skirt for the life of me, so I had to snare one of hers. It is, of course, an inch or so too short, and I can't get the button to close, but it'll have to do.

Elijah came through for me. He brought me an old *Star Wars* comforter with Yoda front and center. He brought a large brown paper bag containing a few books of matches, two pillar candles, some snacks, two packs of smokes, and toiletries. Additionally, he lent me a heavy, wooden baseball bat that I'm supposed to keep next to the door when I'm out and next to me while I'm in. Now that I have my small reserve of cash, clothes, and my most recent notebooks, I'm set for a while.

I stow my coat in my locker and head to homeroom. Along the way, a group of girls laughs as I pass. I have the distinct feeling they're laughing at me. Maybe they're amused that I took a Pace bus to get here today, when they're all driving Daddy's luxury sedans. Maybe they're snickering because I'm showing more thigh than Jesus in his loincloth. But I have bigger worries.

By the time I arrive at homeroom, however, I've dodged more than a few dirty looks. It seems Lindsey's done some damage in the twenty-four hours I've been gone from her life.

"Where've you been?" John's inquiry is upon me before I even take my seat.

"Surviving. What's going on here?"

"If you'd return a damn text, you'd know by now. Damn it, Callie, people worry about you, you know."

Marta Atwood is whispering to Gianna Watson behind me. I hear my name: "Lindsey says she's a lesbo. She tries to crawl into Lindsey's bed all the time."

Gianna retorts, not so quietly: "I hear lots of lesbians, if they're trying not be a lesbian, sleep with lots of guys. You know, to snap themselves out of it."

"Well, that certainly fits the description of her."

One guy.

I've slept with one guy at Carmel, and one guy before him, and these idiots classify that as "lots." Not to mention, wasn't I the only girl on the boat not acting like a lesbian this past weekend?

I'm not surprised at their feeble attempts to bully me. Lindsey's queen to their court, after all, and she doesn't do her own dirty work. I dart a glare in Marta's direction.

She presses her lips together, but when I turn away, the two of them giggle at my expense.

I sigh. Finally meet John's gaze.

He subtly brushes the back of my hand. "I've been worried, you know. I didn't hear from you at all last night, and I called you a hundred times."

"I've been a little confused." It's my best attempt at explaining, but I know to unknowledgeable people, it appears I'm talking about the one thing about which I'm not confused: my sexuality. Marta's giggle erupts into a boisterous laugh.

John's blue eyes penetrate me. Memories bedazzle my

every nerve, flushing my system with warmth, like a fluffy blanket and a blazing fireplace.

"See me tonight," he whispers.

I part my lips to answer in the affirmative, but the bell tolls, silencing everyone.

Mrs. Kenilworth gives me a slip at attendance. Dean Ritchie wants to see me. Big fucking surprise.

"During your study hall," she tells me.

Cleanse.

God, not another day of this. Sweat breaks on my brow as the familiar drumming inside my head commences. Black spots float in my line of vision. It hurts to keep my eyes open.

I feel seasick, as if I'm bobbing and swaying in the middle of a whitecapped lake in a tiny boat.

"Callie, come on!" Yasmin Hayes taps me on the elbow. I follow her to chapel.

I sit for the welcome message. The word pounds my brain: *cleanse.*

The chapel fades, overtaken by the image of a vast, silvery lake. The waves spray against the side of the boat. I'm lying against my mother's belly. She's sniffling, maybe crying, while someone rows the boat closer to shore. I fixate on the dark blue duffel bag near his feet. What's in the bag? I want to ask. What's in the bag?

Nausea hits, and blinding pain cracks through my brain like lightning, jolting me back to the chapel at Carmel

Catholic. I look down at my notebook, which is open on my lap:

Cleanse the body, the mind, the soul. Cleanse cleanse cleanse.

A note folded into a tight square lands atop the words.

John discreetly withdraws.

In French class, Gianna Watson raises her hand. "Madame? What's the French word for lesbian?"

Hushed giggles and chuckles follow.

I know the snarky comment is meant to seclude and humiliate me, even before Gianna purses her lips and raises her brows at me.

I open the note John chucked over the pew at me. It says:

> *Calliope,*
> *Meet after school. Strictly business.*
> *John*

I wonder if there is such a thing as strictly business between us. Maybe he wants to break it off with me. After all, he isn't into the lesbian scene.

I write back—

> *John,*
> *Can't. Appointment with Ewing.*
> *Callie*

—and hand it to him during the passing period between French class and what should be my study hall.

Today, however, I don't have a study hall. Dean Ritchie has summonsed me to appear in his office in lieu of practicing the conjugation of French verbs, and staring at theorems I don't understand.

The words won't leave my head, even though I've written them down:

Christen the flesh with heavenly rain.

When I arrive, Ritchie's pacing his office, patting his belly, studying me. "You know your skirt isn't regulation length."

Cleanse cleanse cleanse.

"Callie."

I blink up at him, away from my notebook, although I'm still forming letters with the pen in my hand.

"Is this insubordination going to become a habit?" He reaches for a file on his desk. "It seems you were missing from some of your classes the other day."

Cleanse the body, cleanse the mind, cleanse the spirit. Bodymindspirit. Cleanse cleanse cleanse cleanse cleanse cleanse.

"Callie." Ritchie slaps a hand onto my notebook and yanks it away.

"I need it," I tell him.

"I need your attention, Callie."

It feels as if my heart is sinking in my chest, bottoming out in my gut. My fingertips tingle. "Please. I really don't

237

feel well." I'm sweating, clammy. It's as if the words are stirring up the sins sleeping inside me, as if the sins are bleeding through my skin, desperate to escape me. "I need my notebook."

"I. Need. Your. Attention."

Sobbing now, I shove up my sleeve, press the tip of my pen to my forearm, and let the words go. I draw in a breath, but Ritchie pulls the pen from my hand before I exhale. "Please." The word comes out on a wheeze. I fumble through the caddy of pens on his desk. Please have a red felt-tip, please. "I need it. Going to be sick. Going to be sick."

"What's wrong with you?"

I'm tearing through my backpack now, in search of my spare pen. "It's my condition." Pen! I bite off the cap and continue to write on my arm.

CLEANSE YOUR SOUL SINNER SINNER SINNER SINNER CLEANSE YOUR SOUL CLEA

Ritchie disarms me again.

"No!" I reach for the pen, and while I can't reach it, neither can I stop staring at it.

"Look at me, young lady."

"I . . . I'm going to be sick if I can't—"

"Graphomania makes you queasy." Ritchie's lips curl up at the corners.

It does, actually.

"I've had it with this excuse! I wasn't born yesterday."

He glances in my direction before opening the file he now holds. "I spoke with the Hutches. They said they'd deal with you at home, but there also will be a consequence here at Carmel."

"I'll pay it. Just give me my pen. Please, I have to. I need it." I try to hold his glance, but the room is spinning out of control. It doesn't help with the impulse to upchuck, but I manage to hold it off.

After a few moments of silence, he admits, "You don't look well."

I'm spiraling down into the dark place again. Already I'm not sleeping much. Food will be the next sacrifice, if the words keep tormenting me this way.

Even when Ritchie places the back of his hand on my forehead, I'm too numb to flinch away from his touch. "You aren't warm."

"Can I just . . ." I have to lick my lips mid-sentence to continue. I'm so parched. "If you won't let me write, can I lie down?"

"Are you drunk?"

"I don't drink."

"Hungover?"

"I don't drink. Just want my pen. Just have to write."

"Do you want to go home?"

I shake my head and slouch farther down in the chair. I can't imagine going home to the place above the Vagabond, where I'll shiver and breathe in decades of mildew, and I know I'm not welcome at Lindsey's. "I just need to . . . I need to write. Please." The room is spinning out of control, becoming a swish of navy blue and green, and a bright white light flashes at intervals. I'm going. I'm going. Going. I allow my eyes to flutter closed.

"Let's get you to the nurse."

With the pressure of Ritchie's hand under my elbow, I stand. Walk. But I'm not really here. Not really present. Numb. Cloudy.

I hear, if only in the recesses of my mind, my mother's bracelets clanging. Someone strums a guitar. She's singing. *Let my love open the door.*

God, I miss her.

Her song swirls inside me.

I sway to the rhythm.

She's turning Tarot over her swollen belly.

Candles burn, masking the lake water scent of the old building with vanilla and cinnamon. A breath of lake breeze whips through the white sheers in a white room. I'm falling asleep in a mound of yellow and pink pillows.

Gripping a rosary in my tiny, two-year-old hands, worrying at the center stone until it falls out.

I'm lying on a cot.

Someone's looking at me.

Palmer.

I scramble to sit, struggle to open my eyes.

But I've been in such a deep sleep that it's hard to stir.

"Easy, Callie."

"No!"

"Callie." An index finger strokes my right knee.

"No, no, no!"

"Callie. Callie, it's me."

John.

His voice is distant, and my body is numb everywhere, save the hot space on the inside of my right knee where he touched me. I concentrate on the spot, willing its warmth to spread over me. I wiggle my toes, and some feeling returns. Do the same with my fingers.

Eventually, I manage to peel my eyes open.

I'm in the nurse's office at Carmel.

He cracks a smile. "You okay?"

"Yeah." And I do feel better. I wonder if I only needed a decent rest. "Yeah." I lick my lips. "I'm okay."

"That's good," he says. "You want a ride to your appointment?"

"Ride?"

"Well, yeah. Lindsey left already, so I thought—"

I tuck a few fingers beneath the cuff of my sweater and twist the face of John's watch toward me. "Jesus!" It's three fifteen. School's over. I slept the entire afternoon.

"You must've been tired."

"I was." I rub sleep from my eyes.

"Come on." He juts his chin toward the door. "I'll get you to your appointment."

"You have practice."

"Screw practice."

"I can take a bus."

"Callie, did I do something wrong?"

I reach for my penny loafers. "Yeah. You neglected to respond to the mating calls of Lindsey Hutch."

He sighs. "With us, I mean."

"No." I shove my feet into Lindsey's old shoes.

"Then stop avoiding me." He flattens his palm against my thigh. "Let me help you."

Ten minutes later, we're on our way to Ewing's office. I'm sucking on a butterscotch Dum Dums pop, one John had tucked in his glove box from his last visit to the bank.

He glances at me. "Are you . . ."

"I'm fine."

"No, I mean, is there a chance you could . . ." He brings the car to a stop at a light and burns me with a steady stare.

I pull the candy from my mouth and try not to sound irritated. "I could . . . what?"

"Lindsey's telling people you're pregnant."

My heart bottoms out in my gut. "Really?"

"I hear she posted something on Facebook about being excited to be an aunt. Tons of people saw it before they even got to school." He licks his lips and hesitantly continues. "Then you were sick today, and—"

"God, can she ever be a bitch!" A cavern hollows out in my chest.

"If you are, it means something about you and Elijah because—"

"Are you kidding me?" I can't look at him. The hollow spot deepens. "I'm not."

"I'm just saying. We used a Trojan, so . . ."

"Why are you acting like this rumor is true?"

The car begins to roll. "I said *if*."

"Well, stop wondering what if. I'm not!"

"Sorry."

"I'm sure you are. I'm sure you're sorry you ever laid eyes on me."

"No. God, Callie . . ."

I turn up the radio and allow Eminem's tortured commentary to fill the space between John and me. Memories of a masculine hand feathering over a pregnant belly flash in my mind. I see it, plain as day. As quickly as the image startles me, it fades.

After a few measures, he punches the dial with his thumb, silencing the music. "Listen, I just think I deserve to know. If you're still . . . you know . . . with Elijah . . ."

"I have a hard time thinking that's any of your business, anyway. We hooked up. Maybe we shouldn't have. But regardless, what happened homecoming night doesn't obligate you, doesn't have to change what I am to you."

"Hey . . . relax."

"I'm a mess. I know that. You don't have to be part of it, and considering Lindsey, maybe you shouldn't be."

"I just asked a question, if there's a chance this rumor is true—"

"You *didn't* ask—you assumed it was—but it isn't."

"Okay." His hand falls on my thigh.

It feels comforting.

Silence hangs between us. Finally, he speaks up: "Can you try to understand that I wasn't asking to accuse you, but because . . . If Elijah's still hanging around, that means something. Not judging you. Just want to know where I stand, you know?"

I soften a little. "Okay."

He's nodding.

"Lindsey's a bitch. Who saw the post?"

He glances at me out of the corner of his eye. "Pretty much everyone, but don't worry. I'll set the record straight."

I'm alone with the words, with fragmented memories that don't make sense, with the fear that Hannah's gone because I couldn't save her. But suddenly . . .

I drop my hand atop John's.

Suddenly, I don't feel as alone as I used to.

TWENTY-TWO

There are certain times I'm reminded of the benefits of having a mother. Bundled in a stadium blanket, half lying, half sitting on Dr. Warren Ewing's leather sofa whilst he counsels me is one of them.

The chills and queasiness have returned, and the words are dancing in my brain like a club beat. My notebook is open, propped against my thighs, and my pen moves, as if of its own volition while I speak. It's never been this bad before.

If my mother were here, she'd be feeding me crackers and tea. Singing. Turning her cards.

"I won't quit until we know, Callie," Ewing says.

That makes two of us. Only where I don't have a choice, he does.

"So," he continues. "Where've you been staying, if not at the Hutches'?"

"If I tell you, you have to report it."

"The place above the Vagabond?"

I write—*Stripped yellow linens dried with the breeze of the sea*—and exhale a deeply held breath. "Yes."

He nods. "Callie, the state has provided ample accommodations for you."

"Lindsey and I are in the middle of something." I place a hand over my forehead and swear I can feel the words vibrating beneath my flesh. "She's telling everyone I'm a lesbian. And pregnant."

"Pregnant lesbian." When he says it, it sounds so absurd that I wonder how anyone at school is buying it. "Are you?"

"If I am, I've sure wasted a lot of time with Elijah, haven't I?" I try to laugh, but it hurts my head too much.

His fingers become a steeple, which supports his chin. "I meant pregnant."

"No!"

"Hmm. Why is she saying these things? What happened?"

"John happened. We sort of . . . hooked up." I yank up my sleeve and present John's watch. I don't want him to think I irresponsibly fell into bed with John; he needs to understand the circumstances, although he'd tell me that he isn't judging me, anyway. "This fits into the puzzle somehow." I reiterate what John said at Lake County PD, about my knowing the inscription, about my remembering it, as if I'd seen it. I tell

246

him about my mother's reading John's aura and fortune.

"Do you . . . this may seem unorthodox, but . . . can we call him in here?"

After I give half a nod of consent, Ewing is already at the door, inviting John into another of my private realms. At this rate, he'll know more about me than he ever bargained for. Before John even takes a seat next to me, Ewing's on him: "Tell me about the day you found the rosary."

John lowers himself to the sofa, licks his lips, and glances at me, as if I breached his secret about his believing in otherworldly energies and distinctly anti-Catholic ideologies.

I shrug an apology, although I don't feel as if I owe him one. This is the one place I shouldn't have to censor or explain myself.

After a brief pause, John answers, "I'd been thinking about it, you know, since I met the mystic—Callie's mom— at the Vagabond."

"Serena told you where to find it?"

"A little over a year ago, yeah. She told me where to dig, and when Hannah went missing, I dug. There it was."

Ewing squints at him. "And why were you looking for it?"

"I took her seriously, I guess. Because of the watch, what she knew about the watch."

"He wasn't really looking for the rosary," I say. "He was looking for Hannah Rynes."

"I was looking for both," he corrects me.

"Hmm." Ewing nods.

"It was worth a look. I mean, what if I'd been given this information, and Hannah had been there the whole time, and I hadn't looked?"

"You think the mystic was leading you to a missing person."

"I did think that." John leans back and pulls my feet across his lap. "It's crazy how much she knew, and she said I'd find the body of an angel there, too."

"Did you go to the police with this lead?"

"After I found the rosary, absolutely. They said they'd follow up on it."

"Following up on it probably meant asking my mother what she meant," I interject. "And she probably couldn't explain herself."

Ewing rises from his chair, walks to the door, which he opens. "Thank you for your time. She'll be out in twenty minutes, give or take."

After John makes his exit, Ewing resumes his seat, cocks his head to the right, and says, "On the record: I want you to take the Ativan."

I begin to nod.

"But off the record . . . you're remembering things. I feel like you're on the brink of a breakthrough, and if you think the medication will quash it . . ." He shakes his head. "Use your best judgment, all right? I'm going to trust you to know what you need to do—take it if it's unbearable. Don't, if you feel like you're getting somewhere."

"Okay."

"And there's no wiggle room on this. Go back to the Hutches'."

"I can't. She's telling people—"

"You said it isn't true."

"It's not so much that she's lying. It's that people will believe it if she says it. I don't like people thinking that way about me."

"Is there any part of you that thinks that way about yourself?"

My first impulse is to shake my head, but now that I think about it . . . "Maybe. I mean, there's Elijah, and there's John, and not much room in between."

"When you and Elijah first got together, did you ever assume he'd be the only guy you'd love?"

I shrug a shoulder. "I don't know. Maybe."

"Statistically, that would've been rare. The expectation that we'll end up with the very first people who cross our paths is unrealistic. So, in that vein, what you're doing with John is very, very normal. You're moving on. Creating distance between you and Elijah. You're not a bad person for doing it."

Tears threaten to well in my eyes. There's a tickle in my nose. "That's rational. But Lindsey isn't."

"What Lindsey thinks of you can't concern you."

"Easy for you to say. You're not the resident pregnant lesbian of Carmel Catholic."

"Has your perception of Palmer changed based on what the congregation insists is true about him?"

I shake my head.

"Then why would your perception of yourself change, just because Lindsey's spreading a ridiculous rumor?"

I'm lying on the itchy carpeting in the apartment above the Vagabond. The establishment below me is closed now, so the place is deathly, eerily quiet. I don't like the quiet any more than I like the solitude.

Not that I'm alone. Someone else lingers, someone knows I'm here. Someone's waiting for me to exit.

I steal a glance out the window every now and again, but I can't see anyone amongst the harbor lights.

By candlelight, I read the hands of John's watch. It's almost two in the morning. Something won't leave my mind—something I felt on the way to my appointment with Dr. Ewing, something I remember seeing in my mind before I fell asleep at school:

My mother's pregnant belly.

Palmer's hand pressed against it.

When I close my eyes, I feel the icy pelting of rain on my back, dirt encrusted under my fingernails, wood planks beneath my feet.

There's a door buried in the loam.

A crimson door.

I wedge the blade of the shovel beneath the door.

My breath catches in my throat, and my eyes snap open.

I listen hard, but only the hum of neon lights buzzes in my ears. It's a far cry less comforting than the sounds of Lindsey's feet swishing beneath her covers.

TWENTY-THREE

Fuck.

It's an overcast day. No bright sunrise awakened me. I'm going to be late to school.

And double fuck, I'm still in possession of only one Carmel skirt, which is too short for me. If I keep screwing up at school, I'm going to be in deep shit with the Hutches.

After an ice-cold shower, I suck it in to zip the skirt, and use a rubber band to secure the button to the buttonhole. Damn Lindsey and her tiny waist. Why can't she have a plump ass like the rest of us?

Lindsey.

Despite everything she's said about me, I miss her. If I'd

never slept with John Fogel, Lindsey and I would be laughing over Pop-Tarts right now. I'd be cautioning her about her tendency to overuse eyeliner, and she'd be braiding a small section of hair across the crown of my head.

I unplug my phone from the charger. I have to find a ride to school. I missed the Pace bus.

A text from Elijah greets me: *c u at harbor 2nite*.

Good. I'm glad he's coming. I have a few hundred questions to ask him. I reply: *will b here*. Then I dial the other man in my life.

John answers on the first ring: "Well, good morning, beautiful."

"Have you left yet?"

"So, it's official."

I flinch when I hear Lindsey's voice at my back. I turn from my locker to face her. She is flawlessly made up, wearing false eyelashes and my Pinkalicious lipstick. Both make her look like she belongs on the cover of a fashion mag. "Hi."

"Is it true?"

"Is what true?"

"That you and Jon are a couple."

"Who's saying that?"

"Everyone saw you get out of his car this morning."

"Relax." I pull my calc text from the shelf and stifle a yawn. "He just drove me to school."

"Why don't you ask your own man to drive you to school?"

"Why do you insist on claiming someone who doesn't want you?"

"You bitch!"

"I'm a bitch?" I kick my locker door shut and lower my voice to a whisper as I hone in on her space. "You're telling people I'm a pregnant lesbian slut, and I'm a bitch?"

"I've never said anything that isn't true. People draw their own conclusions. If the shoe fits, Calliope . . ." She smirks up at me, only inches of air separating us.

"Hey, cool it!" John nudges his way between us and physically separates us, pressing me toward my locker and my sister a few feet farther into the hallway.

Lindsey sneers at him. "Do you like taking my clothes off her body?" She then turns back to me. "Does he know you're wearing my clothes to seduce him?"

"He knows you used my words to snag him," I retort.

"How hot do you think she'll be in rags, loverboy?"

"Cool it, Lindsey," he says.

"Fuck you, Fogel." She glances down at his fly. "Truth is, if it was worth anything, I'd probably be missing it right now, but it was so small I don't remember feeling it." She grins, tosses her hair over her shoulder, and heads to homeroom.

My head spins. "What did she say?" I meet John's glance. "Did she mean that you . . ."

"Are you okay?" John drags a finger along the contour of my cheek.

I feel like someone dug a bottomless pit in my stomach. "Did you . . . did you sleep with her, too?"

He brushes a hair from my forehead, his gaze focused there, and his jaw is set and determined.

"Did you?"

His shoulders drop and, at last, he meets my stare. "Callie . . ."

I shove his hand away and walk to homeroom.

"Callie, come on."

Instantly, the desire to rip the rosary from my neck and his watch from my wrist comes over me. I should slip them off and drop them to the floor the way he just dropped my trust.

I have to see my mother. I'm going, I decide. Immediately after school today.

When today's orderly opens the door, my mother is turning cards and humming. I can't place the song, but I think she used to sing it to me when I was small.

A sly smile turns up her lips when she sees me, but she quickly turns back to her cards.

Once we're alone, I clear my throat. "Hi, Mom."

She raises a finger to delay me and lays out the last cards in a formation I've never seen her use before. This one is more an H than a cross. Her eyes shift over the cards as she studies the supposed meaning hidden there.

"My, my, Calliope." She shakes her head and at last meets my glance. "What have you gotten yourself into?"

Instantly, my mouth feels dry.

"I see two male figures, but neither is competent. One of them is lying to you. The other is hiding something big."

I burst into tears. Shoulders shaking, and with a heavy head, I find support only in the wall behind me. I lean against it and sink to the floor.

"Callie."

I sniffle and take in breath enough to reply. "Yeah."

"Look at me."

I lift my head, but it hurts too much to hold it high. Instead, I rest my cheek on my knee and hold my mother's stare.

"I love you," she says.

"I love you, too." I can tell she wants to ask me what I'm hiding from her.

She tilts her head and raises an eyebrow, but her expression is soft. She's looking at me the way she looked at me after the first time Palmer whipped me, the first time Drake and I kissed. She's looking at me as if she's sorry for putting me in this position.

"Where did you get the watch?"

"It belongs to John Fogel."

If she's ever heard the name, or if she remembers him from the Vagabond, no recognition lights in her eyes. "Can

I see it?" Slowly, she approaches me, crouches to my level.

I hold my hand out to her.

She trails the pad of a finger beneath the face of the watch and smiles. "This boy . . . he's good for you. Better intentions than that boy from County."

Elijah never slept with my best friend.

"Elijah's there for me when no one else is. I know you don't like him, Mom, but I love him. I always will."

She presses her lips together and stands.

"Mom?" I lick my lips and straighten. "Did Palmer take Hannah Rynes?"

"I know he's capable. He took you from me, didn't he?" She shrugs a shoulder and turns back to her cards. "There's uncertainty here. Warning signs. Death."

"You think she's dead?"

This time, when my mother glances up at me, her eyes are vacant. "It doesn't matter, baby. She's gone." She twists a few cards on her snack tray. "Every time I read for you, key cards are upside down." She picks one up and shows it to me. "The World. Your world is upside down."

I wonder what her first clue was.

"Do you remember John Fogel?"

She's busy with her cards. If she heard me, she isn't letting on.

"You met him at the Vagabond. You described his watch. Told him about the rosary."

At this, her head shoots up. "Do you have it?"

257

I hesitate, but nod.

"Where is it?" She shoves aside her tray and takes a few steps toward me.

There's a gleam in her eye. Maniacal. For the first time, she looks as crazy as they tell me she is. I press my hands against the wall and use it to push myself to my feet. I glance at the button near the door, the one that will ring an orderly when I'm ready to leave. But I don't need it, do I? She's my mother. She won't hurt me.

But if that's true, why am I so scared?

"Calliope!"

My heart is kicking up pace, as if I'm running. In the periphery of my mind, I hear the crunch of stones beneath my feet, feel the scratch of juniper branches against my arms, taste holy water. Words scrawl in the air before me. I pull my notebook from my bag and write:

bubbling into oblivion bubbling into oblivion bubbling into oblivion.

"Callie."

"You wanted me to have it, didn't you?" My words are shaky.

"Of course. It's yours. Where is it?"

Slowly, I pull the scarf from my neck and expose the crucifix.

"Something about it is supposed to help me remember." Her hands close around my biceps; she squeezes too tightly as she stares at the pendant, or maybe at my baby ring beneath it. "You shouldn't have gone digging. Palmer . . . he'll be waiting. Watching."

"No, Mom. John gave it to me. Do you remember him? You met him at the Vagabond."

She's shaking her head. Her grip gets tighter.

"The boy with the watch," I remind her. "You told him he'd know me—"

"By your voice. Yes." Slowly, she loosens her grip on my arms. "One of them listened."

"One of them?"

"You know how it works. Read the aura, hook the prospect. I gave the same reading to all of them."

"Every one?"

"The spiel about the watch, the thing with the rosary, the voice, she'll look like me . . . I told them all, hoping one would listen. And this one did. Did he find the door, too?"

I'm dizzy. "The door?"

"Didn't he tell you?"

"Mom, why don't you tell me? Why did you plant the information with strangers instead of just telling me?"

"I kept you safe."

"From Palmer? He's gone now—"

"He's never gone." Her index finger lands gently on my lips. "You could run a thousand miles, and he'll always come for you. You don't know what he's capable of."

"But I'm starting to remember, Mom. It's only a matter

of time until I do, and time is of the essence. If there's any chance Hannah is alive—"

"Alive or dead, she's gone, baby."

"What, according to the cards? Stop pretending you believe in that bullshit, Mom. No one knows she's gone until we find her. No one but the person who took her."

"It's over, if you have your rosary. Something about it's supposed to remind me . . . of something . . ."

"Where did you get it? Did you make it?"

"Maybe. I don't remember."

"Did you make it for a girl named Lorraine?"

"Maybe."

"Do you know who Lorraine is?"

"Who?"

"It's etched on the back. Lorraine Oh."

She gives her head a minute shake. "I don't remember."

"Is she someone you knew before, maybe?"

"It'll help you find your family."

"You're my family!"

"Your other family."

"The Hutches? Mom, this is important. Hannah's life—"

"It's over." She applies more pressure with her finger against my lips, and her eyes glow with insanity. Her lips peel back, baring her teeth, like a tiger about to pierce my jugular. "Shh!"

Her forearm is braced across my neck.

"I want you to listen to me. You have to stop this,

Calliope. Let it go. Go home, baby, get far away from here, and let this place go."

"Where's home? The Hutches'?" I'm prying at her arm, but she won't move it from my neck.

I can't breathe, but I don't know if it's because she's choking me, or because I'm starting to hyperventilate in nervousness. I reach toward the button. Depress it madly as if it flings the paddles of a pinball machine.

"Where's home?"

"It's where you came from. Don't forget where you came from."

"I don't know where I came from! You won't tell me!"

"I can't remember." Her voice is more a hiss than a whisper. "Whatever you do, don't take that rosary from your body. Keep it on you at all times. It'll keep you safe, when I can't. It will take you home."

I hear my sobs, smell her antiseptic breath, taste the salt of my tears.

"You don't want to remember what you've forgotten," she says. "Ignorance is perpetual bliss."

TWENTY-FOUR

There's a red mark on the side of my neck where my mother held me against the wall. With my scarf, I'd hidden it from the orderlies. I have to believe she hadn't meant to hurt me, she hadn't meant to scare me, except maybe to scare me off my quest for information. That's why, when the orderlies asked why I'd hit the button so many times, I told them my mother simply hadn't been herself today.

My mother.

Rather, the woman who stabbed Palmer Prescott in the thigh.

They're two different people in my mind, and they have to remain so, if I'm going to get through this with a modicum of sanity. There's my mother—the one whose hair looks like mine, the one who creates and turns Tarot cards for cash and sings. And then there's the woman who's responsible for the mark on my neck.

Serena and I have always been a team. Us against Palmer. Us against the rent check. Us against the world. The woman who bruised me is not the same woman who birthed me.

I want to head back to the Vagabond, curl into a ball, and cry myself to sleep, but I have homework to do and the answers to a million questions to research. I exit the bus at the library and hurry down a long, winding path from the road through sprinkling rain to the portico, which welcomes visitors like open arms.

The Lehmann Public Library is a Victorian, if not Gothic, structure, situated inland from Lake Nippersink, near Carmel Catholic, built in a grove of willow trees. The Lehmann building is complete with a spire-topped turret and a stone façade. Whether it was meant to look holy or not, it demands respect.

Obeying the rules, I turn off my ringer on my cell phone. I don't need the distraction of texts anyway, not that Lindsey's doing much to communicate with me. I wonder how long it will take her parents to realize I'm gone. My foster sister has been covering for my absences for so long that the space I leave behind must no longer be a void. I wonder how long I'll be gone from John's life before he stops missing me, too.

I take a seat at a computer table near the back of the building and stare out the leaded-glassed window at the rain amassing outside. The droplets streaming down the windows further distort the lake in the distance; it looks like a ferocious beast of blue-silver waves. I'm far from the shore, but I smell it here, as if the lake air is embedded in the old wood slats beneath my feet.

The library feels like home, but more than the scent of it comforts me. I eventually realize it's because it reminds me of Holy Promise: the Gothic archways and corbels, the leaded glass, the polished mahogany benches. If I close my eyes, I might even be able to fool myself into believing that I'm praying in the nave, instead of traveling the stacks in search of sources. Even the book-lined paths remind me of the corridors I used to explore as a child.

A presence looms behind me. Hair pricks on the back of my neck, and a chill races up my spine, the type of sensation I feel when someone's breathing too close to me. I'm afraid to turn around, but I manage to brave a glance over my shoulder.

Of course, no one's there.

Heads bend over notebooks and keyboards. Everyone's writing here. Maybe not the way I write, but they're writing. A sense of normality filters through me. Maybe there's a chance I can belong somewhere, after all.

And then I see him: John, looking a few minutes past a shower, a little fatigued, which makes sense because he's just come from football practice. He's wearing black insulated athletic pants, the kind with white stripes down the sides, and a gray hoodie over a white T-shirt. He offers a wave. Smiles.

I give him a nod, but quickly turn away.

I wonder if he's here to write the same twelve-page paper for Mr. Willis I have to catch up on, seeing as I missed a couple days of school—having cut once with John last week, and spent yesterday sleeping off a graphomania attack in the nurse's office.

But I don't have time for school assignments right now. I pull up the Internet and type in a search: Reverend Palmer Prescott.

There are a few new articles listed on the search page— "One Year Later: Authorities No Closer to Answers in Hannah Rynes Kidnapping"—but I'm more interested in reading the old news.

I click on an old story: "Reverend or Madman: Two sides of Palmer Prescott." I've read this one a million times, but I reread everything. Maybe I've missed something, a clue, a detail . . .

According to police, a source, unnamed, says the founder of the Church of the Holy Promise and the missing suspect in Hannah Rynes's disappearance, Palmer Prescott, is not who he appears to be. If allegations are correct, this information may give credence to the police's theory that Prescott is solely responsible for Rynes's kidnapping. The source alleges physical and emotional abuse against unnamed parishioners, painting a grotesque picture of the man beneath the cloth, yet a great percentage of the Holy Promise congregation contends the reverend is incapable of committing the abusive acts, let alone carrying out a kidnapping. Prescott's followers insist if he's involved, it is due to foul play, to which perhaps Prescott himself fell prey. According to parishioner James Brandiwyne: "He was a man of God, a good man. He baptized my children, held them in his arms. If these people are telling the truth, that the reverend did these unspeakable things, why are they hiding behind anonymity?" This isn't the first time Prescott faces allegations of abuse. The first accusations came a year before Rynes's disappearance; the accuser is now a resident of the Meadows Mental Health and Rehabilitation Center.

I'm the unnamed source in this article. Mr. Brandiwyne wasn't the only one to contradict my statements. Considering my graphomania, the blackouts, I have to wonder if maybe Mr. Brandiwyne is right. Maybe I don't know what really happened. Am I as crazy as my mother? Did I imagine hearing my mother's cries from the confessional? Did I invent the story about the fountain, and conjure the belt slashing and biting into my flesh?

Tears rise before I can stop them. I bring a hand to the scar on my shoulder. Is Palmer really responsible for it? Maybe nothing is real, maybe I'm as insane as I feel, maybe—

"Hey." A hand on mine shocks me more than comforts me at first. John.

I wrap my fingers around his.

But I can't stop the revelation spinning in my mind: he slept with my sister, he slept with my sister, *he slept with my sister*. I pull away. Turn back to the computer screen.

"I don't blame you for being mad. I should've told you." He takes the chair next to mine and pulls a chunk of hair away from my face.

I give him a quick glance from the corner of my eye. "Why didn't you?"

"Why didn't she?"

"She doesn't have to tell me, John." But I've been wondering the same thing. She tells me everything. Why wouldn't she have told me about this?

"Okay." When he sighs, his cheeks puff up a little. "Okay, it was last spring, end of March."

Before me. Late March. That's why Lindsey didn't tell me about it. It was right around the time I came to live with the Hutches. She didn't know me yet, let alone trust me enough to tell me who she'd slept with. And I didn't know any of her friends.

"We were on my boat, a bunch of us, and—"

"Shh!" A librarian gives us a threatening stare.

I roll my eyes, refocus on the screen, on a black-and-white candid of Palmer with hands raised to heaven on the altar at Holy Promise.

John whispers: "Listen, that night, I wasn't quite . . . you notice I don't drink. Or smoke." His tongue touches his lower lip as his eyes narrow in an expression between frustration and contemplation. "Lindsey and I, we're friends . . . sort of. I wouldn't have . . . I didn't use her."

"You had sex with her."

The nearly imperceptible bob of his head can pass for a confirmation.

"And you weren't planning on dating her."

"No."

"So how is that not using her?"

"Because it was her idea, all right?" His blue eyes harden. "I'm not blaming her, I'm not, but I was sort of drunk—it's one reason I don't drink anymore, not that I ever drank too much—and she kept making moves, she had . . . you know . . . protection, and it just kind of . . . happened."

"The way it just kind of happened between us? I had protection, too."

"God, Callie, no."

"And I played right into your hands."

He slumps back in his chair. "Is that what you think of

me? You think I just go around screwing girls I don't care about?"

"If the shoe fits . . ."

"So that's what you think." He knots his fingers in his hair. "You think I just . . . do this . . . with other girls."

I don't think that, not entirely. Blood buzzes as it rushes through my veins. Every nerve in my body hums, but as much as I want to cave, as much as I want to put stock in what he's trying to say, I force myself to remain stoic. It's one thing to be put over by Elijah, but I refuse to let John snow me, too. I raise an eyebrow and repeat, "If the shoe fits . . ."

"Fine," he says. "But you're wrong."

"Two girls living in the same house say I'm right. Odds are—"

"I made one mistake, and I made one decision. There hasn't been anyone else, Calliope, and I don't want anyone else."

Butterflies kick up in my gut. I meet his glance.

"That's right. Once with Lindsey, once with you. That's about the size of it. And if that makes me a guy who just screws girls he doesn't care about . . . okay."

I feel my shoulders sag a little, feel tension releasing in my jaw. "You should've told me about you and Lindsey."

"Yeah, I should've, but would it have changed anything?"

"We'll never know."

"Callie, I wish Lindsey and I hadn't—believe me, I wish we hadn't—but I can't change the past."

I glance again at the picture of my father on the computer screen. "No one can."

He touches me on the neck, fingers the mark my mother left there.

The Lehmann Library blackens in my peripheral vision— "I need a pen"—and suddenly I'm throttled through avenues of my memory bank.

There's a blue duffel bag in the rowboat.

A man digs on the Point.

Someone's crying, muttering three imperceptible words over and over again.

I can't make out what she's saying. Listen hard. Harder. She's crying. I can't hear her. Can't hear.

What's in that duffel bag?

"Callie?"

I look again over my shoulder, toward the rowboat, but there's nothing there. Nothing there. Black night. The piney odor of Palmer's aftershave looms behind me.

I gasp for breath, collapse into the earth.

"Callie."

The gluey scent of fresh felt-tip meets my nostrils.

I lift my head, take in the sight of Lehmann Library, then look to my notebook:

Strangled by the cords of daisies I Killed him I Killed him I Killed him. I Killed him. Killed him.

John's hand is warm against my neck.

I've been craving his touch all day, and at the same time wishing I wasn't. Still at odds, I now stiffen with the contact.

I close my eyes and again bury my head in my arms. "Johnny?"

"Yeah?" His fingers are now caressing the tender flesh my mother marred.

I twist my head just enough to meet his glance. "I think I remember something."

His fingers still. "What?"

"A blue duffel bag. On Highland Point. There are things—other things—buried up there."

He's nodding. "Want to call that detective?"

"You heard what he said. Tangible evidence. All these snippets of memories aren't going to help without tangible evidence."

"Thousands of leads."

"Not enough time, not enough man power, to follow all the leads that come in."

"Go after dinner?"

"Yeah."

"Pick you up at Lindsey's?"

"I can't go home tonight."

He pulls his cell phone from the pocket of his sweatshirt, and punches in a text. "Wanna have dinner at my place, then?"

Despite the initial elation fluttering in my heart, I'm still not sure how I feel about Lindsey and him. "No."

"You gotta eat, right?"

The closest I've come to the whole meet-the-family thing was the day Elijah and I went AWOL from County and hopped a train to hit a rave in North Chicago. His biological mother lived on the way, he'd said, in the ineptly named Bel Air Motel. I'd stared at the drab stucco façade, so dirty, and the half-lit neon sign with Vegas-style bulbs blinking an unwelcoming beckon.

"You want to stop to say hello?" I'd asked.

He'd replied with two words—"Hell no"—and quickened his pace.

It was the only time we'd ever discussed his mom, whom he said he hadn't seen in a few years.

His dad was another story. He'd *never* seen him, save a mug shot posted online.

So it's safe to say I'm a little less than practiced in this regard.

"Relax," John says.

Impossible. My fingertips feel numb, my heart races, and I can't keep my feet still for the life of me.

Out the car window, along the winding driveway to the mini-mansion John calls home, the trees blur in dizzying palettes of yellow and green amidst the misty rain. I imagine I'm going to feel just as shaky when I come face-to-face with the Fogels as I do now.

What if I graph out in the middle of dinner? God, they're going to think I'm crazy.

John brings the SUV to a gentle stop in a circle drive before the home, which backs to one of the nine inter-connected lakes along the Chain. I couldn't tell you which—we've twisted and turned too many times to keep track—but I already smell the water.

The distinct sound of a basketball repeatedly hitting pavement rises the moment he kills the engine.

On a brick-paved section of the driveway, a girl bearing a striking resemblance to the guy who slept with my sister shoots hoops. As soon as John opens his door to get out of the car, I follow suit and wait while he gathers his school bag and practice gear from the backseat.

He saunters not toward the main entrance to the place, but toward a door near the garage. "Hey, Abby. It's raining."

"Hey, John-boy." Bounce, bounce, bounce. Shoot. "I won't melt."

He tosses his head in my direction. "This is Callie."

She gives me a smile. Bounce, bounce. "Hi, Callie."

"Hi."

She lifts her chin—"What do you see in this guy, any-way?"—and shoots again.

"Funny. Real funny." Once we're beyond hearing dis-tance and entering a laundry room, John leans in a bit closer. "Not so hard, is it?"

"Not so far." But what am I going to do if the impulse to write overcomes me at the dinner table?

273

"John, is that you?" a female voice calls from deeper within the house.

"Yeah." He deposits his athletic bag atop the counter, near the washing machine.

"Would you mind putting the wet clothes in the dryer?"

"Already on it."

And he is. Adeptly, he's tossing clothes from the washer into the dryer, while shoving the slightly wet shoes from his feet. It's clearly part of his daily routine. I soften a little to see him in his natural habitat.

"You can hang your coat on one of the hooks behind you."

No sooner do I accomplish the task—I opt to keep my scarf on to hide the mark on my neck—than he's handing me his coat, too. When I turn to hang his coat on the hook next to mine, I hear the slam of the dryer door, and the rush of water filling the washing machine.

I tumble through archives in my mind. Scrape my shins against jagged rocks. Land at the flat bottom of a rowboat. Push, pull. Push, pull. Push, pull.

In the black of night, I'm rowing. Water is too choppy. I'll never make it. Never make it. Never make it. Have to swim to shore.

I'm gasping for breath.

I feel the water rushing past my face.

Cold. So cold.

And muddy. The shore is muddy. My feet squish into the soft ground.

Branches rip at my flesh as I pound my feet against the earth, fall, get up, fall, get up again. Fall.

"Callie."

"Yeah."

"Hey."

I feel the back of John's hand against my cheek moments before my surroundings reemerge from the clouds in my mind. I'm sitting on the blue slate floor of the Fogels' laundry room, backpack open to my right, notebook open and propped on my knees. John is crouching in front of me.

"You okay?"

I'm holding one of my red pens.

I focus on his eyes. Swallow hard. Brave a glance at my notebook:

Let my love open the door let my love let my love open open the door the door the door the crimson door in your mind.

"I like that song." He twitches a smile. "Classic. Good rhythm. Great lyrics."

"Yeah."

"I remember it a little different than you've written it."

I chuckle, although it isn't funny. "Yeah."

"John, are you—"

A woman is standing in the doorway.

"Mom." He stands in a liquidlike motion, helping me to my feet along the way. "This is Callie."

She's drying her hands on a dish towel, then extends her right hand for a shake. "Welcome. I hope you like lasagna."

"Yes." I shift the pen to my left, then take her hand. "Thanks."

"She's a writer," John says. "A poet, actually."

"Is that right?"

"Yes," I say because even if it isn't wholly true, it's easier than explaining. "I write." I only hope I don't write much more this evening. I busy myself with removing my penny loafers, thankful for the excuse to break the gaze.

"Listen," Mrs. Fogel says as she inches out of the laundry room, "are you free to pick up your nephew from day care next Tuesday after practice? I have an appointment."

Nephew. He's an uncle. Something warm and comforting filters through my system.

"Six o'clock?" He gives me a wink, and leads me farther into the home. "We can probably do that, can't we?"

We?

"Great." Her voice reverberates in the hallway. "I'll tell Tracy to leave a car seat when she drops him off . . ."

An old, acoustic guitar propped on a stand in the corner of the family room catches my eye. As desperately as I try to focus on the conversation, I can't take my eyes from it. Amber in color, with a burgundy swirl hand-painted along the arc. Shaped like a woman's body. I've seen it before. At least I think I have. Maybe at the Vagabond.

"Who plays?" God, I just interrupted his mother.

"Pardon?" She glances at me over her shoulder. If she's irritated with my interruption, she doesn't show it.

"I'm sorry . . . that guitar." I glance up at John. "Do you play?"

"Yeah." He smiles. "A bit."

"It looks . . ." Will I sound like an idiot if I say the guitar looks familiar? Who says that sort of thing? "Looks old."

"Family heirloom of sorts." Her lips press together as she curtly nods.

"I'm sorry." I shake my head, manage to redirect my attention. "Can I help with dinner?"

"Sure."

Before I know it, I'm chopping radishes and carrots, but I can't shake the feeling. I've seen that guitar before.

TWENTY-FIVE

With the exception of six words, which I'd written on a paper napkin at the table—*Trip me with your benevolent intentions*—dinner with John's parents, and the two youngest of his four sisters, went well. I'm sure they thought it was weird the moment I cracked out a felt-tip and, in the midst of a panic attack and a side of steamed green beans, started writing. But no one stared, no one asked, no one commented.

And now, I've brought John home, to the apartment of the Vagabond, where I'm getting ready for tonight's trek out to the Point.

Red words spin around me, but I can't take my eyes off John, who looks rugged in layered flannel, ripped jeans, and Carhartt work boots.

John's eyes are wide as he slowly turns in a circle, staring at the bathroom walls, seemingly spellbound with my graffiti. "So this is where you were? This is what you were doing for the day and a half after Hannah disappeared?"

"Yeah."

"What did the police say about what you'd written?"

My glance goes directly to the space two inches from the doorknob, where I'd written: I KILLED HIM. His blood is on my hands. His heart is in my soul. I KILLED HIM.

"I contradict myself a lot on these walls, so they assumed it's gibberish, at first. But Ewing thinks I'm interpreting what I remember. Morphing it into a shape I can handle, because I can't handle it in its rawest form . . . not yet."

I have to change clothes. I feel sort of self-conscious doing it in front of him—which is silly, as he's seen all there is to see of me—but as the words on the walls have garnered his attention, at least for the time being, and we're in a race against sunset . . . I pull off my sweater, then the polo beneath it. After hanging the uniform over the shower bar, I yank on an old pair of jeans, a T-shirt, and one of John's old sweatshirts, which I'm borrowing for tonight's quest.

"You know, you wrote a lot of this in your notebooks. This passage here: *abiding like the tide*. And this one: *amber ashes in her hourglass*. Lots about water. Lots about death. Choruses, if you will, followed by contrasting bridges. You're not just remembering here. You're creating. Poems. Lyrics."

"Ain't it grand being me." I cough. Cough again. It's coming on. With a vengeance. I dart for my backpack. Tear it open. Suddenly, I can't breathe. I'm underwater, groping for something, anything to push against to resurface.

I open my eyes, feel the sting of the icy cold water against my eyeballs. I see him—Palmer—through the rippling surface. My hand meets something hard and blunt, like the edge of the fountain, but even when I attempt to pull myself to the surface, no relief comes. He pushes me down again.

"Callie!"

I feel the earth slipping away, receding like the tide. I cling to the shore, only to be washed away on the ebb.

I gasp.

Allow my lungs to fill with air, only to choke on more water.

He's turning me over, holding my hair back, as I spew the water back into the fountain.

Only it isn't the fountain anymore, and nothing's coming up. It's the pink bathtub in the place above the Vagabond. I press my cheek to the cool porcelain and study what I've just written:

Bubbling into oblivion bubbling bubbling bubbling into oblivion.

"That's what it means," I say. "Drowning."

"You okay?"

I struggle to catch my breath. Maybe to him, I was simply dry heaving thirty seconds ago. But in my mind, I was fighting for my life last year. "Why do they call drowning a sweet death?"

"Sounds sweeter than some of the other things written here: buried alive, burned, crucified, quartered, stoned, pressed . . ." He's sitting on the bathroom floor next to me, raking through my hair. He flashes a smile. "Hey, you."

"Hi." My head still rests on the edge of the tub. I try to smile back.

"Went well tonight with my family. They like you."

"Only because your family's far too polite to call me out at the dinner table."

"What, that little writing stint? Don't worry about it."

"Easy for you to say."

"I've bolted out of Christmas dinner before to write music. This isn't any different."

"You write music?"

"It makes sense to me, you know?" A faint smile warms his eyes. "Words come to you; notes come to me. I mean, I get it from my dad. He taught himself how to play piano and guitar."

"The guitar." I straighten. "It's his. Your dad's."

"It used to be. He gave it to my cousin before I was born." He squints for a split second. "That's another reason we know he didn't run away. He would've taken that guitar with him."

I hear the song, see the white room in a distant corner

of my mind: *Let my love open the door.* "I'm not crazy, but—"

"No one thinks you are."

"—but I know that guitar. From the Vagabond, maybe. Did your cousin ever go there?"

"Maybe. I'll text my dad."

"It's getting darker." I move to stand and brush past him on my way toward the door.

"Hey." He catches me, holds me against his chest. "I'm sorry I didn't tell you about Lindsey."

I breathe in the clean scent of him. "Okay."

"I know it doesn't fix things, but . . . I'm sorry I didn't tell you."

"She's my sister, Johnny."

"She doesn't care about me as much as about getting everything she wants. She'll get over the insult to her ego, and I'm going to fix this rumor."

"Can you tell me something? I mean, I guess I understand how it happened, but if you don't do that sort of thing with girls . . . don't, you know, sleep around . . . didn't you want to make it right? Try dating her? You could've done a lot worse, right?"

"Yeah, I guess I could've." He rocks back, puts some space between us, drags a few fingers through his hair. "Maybe I would've. I was going to call her the next day. Thought about taking her to lunch. But, I don't know . . . there's something about the way it happened. I just didn't see how we could recover from it, how we could ever be more than what happened. Cheap. On the surface. And then she kept throwing herself at me, and I just . . . couldn't do it."

I'm massaging the writer's cramp in my palm.

John reaches for my hand, takes up the task.

I'm staring into his navy blue eyes. I think he's telling the truth. But the truth will always be there, and soon, the sun will set. "We have to go."

He nods in agreement. "Burning daylight."

"We have shovels?"

"Yeah, I brought a couple."

TWENTY-SIX

Rain pelts my back like icy daggers, and my arms ache. The scent of the lake fills my nostrils, and I shiver with the cold. Yet still, I toil on. Dig. Chink. Sift. Talk about déjà vu. How many times have I contemplated performing this task?

A crescent moon is on the rise, yet we can't see it through the mask of clouds canvasing the sky. A watery, pink filtering of setting sun is low on the horizon. It's a terrible day to be outside. Even worse day to be digging.

But I have to know if the door is where I envision it, I have to know what else is buried up here. I have to know what's real, and what's only imagined.

Images of that night haunt me. The sounds of the shovel.

The cool, flat bottom of the rowboat. Hannah's cold body lying next to mine, her fingers wrapped around my hand.

I dig into the earth again. My shovel hits something hard.

"What was that?" John turns the beam of his flashlight to the land beneath my feet. A tiny patch of red reflects in the beam.

I tap the blade of the shovel against the dirt. *Thunk*. "This is it!"

"That's it," John agrees. "Find the edges."

I'm exhausted, covered in dirt and muck, freezing . . . but I keep digging alongside John, who heaves two shovels of dirt to my one out of the hole in which we're standing.

When we've cleared the surface, he climbs out of the muddy hole, pulls me out after him, and we shine our flashlights into it. We stare down at a door. Crimson in color, it's beautiful from an architectural standpoint—arched to a Gothic point, as if it belongs at the Church of the Holy Promise. Wide-grained wood—hickory, maybe—with red paint peeling from its edges. There's a minute window, about eight inches square, in the peak of the arch. Most of the diamond-shaped panes have broken free from it, but it's gorgeous.

They say life flashes before your eyes when you're about to die, and mine now becomes a slide show in my mind so vivid that I wonder if I'm about to meet my maker, too. The last time I saw this door, I was certainly close enough.

When I close my eyes, I see linens drying in the breeze

off the lake. Hands clutching a rosary. Then the pictures come more quickly. The Vagabond. My mother, the mystic. The labyrinth at the Church of the Holy Promise. The fountain. The garden house and the panties. The rowboat. The shovel. The dirt . . . the door.

I remember everything. From the moment Palmer pulled me out of that fountain, until the police shoved me into the interrogation room two days later. From the day I arrived at County Juvenile Hall to the day the Hutches came for me.

No! I attempt to scream the word, but it comes out only as a shrill, and I can't stop screaming. I gravitate away from the hole we dug.

No.

No, it isn't true. It can't be true!

I break into a run, heading back toward John's SUV.

"Callie!"

I hear him behind me, but I keep running.

"Callie, wait!"

I skid to a halt at the vehicle and tear off my muddy clothes. Have to get the filth of it off me. Have to leave the earth where I found it. Have to respect the dead.

The rain is a downpour now, cleansing my flesh.

But nothing will cleanse my mind.

I left her there with a madman.

I didn't save her.

I saved only myself.

I lift my face to the heavens and breathe in the rain.

Drown me now, Lord. Drown me now.

"Get in the car," John says.

No. But I can't speak over my stifling tears.

"Get in the car!" He's shedding his muddy clothes, too.

I hear doors opening and closing. I guess he's putting on his spare clothes.

Flashes of blue and red lights cross over my closed eyes, but I know they're only memories of the night the police found me writing on the walls.

"Damn it, Calliope! Get in the goddamn car!"

Rain washes over me, masking my tears.

Something fluffy and warm surrounds me.

John pulls me into the car.

I shudder out another sob and wipe my tears on the sweater he wrapped me in.

"What the hell happened back there? We finally find it, and you run?"

At last I turn my head toward him. "Johnny?" The rosary is cold against my skin. My fingers close around it.

"What happened?"

I'm bawling violently, trembling, hyperventilating.

"Calliope, talk to me!"

"I remember," I whisper.

"What?"

"I remember!"

He's silent for a few seconds. "Well," he finally says.

"That's good. That's what you wanted, right?"

I didn't want to remember this. I wanted to remember that she'd gotten away, or even that he was keeping her someplace safe, or . . . or . . . anything but this! I shove my arms into the sweater and curl into a ball on the seat, resting my head on the consul. A red felt-tip and my notebook taunt me from the floor. I grab them both.

"We'll get through this." He massages my head a moment before he reaches for his cell phone. "I'm going to call Guidry, okay? Have them look at what we found."

I uncap the pen, open my notebook, and write:

Unearth her. Fitting tomb. Unearth her. Fitting tomb for a beautiful girl. Unearth her unearth her unearth her.

"John?"

"Hmm?"

"Hannah Rynes is buried under that door."

He inhales sharply, as if sucking back in the wind my words just knocked out of him. "Anything else I should know?"

Plenty.

For starters, she was alive when Palmer put her there.

TWENTY-SEVEN

The jury is out on whether we are heading to the Vagabond to drop me off, or to grab some things so I can stay with John and his family. I can't imagine the latter, and he can't imagine the former—leaving me there, above the Vagabond, alone.

By the time we arrive, a third option presents itself; although calling it an option is like calling one's own birth a choice, as I'm certain neither of us will have a voice in the matter.

Three squad cars and one plain black sedan with civilian plates—all with flashing lights—are parked in the lot at the harbor near the walk leading to the iron staircase.

"I'll be going back to the Hutches'." And if they let me go tonight, I'll consider myself lucky.

"I'll talk to them," John says. "See if they'll let me bring you home, and you'll just come with me."

Before I can tell John it won't make a difference, Elijah appears, hands cuffed behind his back, squinting into the blazing headlights of the patrol cars, as an officer leads him toward the backseat of one of them.

I bolt out of the SUV, wearing only John's Carmel-issue, Land's End V-neck sweater. "No!"

I'm in a room at the Lake County Police Department, wearing sweats with *LCPD* scrawled down the left leg. They're too large, but at least they're warmer than wet underwear and a damp sweater, all of which I'm pretty certain has made its way into evidence bags, along with the digging clothes, which John had balled in the back of the car.

I've been in this room before, and it's just as chilly now as it was last year. Still, it's comfortable, as waiting rooms go. I'm sitting on a vinyl-tufted bench the color of rotten kiwi and leaning against the cinder block wall behind me, waiting for the Hutches to come take me home. This time, I knew the answers to the department's questions, and even to those they didn't ask. I know rounds two and three and four of questions will follow in the weeks to come, but for now, they're satisfied. They'd call, they said, to tell me if Hannah's remains are under the door.

The interview didn't take as long this time around . . . for any of us, apparently, as John's already been permitted to leave—which he did, with some persuasion, although he'd wanted to wait around for me—and Elijah just walked through the door to join me. Without handcuffs this time.

He takes the seat across the room on an equally putrid-looking bench, upholstered in burnt orange, and does everything in his power not to look directly at me. "Thanks," Elijah says. "They were going to book me for breaking and entering, until you showed up. It's the difference between staying with the fosters or heading back to County, so . . . thanks."

"They won't send you back to County."

"If they'd arrested me, they would've. But . . . no. Looks like I'm good."

"Glad I helped for a change."

"Well, I had a legitimate excuse for being there. You. That's why the cops showed up. Someone saw me go in. We had a date, remember." He zaps me with a look to kill. "Or do you?"

The steady stare between us is cool enough to freeze water. I raise an eyebrow but don't break the glance . . . or the silence.

A few seconds, which feel like hours later, he blinks away. "Don't you think I was better suited for that jaunt out to Highland Point than that mannequin?"

"Maybe you were."

"Callie, I've been there since the start." Elijah casts his eyes downward. He nods toward the watch on my right wrist. "That his?"

I hesitate, but eventually sigh. I don't know how to tell him I'm not wearing the watch because it's John's but because of its mysterious connection to my past. "Yeah."

"That's some hickey."

"It's a bruise. My mom sort of freaked out on me." He's the only person I'll tell.

He shrugs, as if he expected it would be only a matter of time before she lost it on me. "You okay?"

"I guess so."

He holds my gaze for a long time, as if determining whether or not I'm telling the truth. "Don't tell me you're falling for him."

"Fine. I won't."

"What kind of a fucking prince is this guy? Making you dig!" He drags a few fingers through the wavy chocolate mop atop his head. "Christ, I would've dug that hole for you, you know—"

"I wanted to dig."

"—so you wouldn't have had to see it."

"I needed to see it! I've been digging in my mind for a year, and not just metaphorically."

"Was she . . ." He drums his fingers against his knee. "Was she there?"

"I think so. I don't know. We found a door, and that was all I could handle."

He's nodding. "Why'd you dig there? I mean . . . how'd you decide?"

"I wrote something about daisies a few weeks ago. I remembered there used to a patch of them, and I wondered—"

"What do you remember? What exactly do you—"

"That night, the night it all happened."

His jaw clenches, and after a time, he glances around the room and gives his wavy hair a tousle with a sharp toss of his head. "Come here."

I cross the room; he stands to meet me in the middle of it.

His arms close around my body. He whispers in my ear, in case we're being watched: "Did you kill him, like you thought?"

"No," I whisper. "He almost killed me."

Nearly instantly, he backs away. "Some things are worth forgetting, Callie. Your father trying to kill you is one of them." He pinches the bridge of his nose, then strikes me with a stare.

An exasperated sigh escapes me. "Elijah, I had to know." Absently, I fiddle with the watch. "I can't move on, can't leave it in the past until I understand it all."

He chews at the cuticle on his thumb and resumes his seat. "So . . . you happy with this guy?"

"I don't know." I shrug. "I'm not really with him, not officially."

"I'm just asking because I think maybe it's time, you know? Time to leave *us* in the past."

Here it comes. My eyes glaze with tears. I can't imagine life without Elijah.

"I love you, baby."

I nod. "I know."

"And I know you love me."

Still nodding: "I do."

"I think I could hang out with you forever, but I don't know if that's what you need anymore."

"Elijah, don't." A few tears escape my lashes. My gaze locks on his four crooked bottom teeth. Such an intimate detail. And I can feel those teeth against my tongue if I so much as glimpse a memory of his kiss. "Don't."

"Hey, nothing's changed, Callie. Not really."

Except everything. And as much as I know he's right, that these words have to be said, part of me wants to grasp on to him, hold him tight, keep things the way they used to be.

"I'm still gonna love you. I'm still gonna be here whenever you need me, okay? I'm still gonna kick anyone's ass out of your way, and I'd still fight to the death for you."

I wonder how his new girlfriends are going to feel about that, but I don't ruin the moment by asking.

"I'm just letting you go," he says. "Letting you find your way, and I'm gonna start looking for mine."

As if magnetized, I'm moving toward him. I'm on my knees before him, my head in his lap, my arms grasping him about the waist.

"You're pretty fucking amazing, you know that?" he says, nudging my chin upward.

"So are you." When I look up, I see his eyes are glossy, too.

He chucks me under the chin. "Any time. Any time you need me, I'm there."

"Ms. Knowles?"

I peel myself up from the floor and face the officer in the doorway.

"Mr. Hutch is here to take you home."

Elijah wraps me in a bear hug, kisses me on the cheek, and whispers, "Don't forget me, baby."

Impossible not to remember him. He's part of me.

TWENTY-EIGHT

Lindsey's in her bedroom with her iPod speakers cranked up so loudly that she doesn't hear me step in, even when I rap on the door. She's wearing a white cotton tank, a matching fleece hoodie, and camouflage flannel pajama pants adorned with *Booty Camp* across the rear—which I see because she's lying on her stomach, kicking her feet to and fro. Her phone is in her hands; thumbs busy at work, texting.

Grass.

I'm certain she's gossiping about me. It's a good guess that the student body will be afire tomorrow with all sorts of unreliable theories as to why I was detained at the police station tonight wearing only John Fogel's sweater and wet undergarments.

I knock again. Louder this time.

Grass.

When Lindsey looks up, her black tresses fall over her turquoise eyes. For a moment, an expression of pure vulnerability is present in her pained stare, but then I decide she only looks sort of stunned to see me, as if she expected her parents to abandon me simply because I've pissed her off. Still, I'm struck with her natural beauty, with her ability to command a room simply by being in it.

"I need a uniform for tomorrow," I say. "Just tell me where you put my skirts, and I'll get out of your hair."

She pulls a plastic sweater box out from under her bed, gives it a shove in my direction, and turns up her speakers.

The grass grew grew grew.

I take my skirts, my oxfords, and my sweaters, and marvel at her premeditation in hiding my things. She's sneakier than I knew—and I already knew quite a bit. After mumbling thanks she can't hear, and doesn't want to acknowledge anyway, I turn away.

Mr. Hutch peeks in just as I'm heading out.

I nearly drop my stack of clothing, when I press my back against the door to make room for his imposing frame.

"Turn it down," he says. Then yelling: "Turn! It! Down!"

Lindsey obeys.

"We'll talk about this tomorrow, young lady."

I say, "Yes, sir," as Lindsey says, "Okay."

With our simultaneous replies, we share a surprised glance. What does he want to talk to her about? I guess

Lindsey must be thinking the same thing, judging by the confused knit of her brow. Slowly, she lowers her glance back to her cell phone.

Mr. Hutch, wearing the same expression as Lindsey, darts a look in my direction, but quickly turns back to his daughter. "Don't make plans for after dinner tomorrow."

She nods. "Okay."

He awards me—or rather my neck—one last glance, but he doesn't ask about the mark there before he walks toward the master suite. I'm sure the police have told him what I reluctantly told them—that my mother can be dangerous. I appreciate his not delving into the conversation today. It's been a long enough day already.

I walk down the hallway and spill into my warm bed. There's still a trace of John Fogel in the sheets, as the last time I slept here, I slept here with him. I picture the two of us holding hands on Highland Point, then imagine roots pushing down from our heels into the earth, tangling and webbing together until one can't be discerned from the next.

My phone buzzes with a text from John: *can u talk?*

I text back: *2 tired*.

John: *sleep well*.

My eyes are already heavy.

Grass grows.

I follow the roots into the earth, tunneling deep, and surrender to the quiet.

"Callie?"

I startle awake to see a Lindsey-shaped silhouette standing over me. The clock glares 2:18 at me. "Wh—"

"My dad found my stash."

"Oh."

"He's pissed."

"Tell him it's mine."

"Really?"

"Yeah. Tell him it's mine."

"Why would you do that?"

"Didn't turn out too bad when he found my smokes. I can take it."

"But . . . why would you?"

"You're my sister."

"No, I'm not." She nudges her way into my bed. "Cuddle up."

I scoot over and share my covers.

One of her feet grazes mine, when she begins to swish them against the sheets.

She's freezing.

The aroma of potting soil and grass seed overwhelms me.

"Honor thy father."

"No, no, no, no!"

"Nymph," he hisses. "Lucifer's temptress. She'll get her due, she'll get it!"

Through the spaces between my fingers, I see him reach for his belt. I think he's about to buckle it, but he yanks it from its station and slashes it over a pale-skinned shoulder. "Why do you make me do this?"

I can't speak to stop him.

Slash.

"Why?" he prods.

Slash.

"This is the devil's work," he growls. "The devil's!" Slash. "And you do his bidding!"

I flinch when my blueberry tarts pop from the toaster, and I cringe with the haunting images. I glance at my notebook, open on the counter:

The grass grows grows grows grows grass grows grass grass grass grows grows.

"You're looking a little pale." Mr. Hutch, wearing khakis and a brown cable-knit sweater, pours himself a mug of coffee and heads, newspaper in hand, to the breakfast table, where Lindsey's already nibbling on a granola bar.

"She does look pale," Lindsey says. "It's almost like she's going to spend the day vomiting."

I thought we'd gotten past this last night, but apparently, I'm still the ritual sacrifice for the bruise to her ego. I shoot her a glare.

She mouths: *No one fucks with me.*

I roll my eyes. Seriously? *The grass grows.*

"Nice turtleneck," Lindsey says.

It's hers. I'm wearing it under my Land's End V-neck to hide the bruise my mother left on my neck. "Thanks."

"Are you feeling okay?" Mr. Hutch asks.

"Yes. I'm fine." I fight with the mad-hot pastries to get them onto a plate—staccato movements like pulling legs off spiders—and blow on the tips of my seared fingers as I walk to the table.

As strange as it is that Lindsey's talking at and around me, instead of to me, it's stranger still to have Lindsey's dad underfoot. The entire six months I've lived with the Hutches, I've never seen him in the mornings. I wonder why he isn't already at work and doesn't appear to be heading there. I wonder why I haven't seen Mrs. Hutch, or her car, since before the homecoming dance. Something's going on.

"You're okay?" he asks again.

Lindsey raises her brows.

I wonder if Lindsey's shared her rumor with him. "Yes, fine."

"Good. I feel like you've missed enough school." It's the first, and I suspect last, time he'll raise the issue of my cutting class.

"Yes, I have."

"And we understand that Lake Nippersink has a police department, and detectives and specialists, to do what you were doing last night."

301

"Yes, we do."

"Then we understand each other." He shakes open the paper. "And from what I hear, the two of you haven't been reporting for charity work. If we don't pick up the pace, we'll start looking for paying positions. Clear?"

"Clear," Lindsey and I say together.

So this is what it's like to have a real dad.

My gaze locks on the front-page headline, and I gasp: "Infant Remains Found on Highland Point."

Infant?

That means three things:

One: a baby died.

Two: alive or dead, Hannah's out there somewhere.

And three: my memories, however vivid, aren't valid. I'm back to square one.

Lindsey parks the car in the student lot. She hasn't said much to me since I've been back home, but she hasn't seemed to be seething with anger, either. On the contrary, judging by her crawling into my bed last night, I'd guess she needs me. But why?

Once we're both out of the car and heading toward the building, she quickens her pace, as if anxious to leave me behind.

I don't know if this is any of my business, but I decide to brave a question: "Where's your mom been?"

"I've been wondering how long it was going to take you

to ask." With a stomp of her foot, she turns to face me. Her chest is heaving, and a blush is crawling from her neck into her cheeks. "You've been so busy in bed with Jon Fogel that you haven't even noticed."

I've been busy. Not so much in bed. But that's beside the point. "I'm asking now, Linds."

"Like you care. You knew how I felt about Jon, and you—"

"That's not true, Lindsey. I didn't know how you felt about him. You had some interest, that's all. That's all I knew. I didn't know you and he had . . . you know . . ."

"Wish we hadn't."

"You should've told me."

"Would it have made a difference?"

An unbearable silence hangs between us. So unbearable that I fill it: "What's going on with your mom?"

With a minute shake of her head and a roll of her eyes, she says, "She left."

"Left?"

"She's gone overboard with the children's charity. She's on a two-month-long retreat. She'll be gone till after Christmas, and my dad's pissed. Says she's putting charity before our family, and considering *you*, I have to agree with him."

"I'm sorry. I didn't ask to be put into the foster system, you know."

Lindsey shrugs. "Do you think anyone cares that she's

skipping out on Christmas? Or just that she's skipping out on our first Christmas with *you*?"

"That's awful. I'm so sor—"

"Ironic thing is, I feel like my dad's making too big a deal of this. Do you know how much shit they've missed in *my* life? No one makes an issue out of that, but she leaves during all this Callie drama, and my dad threatens divorce. Sort of tells you something about his unnatural attachment to you, doesn't it?"

I stop in my tracks. I don't feel very attached to her dad at all, let alone overly attached.

She grins. "*C'est la vie.*"

I hang back and watch her walk on without me. God, she's vicious when she's angry, blaming me for everything— including my existence. She's obviously less worried about taking the heat for her stash than she is about getting me back for spending time with John Fogel.

"Maybe you don't know me as well as you thought," she says over her shoulder. "No one fucks with me."

Numb, I walk to my locker. Stow my coat. Grab my calc text. Head to homeroom.

"An infant." John falls in step beside me. "Did you hear the report?"

I swallow over tears building inside me. "Saw the article. Didn't have a chance to read it."

"Hey . . ." He touches me on the elbow. "Are you okay?"

"It's just, you know, Lindsey."

"I'm taking care of that rumor."

It goes beyond the rumor. She hates me. The thought of it stings, cuts through me. No matter what I do to stifle the tears, I feel them coming.

"So." He reaches for my hand.

I let him take it, and although it feels natural to be close to him, it doesn't feel normal to be holding hands, walking down a high school hallway with a boy. Such an easy, carefree gesture. My life is anything but easy and carefree these days, and never has been.

Just as we're passing Gianna Watson, he asks, "So, whose baby do you think it is?"

Gianna yelps with delight and says, "We assumed it was yours!"

The hushed sob I've been withholding escapes me. Great. Just great.

John slows his pace and turns to face her. "Hey, I was talking about the news—"

"Don't bother." I tug on his hand. "It won't matter what you say."

A few steps closer to homeroom, he says softly, "God, I'm sorry. Stupid thing to say. Bad timing."

He brushes a kiss over my lips, although the Carmel Catholic code of conduct states there ought to be no public displays of affection beyond holding hands on school property or at school events. He casts a concerned gaze down into my eyes. "There was a baby under that door."

"Yeah, I saw the headline."

"Do you know whose baby that was? On the Point?"

I don't, but memories are swirling. *Grass grows.*

"Oh, and I asked my dad. He thinks my cousin probably did hang out at the Vagabond from time to time. He says they used to have open mic every night, not just on Tuesdays, back then. Fewer professional bands, more amateurs."

White room, guitar, my mother's laughter. The watch, the rosary . . . "I think you should meet my mom."

A smile brightens his eyes. "I think you should get to know mine better, too. How do you feel about coming to their anniversary party?"

I don't mean it the way he does.

"Or maybe dinner tomorrow?" John asks.

I sniffle, wipe away tears. "Ask me tomorrow, okay?"

TWENTY-NINE

'm looking up today's news on John's phone while he's driving me to my appointment with Ewing. While I was in French class, Detective Guidry left a message to confirm they'd found human remains, but he couldn't give me details. He said they'd call to schedule another conference soon. They didn't find Hannah, but they found someone up on the Point. Although I all but marked the spot with an *x* for them, I'm left to scrounge information online, like everyone else.

"It says here the remains appear to be of an infant girl, estimated at three months of age," I say.

"So young."

I nod, but keep reading.

"I don't remember reading about any missing babies from the area." And he would know, given his self-proclaimed addiction to missing child cases. "Do they know how she died?"

"If they do, they're not saying." When I scan the next line, I understand why Detective Guidry hasn't offered me much information: I can't have had anything to do with her death, and it's unlikely that I knew anything about her circumstances. She's been there since I was a small child. Slowly, I lift my gaze to the road ahead of us. She's been there the whole time—near my rosary.

How on earth did I know about it, then?

A memory nags at me from the back of my mind. I follow its pull until I'm back there again, in a white room with my mom. I'm rubbing the stone at the heart of the crucifix. My mother is turning cards. Laughing, she rests one on her pregnant belly.

Pregnant.

What happened to that baby?

"Maybe nothing." I look at Ewing and expect to see three eyes or a spiked tail protruding from his body. Nothing? Is he whacked? He's pacing his office floor. I'm on the sofa with my feet curled under my rear.

"Something must've happened to it," I say. "I'm an only child, aren't I?"

"Maybe there was no baby." Ewing taps his fingertips

together. "The thing about memories, particularly memories of very young ages, is that often they're unreliable. There was representation of a baby, no doubt about it, but whether or not there was actually a baby remains to be seen. It's convenient that remains of a baby turn up simultaneously with these memories, but until we know otherwise, it's a coincidence, and nothing more. Maybe it's something you've conjured to help explain things to yourself, to sort things out in your mind."

"You think I'm making it up?"

"That phrase indicates you're lying, and I don't think you're lying. You honestly believe you saw your mother pregnant. But that doesn't mean she was. Your graphomania is a perfect illustration of how mangled information can come to be, especially in traumatic situations."

This makes sense. The yellow dress in the rowboat, for example, was a melding of suggested memories. Guidry's already ruled out the possibility the sundress was Hannah's, but I still associate it with her.

"I spoke with Detective Guidry this morning. He'll be calling you to schedule another conference. I'll relay this memory about a baby, and maybe he'll collect some samples from you, Serena . . . you know, to test against the remains. If that baby was your sister, DNA tests can confirm it." Ewing massages his chin as he walks back and forth, back and forth. "But I want to deal with the entire scope of this situation, not just the remains of a baby on Highland Point.

Some pretty distinct memories led you to that door."

"Hannah was still alive, at least I think she was. He rolled her into the hole. He dropped the door again, and . . ." My head is pounding. "But she wasn't there. Why wasn't she there when they dug up the door?" *Imprisoned obsession.* I rub my temples and reach for my notebook. "I swear it happened."

"We'll sort through it, what these memories may mean," Ewing says. "One step at a time. Write if you have to write, but let's . . ." His words echo, as I tumble down an avenue in my mind.

His voice is distant, as if it's coming to me via tins cans and a string: "You okay, Callie?"

No. It feels as if my head is in a vise, as if the words are pushing out, but all the hands of the world are pressing on my skull to keep them in. Stars dance at the corners of my eyes. I grasp at reality . . . something, anything, to bring me back to the here and now.

But his words are fading, as if he's miles away on a call with a bad connection.

The grass grows grows grows. Blisssssssssss

The room whirls about me, as if I'm holding fast on to the hub of a carousel.

Keep digging. Keep digging. Keep digging.

The corners of the space darken, until there's only a

tunnel before me.

I smell the earth, feel the grit of dirt accumulating beneath my fingernails and grinding between my molars. My hands ache from digging. My eyes burn. Chunks of earth consume me, swallow me whole. I breathe earth into my lungs. Cough it out again.

My hand breaks through to the other side.

The ground crumbles as I emerge. I gasp when I see the moon against a midnight backdrop.

I stumble over the terrain, trip on the wilting daisies. The grass grows up here, but not down on the rocky shore. "Callie!"

I blink through tears, and the moon fades away, but I can't draw a breath through the sobs racking my body. Ewing's office bleeds back into view. I glance down at my notebook:

The grass grows grows grows. Blisssssssssss Amputate cancer of the folds of years Does the scent of her linger within you Tempt her, break her, make her feel real. Devour her when she begins to bleed

Bleed bleed

bleed her and feed Burn her in an urn Crucify quarter and stone her Buried alive she'll claw at the case Smile as you condone her

. The grass grows grows grows. Bliss Bliss Bliss Bliss Bliss

Bliss Bliss Bliss Bliss Bliss Bliss Bliss Bliss Bliss Bliss Bliss Bliss Bliss Bliss Bliss Bliss

Walk not on the cobblestone paths of her memory in black-veiled grief to relieve you Mourn not for her mind her beauty her mouth drawn down so quick to believe you Pressed like a rose in a book from a lover Sift through as the hours pass Imprisoned obsession She can't escape Amber ashes in her hourglass

"It was me he buried," I whisper. "Not Hannah."

Ewing stops dead in his tracks near his office door, his mouth hanging open a fraction of an inch.

"It was me, Warren," I say with more conviction. "He buried me that night. Under the door. I saw him in the labyrinth. I was in the bell tower, and I saw what he was doing."

"You saw Palmer."

I nod and swallow over a lump in my throat. "And Hannah."

"What was he doing with Hannah?"

"I felt it all. Like it was happening to me, and not Hannah. Like you said at that meeting with Guidry, about survivors assuming they felt things victims felt . . . I felt it, like I switched places with Hannah . . . It should've been me. Would've been me, if I'd been where I should've been."

"I know this is hard. But tell me what you remember."

"I was hiding, crouched down in the bell tower. I was going to run away again, and I knew he'd look for me in

312

the labyrinth, because that's where I was supposed to be—scrubbing the lime deposits off the marble basin of the fountain. I was going to sneak back through the sanctuary when I knew he was outside, and make a break for it, but then . . . I saw he had Hannah. Her parents were coming back. I don't know why they left her, but they were coming back. He didn't have much time." I wipe tears from my eyes. "I accidentally pulled on the bell when I saw him dragging her to the fountain. He looked up, but I don't think he saw me."

I start to tremble a little, and when I breathe in, I sound like a whispering locomotive: *chuff, chuff, chuff.* "I saw what he did, but he didn't do it to me."

Ewing slowly lowers his body to the coffee table before me. His eyes are wet. "This is Palmer's shame, Callie. Not yours."

I focus on his eyes until they become a blur of opaque hazel. I smell juniper and holy water; I feel the crunch of pebbles beneath my feet.

I'm running. Running into the labyrinth. Have to save her. Have to distract him, have to get his hand out of her pants.

Flashes of her fearful expression haunt me. Too frightened even to scream. Faithful that her parents will come for her. Faster. Have to get there faster.

I cut through the hedges to get to her faster, to stop him, but by the time I get there, she's gone. He's locking the gate,

313

swearing at the key that won't turn it. I hold my breath and delve back into the juniper. I know where he put her; she's in the garden house. God, what is he going to do with her? I have to get the key. Have to get it, have to get her out before it happens.

I hear her faint screams for help.

I'm shaking. Bawling. Can't make a sound, can't make a sound, can't make a *sound*.

His labored breathing is getting closer. I hear the subtle limp in his step, the minute drag of his left foot, there courtesy of my mother and a pearl-handled knife. She's been gone at the Meadows thirty-four days. I concentrate on memories of my childhood—the arts and crafts, the homemade jewelry, the songs. *Let my love open the door.*

And suddenly, the step, drag-step of his gait stops.

My heartbeat encompasses my head, pounds in my ears. I can't hear anything but static and the adrenaline pumping through my system. Smell the sweet wine on his breath. He's standing . . . right . . . here. He knows I'm hiding from him.

"Calliope." His hand forms a fist around my wrist.

I plunge deeper into the juniper, yanking free from his hold. I come out on the other side, on another path. Disoriented now. Which way out? Which way, which way, which way?

"Honor thy father."

I'm running—full speed. Skidding on the stones as I

round a corner. Falling.

"Honor thy father."

No!

His hand on my ankle. Pulling me through the juniper. Stones scraping and scratching against my flesh. Branches lacerating.

I'm dizzy. Going to be sick.

Cold marble against my pelvis.

Leather slashing over my back.

Blood dripping into the holy water in the fountain.

His hand on the back of my head. "It's because of you! It's because of you!"

Submerged in the water.

I breathe in a lungful of water. Can't cough it out. Cold. Numb. Can't breathe. Can't move.

Something hard hits the side of my head, near my right temple.

Images flash before my eyes: my mother, the man with the watch, a burgundy-haired baby. Mom sobbing—"I killed him! I killed him!"—digging a hole behind Holy Promise, Palmer paving over the freshly overturned dirt with cobblestones.

The Vagabond, the cards, the late-night escapes from the reverend, only to be found in the morning, dragged back to Holy Promise for penance. The confessional. Her screams. Andrew Drake, the Meadows, Elijah, Lindsey, John, Elijah, Lindsey, John, Elijah, Lindsey, John.

A blinding white light illuminates the backs of my eyes. I know I'm slipping away.

I feel the stones against my raw back, when I hit the ground. Palmer's fingers pressing into my cheeks. "Callie."

I can't answer.

"Callie."

"Callie!"

I flinch. And Ewing's office slowly materializes around me. Tears stream over my cheeks. My eyes burn with mascara.

I look down at my journal:

Buried alive alive alive alive alive alive alive.

I killed him killed killllled killlled killed him.

Ewing squints at me. "Catch your breath."

"He thought he killed me," I say. "He thought he'd drowned me. He put me in the garden house, and he locked the door. Hannah thought I was dead, too. She couldn't get out. The door wouldn't open."

"He brought Hannah to the garden house?"

"Before me." I'm nodding. "She was screaming. His hand

was over her mouth. I saw her panties on the floor. Floral cotton briefs." I can't see through the tears, can't wipe them away fast enough. "And I remember thinking they were little-girl undies. I didn't help her. She was screaming, and I tried, but I couldn't stay awake long enough to get up. I didn't help! God, I didn't help!"

"Couldn't, Callie. You couldn't help. Palmer Prescott is responsible for what he did to Hannah, and he made it so you couldn't help her. You're not responsible."

"I couldn't stay awake." I shudder over an inhalation. "She was the one in the yellow sundress—he made her wear it, it was too small. She was in the boat with me, rowing on the way to Highland Point." I swallow hard. "Where he buried me. They thought I was dead. I couldn't move. Couldn't keep my eyes open."

Ewing offers a hand, palm up.

I slide my hand into his and squeeze. "I think the baby on Highland Point was my sister. I remember a baby girl."

"It's possible. But it's difficult to hide a baby, once she's been spotted around town. The police will be searching the missing children databases."

I know it's possible my mother won't talk about it, or maybe that she won't have her wits about her when I approach her, but I've already decided to ask her about it. "Warren?"

"Hmm?"

"I think I died that night."

His brow scrunches up. He thinks I'm crazy. But he says, "Go on."

"The night in the fountain. The night he buried me. I think that night gave me a glimpse into what I used to be, what I'm supposed to be looking for, who I might someday become. The white room, the guitar, the poetry tumbling in my mind . . . It all came from somewhere. Distant memories, maybe. Mine, or someone else's. Things I saw, but didn't understand, maybe."

He slowly nods his head. "When you're ready, you'll remember, you'll understand."

"Why was I spared, when Hannah wasn't?"

"We don't know she wasn't, Callie. As far as Hannah's concerned, we're back at square one. She isn't pronounced dead until the authorities determine there's no likelihood she's alive. From what you've just told me, she was alive the last time you saw her. There's no body to suggest she's dead."

I nod at his digital recorder. "Are you going to forward this tape to Guidry?"

He chews his bottom lip for a few seconds. "Yes."

"Okay." I grab a tissue and swipe it over my eyes. "That's good."

"We're getting closer. You're doing fine."

THIRTY

I've signed a release form, enabling Ewing to disclose the information I dug up during this afternoon's session, which means the weeks ahead of me are going to be full. Thanks to the day I cut, the one I spent in the nurse's office, our trek out to the Point last night, I didn't finish my twelve-page paper. Mr. Willis gave me a two-day extension, and it'll be at a five-percent penalty. Calc is kicking my ass, and *je ne parle pas le Français*. At least not *bien*.

But instead of planning and studying ahead—midterms are right around the corner—I'm sitting on John's living room floor, staring at unfinished homework, while he, sucking on a Tootsie Pop I offered him, researches missing children on his Carmel-issued iPad. So far, he hasn't found any that definitively fit the description of the remains found on Highland Point. "It's hard to pinpoint," he says. "Until we know exactly how old she was when she died, until we know how long she's been there . . . it's like picking dust out of pepper."

Aromas waft from the kitchen—beef stew—where his sisters Abby and Rachel are cooking. I glance in their direction; they're chatting and laughing.

The guitar propped in the corner keeps drawing my attention. Is it the same one I've seen in my mind?

"The guitar, the rosary, the watch," I say.

"Yeah." He doesn't take his eyes from the iPad right away, but when he does, he pulls the lollipop from his mouth. He's wearing an expression—eyes wide with something that looks like disbelief, slight smile—which tells me we're on the same page.

"All three of them draw a potential connection between your cousin and my mother. And if your cousin was involved with my mom and suddenly disappeared . . . and if it's safe to assume Palmer is responsible for Hannah's kidnapping, it means he's capable . . ." I don't want to draw the conclusion—that John's cousin met with foul play by Palmer's hand—but judging by John's nod, I don't have to. He's already considered the possibility.

"Yeah," he says. "I know."

"I think Guidry listened to you that day you brought me to the station. I think he'll reevaluate your cousin's case."

"It'd be nice to have closure," he says. "Not necessarily for me. I mean, I have glimpses of memories, pieces . . . I was three years old when he disappeared . . . but for, you know, my dad. He chose him to be my godfather. They had to be fairly close."

"Yet your parents know nothing about him having a woman in his life, so maybe we're wrong."

He shrugs a shoulder. "He wasn't living nearby when he left. He'd been staying up the coast of Lake Michigan, at our family's cottage. It's feasible he could've had a girl-friend and no one knew."

"In that case, it's unlikely it was my mom. She never went very far from home." I'm exhausted with attempting to piece together smidgens of an age-old epic, exhausted with not knowing what happened and how it all relates to Hannah.

And I can't, no matter how hard I try, concentrate on calculus with all these bits of information spinning in my head.

"Cottage." Suggestions of memories tumble—the white rug, the gauzy draperies, the fluffy towels in the old, built-in linen cabinet down the hall. I wonder . . . "You wouldn't happen to have any pictures of this cottage, would you?"

"Sure." He reaches across me and pulls a photo album from an end table. He deposits the heavy book in my lap.

I flip through pages. I don't recognize the exterior of the large house, but something about the view of the lake in the distance is familiar to me. I turn another page and study a picture of John's immediate family posing in what appears to be a living room. The floors are dark planks of wood, blanketed with a white area rug. The sofa they're piled on is white-on-white striped. But is it the same place I keep remembering? I can't see enough of it to tell.

John looks to be about eight or nine in the picture. He's adorable. They all are. He's from good-looking stock, and they all look alike. I lean into his space. "So, who's who?"

"Oldest"—he points—"Tracy. Then Christina. And you know Abby and Rachel."

"What?" one of them says from the kitchen.

"Nothing," he calls back.

"I heard my name."

"Hey, I'm studying over here," he says over his shoulder. Then turning back to the album: "And me."

I'm sort of in awe with the size of the clan. Their over-sized house makes sense now that I know he's from such a big brood. Unlike the Hutch estate, this one is filled to the brim—or was at one time. "Your relatives could outnumber the population of Montana. You know that, right?" I look back to the picture. "What's it like? Having such a big family?"

"Compromising is a big part of it." Without turning to look at it, he points to the wall behind the sofa against which we're leaning.

Compromise is lettered directly on the wall.

"I can't imagine."

"You should come to the anniversary party. You can meet Tracy and Chrissy, and my aunts, uncles, cousins . . ."

"I'll never remember everyone's name."

He chuckles. "Hell, even I don't know half my cousins' names."

A sense of warmth surrounds me. Immediately following is a pang of envy. Even if I want to, I can't share this sort of thing with him. I don't have baby pictures, save the occasional grainy snapshot of Mom and me, and I think those are packed away with my mother's belongings at the Meadows, as I haven't seen them since she went away. There are no longer any rooms stamped with my mother's fingerprints; nothing reflects her essence the way the *Compromise* reflects Mrs. Fogel's, if not the place above the Vagabond, and it's empty now. I don't know if I'll ever walk those floors again. Whatever roots I'd managed to vein into Lake Nippersink have been strangled and cut off.

If Hannah's still alive, I think she must feel like I feel right now, as if survival is dependent upon adjustment and adaptation. She's an endangered species, and until we find her, part of me is missing, too.

"I was scared, you know," he says. "That day after Hannah's service, when you disappeared, and you didn't call me back. I thought you'd run away again, that you were missing. I kept seeing that web page in the back of my mind: missing and exploited children. The one with your picture on it."

I fold my hand around his arm, just above the elbow, and I lean into his shoulder.

His eyes fall closed for a long moment, and when he opens them, I feel as if they're staring directly into my soul.

John touches my right wrist, runs his thumb under the band of his watch, still fastened loosely at the cuff of my Land's End sweater.

"When my cousin left, he left the watch behind, and in the note, he'd indicated he wanted to start over, so the police deduced he must've left willingly." He shrugs. "But like I said, lots about that theory doesn't hold water. I know it's crazy, but now that I'm old enough, I keep looking for him, expecting to find him someday."

"It isn't crazy." I shake my head. "I'll keep looking for Hannah until we find her."

"Yeah, but I think Hannah wants to be found." His hand comes to rest on my thigh. "My cousin . . . I don't think you find someone who chooses to disappear. But if he's alive, someone would've seen him by now. Somewhere."

"Maybe. It was a long time ago. He probably doesn't look the same."

"Would you ever run away now? Knowing what it's like on the other side? The waiting? The wondering?"

I've never thought of things this way before, what my mother must've been thinking, when I ran away. "I don't think so. Not anymore."

"Why'd you do it?"

"It was just too hard to stay."

"It must've been hard on your family."

"I'm a ward of the state." I say it as if he knows, as if it's common knowledge, but then I remember that I dodge the question whenever he asks about my relationship with Lindsey. I don't like to go into the explanation—Elijah's the only one who knows everything—but he probably deserves to know. "When Palmer committed my mom, the state placed me with him because his name was listed as father on my birth certificate and because I'd known him my whole life. Paternity tests confirmed it."

"You didn't know he was your father?"

"She'd never told me I had a father, but he'd been in my life since birth. It seemed a logical placement." An aching sensation settles around my heart. He'd been strict with me, with all the children of the congregation, before the state placed me in his care. But he went berserk with power when he had ultimate control over me. The scar on my shoulder burns and itches.

I have to see my mother. I need answers. Answers to questions I've never known to ask.

"Hey, Romeo," Abby calls from the kitchen. "Time to feed your Juliet."

He rolls his eyes. "Sisters."

THIRTY-ONE

While I'm inside my mother's cell-slash-bedroom, thumbing through a notebook, John's in the waiting room, researching on his iPad. I was hoping to bring him in to meet her, but the nurse on staff said she had to clear it with Mom's psychiatrist first. They're going to escort him down in a few minutes.

My mother blends graphite into paper.

"What are you drawing today?" I ask her.

"Palmer."

"God, why?"

She sighs. "Part of my life, baby."

I glance at her sketch. It's a decent likeness. Not necessarily accurate, but decent.

"The police were here, you know. They say you found the door."

My fingers still. "What do you know about the door?"

"I told you to leave it alone." Her gaze flickers up to mine, but quickly returns to her drawing.

"Was that baby yours?"

"You're my baby."

"I know. Doesn't mean there weren't two of us."

"I went crazy, knowing they gave you to him. I told them everything. The police. That detective. I told him not to leave you with him. Crazy man. Thought he was God."

Coming from a crazy person, I can understand why Detective Guidry didn't put much stock in her testimony. "Guidry knows now," I tell her. "He knows you were telling the truth."

"That conclusion comes a little too late, don't you think?"

"Palmer had rights, Mom. As my father. There was no one else to take me."

"Tell me he never . . . took you."

My stomach lurches when I realize what she's getting at. Slowly, I shake my head.

"If you ask me, the man deserved what he had coming, and he's lucky I missed! He's lucky that knife hit his thigh. I aimed to chop it off! So he could never hurt you the way he hurt me!"

"Why would a man . . ." I feel like I'm going to throw

up. I lean against the wall to ward off dizziness. My phone is buzzing with a text message. I ignore it. "He must've known I'm his daughter. He wouldn't have—"

"Not if I'd chopped it off. It was only a matter of time. I knew that. After you were born, Holy Promise cured him for a while. But when I started to notice the way he was looking at you . . ." She sighs. "It was only a matter of time. I made a deal with him."

"What . . . what kind of deal?"

"I promised I'd stay. Do what he wanted. As long as he didn't touch you."

"How did you get messed up with him?"

"The church worked . . . for a while. He was a man of God." There's a faraway look in her eyes, as if she's attempting to grasp something she'd forgotten long ago. "His charisma . . . he captured people, made them believe." She shrugs, as if she's contemplating eating another olive and can't decide whether or not she should.

"Mom, do you remember a man with a guitar? The man with the watch?"

She's shaking her head.

"You don't remember?"

A tear crawls down her cheek.

"What's the earliest thing you remember? How far back can you go?"

Her fingers draw lines around Palmer's features. "I remember the day you were born. Palmer was furious; he blamed me. I'd left him; he let me go. We stayed above the Vagabond." She's gazing into the wall behind me, as if it's a canvas of a starry night. "I remember the day Cleo was born—"

"Cleo?" Slowly I approach her.

"—and I remember the day she died. The day Palmer buried her. The day I climbed up the cliff to give her the only thing I had left of my past. My rosary."

"So, it's true?" I grasp my mother's graphite-stained hands. "That baby was yours?"

"Palmer said she was Satan's spawn, that's why she had to die." Her eyes moisten with tears. "She never had a chance, always belonged to God. Never officially existed. I never went to the hospital."

"I remember you pregnant."

"You do?" My mother's smiling through her tears, as if she dreamt she won the lottery.

"Recently. I haven't always remembered."

"You put your little hands on my belly. You liked to feel her kick. Remember?"

I'm nodding, tears in my eyes, too. I do remember.

"I set the stone from the rosary in a ring for you."

I grasp the ring in question.

"To bond my daughters forever."

"Was Palmer her father, too? Or was there someone else?"

Her smile fades; she turns back to her sketch.

I sigh. "Mom?"

She shakes her head.

It was a lot of information, actually. I shouldn't be disappointed that she's so quickly gone again.

She begins to hum. *Let my love open the door.*

Text from John: *Calliope . . . Greek, muse of poetry. ironic? or is it me?*

I already knew this, but I have to agree. Definitely ironic.

I text back: *check Cleo.*

John: *Cleo or Clio?*

I wonder why it matters.

Me: *both.*

My mother pipes up: "I remember the day I married him, you know. He was supposed to save me."

"Married? You married Palmer?"

I feel a headache coming on. I shouldn't stay here much longer. She's in decline, and I feel the words beginning to stir: *bliss bliss bliss.*

I text: *can we research marriage records?*

As far as I knew, my mother and Palmer had never been married.

John buzzes back: *Cleo . . . Greek. to praise. form of Cleopatra . . . also Greek, glory of the father.*

Well, that sounds like Palmer.

And another: *Clio . . . Greek, muse of history.*

Something inside me clicks, as if I've just tapped another piece of a puzzle into the frame. No matter what the police say, no matter how Ewing cautions me not to believe it, I know now. I had a sister.

330

"Palmer put him under the cobblestones," she says.

I flinch. "Who?"

"He made me dig the hole."

I'm heady. I think I'm going to pass out. I ring for an orderly.

"Who's under the cobblestones?"

"Calliope, you remember him."

My heartbeat is a clamor in my chest. "I don't remember."

"I could never forget."

I lean against the wall and allow myself to sit, while the world spins madly before my eyes. *Bliss.* I reach for a pen. Flip to a blank page in my notebook. The lines on the page begin to blur, then wiggle, until they're pale blue tethers yanking me into a catacomb in my mind.

I'm violently ill, hurling into the sink and leaving muddy, bloody handprints on the pink porcelain. I taste the earth and the soft salty essence of holy water.

My back is raw with lacerations. Leather cuts through skin like a hot knife through butter. And dirt burns when it rubs into the wounds.

Dirt bleeds from my sweatshirt onto the mosaic tile floor, turning the already dingy grout lines black.

The water is running in the tub. I want to lie beneath the stream. I want to die. I step into the tub, let the cool water soak my clothing—my T-shirt, bra, panties, socks . . . but I don't know what's happened to my pants. I watch the fabric meld to my body like a second skin. I want to feel the warmth of the white room. Want to go back there, to the place where I'm safe. I concentrate on the sounds rising up from the Vagabond below me. Someone's singing: *Let my love open the door.*

I know the song. Remember it. From a long time ago.

Muddy water circles the drain. I watch it until it all runs clear.

I'm shivering beneath the chilly stream, but I have no towel to warm me when I step out.

The linoleum is cold beneath my feet, too, but I don't feel it. Not really. I don't feel anything beyond the burn of Palmer's belt against my back.

I listen for the song, but it's not there. The Vagabond is dead below me now. Which means it's late. Too late, even, for the quiet alcoholics and poetic minstrels, and for them, it's never late enough.

God, how long have I been here?

My gaze is stuck to a red felt-tip pen abandoned beneath the sink.

I fish it out. Press the tip to the wall. I write:

I KILLED HIM. I KILLED HIM.

The pen won't stop. I can't make it stop. My words keep flowing over the old, floral wallpaper. I'll cease breathing if I force the pen to still. I can't stop, can't stop, can't stop.

Breathing is writing. Writing is breathing.

The red words spin around me like neon spaghetti. I can't keep up. I'm stumbling, tripping, tumbling.

He's slashing my body with his belt.

I remember the knife resting on the marble ledge of the fountain. It's the same weapon my mother used on him the day he sent her away, the knife with the ivory handle and the ebony cross inset.

I hear the blade cutting through denim.

I'm bleeding.

Blood on my hands.

Dripping to the ground.

So much blood.

I hear her in the distance: Hannah. She's screaming.

"Miss Knowles?"

What? I feel a jarring sensation, as if someone's shaking me.

"Callie!"

"Yeah." Slowly, my mother's room blends into view.

My hand aches. My head pounds.

"Callie."

"John." I focus on the sound of his voice, look up at him.

My mother is staring at him, as if she wants to reach out and touch him, but the orderlies are holding her back.

"You okay?" John asks.

I glance down at my notebook:

Perpetual perpetual perpetual bliss bliss bliss bliss Stripped linens dried in the breeze of the sea strippedstrippedstripped Ignorance is perpetual bliss

THIRTY-TWO

It's dinnertime by the time Detective Guidry drops me off at the Hutches' house. He's taken my notebook—and my testimony, what I know, what I've remembered, what I think it means. I'm exhausted. I just want to sleep. From the front door, down the broad hallway, I see a carry-out pizza box on the center of the round breakfast table. Lindsey and her dad are locked in a stare-down across the table, which I relieve when I close the door.

"You're back." Mr. Hutch smiles. "Are you okay? The detective said there was an incident with your mother."

"Yeah," I say. "I'm okay."

"How is she?"

"She's . . . you know, okay."

"Can we finish this later?" Lindsey asks him.

"No," Mr. Hutch says. "Callie is family, and this involves her, too."

"I can come back later," I offer.

"No," my foster father says again.

"Ohhh-kay." I lower myself to an empty chair between him and Lindsey.

Mr. Hutch offers me a hand and takes up Lindsey's. With a reluctant roll of her eyes, Lindsey takes my outstretched hand, too.

"Dear Father," Mr. Hutch begins to pray, "we humbly accept your sacrifice . . ."

Prayer has been an integral part of my life since I took my first breath. But I'm uncomfortable with this blessing tonight. After the day I've just endured, the grotesque things I heard and remembered, I can't contain my tears. I sniffle through the blessing and bleat out only a meek amen.

None of us touches the pizza.

In silence, save my occasional whimper, we stare at our barren plates. Mr. Hutch holds tight to both our hands.

"I guess I'll start." Mr. Hutch gives a firm nod. "Mom and I are going to be fine. I don't agree with what she's doing, but I respect her calling. Either way, you're my girls. My commitment to you—to both of you—won't falter." At last, he releases our hands. Reaches for a slice. Pops open his can of soda.

Lindsey and I share a glance, then follow his lead in serving ourselves.

"Lindsey, this rumor you posted on Facebook."

Oh, God. We're going to talk about it. All of it. My cheeks flush. My tears intensify. Lindsey looks almost sorry for me.

"You know this could cause us a lot of trouble. Not only for Callie, but for the state to deny our application."

Application? My glance darts to Mr. Hutch, but he's still staring at his daughter.

Lindsey refuses to look at him but shrugs and lifts her slice of pizza. "So could a divorce."

"Not unless it directly, negatively effects Callie's well-being, and—"

I push back from the table. "I should really—"

"Stay," Mr. Hutch says.

I freeze.

"I mentioned the word," he says. "That's true. But mentioning divorce and following through with it are two different things. Now, if the state sees fit to deny our application to adopt Callie because of it—"

Adopt me?

"—well, I think we'd appeal their decision. All should go as planned, if you can manage to keep your hands off the smoke." He lifts his soda to his lips.

I catch Lindsey's glance, the one that's pleading with me to take the heat for her. I offer a subtle shrug. Her family's done a lot for me. I owe her . . . don't I?

Maybe if she hadn't been such a bitch . . .

"So whose is it?" His can clinks against the tabletop.

"Mine," I say. "It's mine." In the periphery, I see Lindsey's shoulders relax a little, as if she's just released a long-held breath.

Her dad is staring at me. I feel it. "Look at me, young lady."

Slowly, I trail my gaze to meet his.

He presses his lips together, refuses to blink. When I can hardly stand it another second, he sighs. "I've been through your file. I know what you've been through, what you're *going* through. I also know you have a tendency not to take your Ativan because you feel detached when you do—yes, I've spoken with Dr. Ewing. So the question is this: why would you partake of a recreational drug with many of the same effects? Why would you risk doing something illegal, when you don't even want to take your pills?"

I'm not good at lying. I don't know what to say. I can't argue with his logic.

"It doesn't add up, Callie." He raises a brow to his daughter. "Lindsey? Anything to add?"

"No." Her voice is nearly a whisper.

"Why I found it in your closet, for starters?"

"I . . . don't know."

"I'd like you to be straight with me."

When she sighs, her breath sort of stutters, like she's trying not to cry.

"In with the marijuana," my foster father says, "I found

a pack of Seasonique. That's birth control."

Lindsey and I share another glance. She's the first to look away.

"So how is it that we assume Callie's pregnant if she's been taking the birth control pill?"

Oh, God. If I'm not red with humiliation, I'm on fire. The silence is deafening. Mr. Hutch's stare won't relent, as if he's attempting to burrow a hole with the power of his gaze in the middle of Lindsey's forehead.

Finally, she lets out an audible sob. "She's taking the heat for me, okay?"

"Okay." Mr. Hutch nods. Reaches for his daughter's hand.

She allows him to take it, but won't look at him. "Okay."

"You'll start counseling next week. The sooner the better, before the adoption application is reviewed."

It's really happening. They're adopting me.

My fingertips tingle, and a new river of tears starts to flow. I've never known how I would feel about this news, even when Lindsey and I were best friends. It feels sort of like a betrayal of my mother, but also like I'm holding magic beans. There's no telling what may sprout from this *bon chance*, and if I'm honest with myself, I know that my mother is traveling another path now, a path she wouldn't expect me to follow.

"But this damn Facebook post," Mr. Hutch continues. "Lindsey, if the social workers catch wind of this, there's going to be an investigation. I'll be questioned, you'll be questioned. Callie will be examined. Even when they learn you lied about her being pregnant—"

I let out a sob, which shakes me to my very core, and pinch my eyes shut, but I know he's looking at me.

After a few dreadful seconds of dead air, he reiterates: "They'll have to determine whether there's any truth to what you've been saying."

"I'll tell them I made it up."

"But why?" Mr. Hutch asks. "Why would you say such a thing?"

I hold my breath. Wait for Lindsey's reply. Our gazes lock.

"They'll want to know," Mr. Hutch says.

"It's . . ." Lindsey's attempt to formulate an answer falls short, but she quickly redirects. "Maybe this just isn't meant to be. Maybe she doesn't want to be in this family."

"Callie?" Mr. Hutch turns to me.

"You've been good to me. I appreciate everything you've done. All of you."

"Nothing will change," Mr. Hutch says, as if he can read my hesitation. "Not your name, not your relationship with your mother. We'll be giving you a permanent address and benefits beyond what the state gives you. Security, if you will."

Translation: college. Opportunity.

"Thank you," I say because I don't know what else to

say. I don't want to sound ungrateful. I hope it's enough of a retort.

"But, Lindsey . . ." Mr. Hutch, shaking his head, drops her hand. "What would possess you to say such a thing?"

I brace myself for whatever may flow from between my sister's lips.

I'm tired. Exhausted. I don't know if I can stomach a tirade about my "stealing" John Fogel out from under her thumb. I don't know if I have the wherewithal to defend my chastity—or lack thereof—or to explain to Mr. Hutch that Lindsey makes a game out of trashing a girl's reputation if she thinks she might be muscling in on her territory. I stare down at my practically untouched dinner.

"Lindsey Michelle Hutch. Do you understand the ramifications of what you've done? If the authorities find just cause to investigate this rumor, Callie goes back to County until the investigation is complete."

My heart pounds with the thought of it. Sure, I survived County once, but I had Elijah there to help me through it.

She smacks an open palm against the table and rises. "She deserved it, okay? She fucking deserved it!"

"Watch your mouth."

"You go out of your way to help her! You don't help me! When do you ever help me? Why is she even here?"

"Sit down."

Defiantly, Lindsey slams back onto her chair.

Mr. Hutch draws in a measured breath. "I got a call

from a dean at Carmel last week. You've spread some pretty nasty rumors about an honor student. And now all this . . . with Callie. Why are you doing this?"

"I want to win," Lindsey says. "Just once, I want to win. I want to be important. Just once. And then Callie comes to Carmel, and she ruins it all, and I can't win anymore."

"I'm not trying to win," I say. "I'm just trying to survive. I'm sorry. I didn't mean to—"

"You didn't mean to be a whore."

"Lindsey!" Mr. Hutch interjects.

"You just were." A sly grin threatens to spread over Lindsey's face.

My head is in my hands now, the flush of embarrassment rushing up the back of my neck, and over my cheeks, like flames. I hear, in the recesses of my memory, Palmer's voice, rising from the confessional: *honor thy father.*

Words fly between Lindsey and her dad, but I can't hear them, can't concentrate on what they're saying because the words are gnawing at my brain, itching in my fingertips: *something in the breeze, something in the breeze.*

"I need . . ." I need another notebook. Guidry took mine. "I need a pen."

But they can't hear me. They aren't paying attention until I push back from the table, the legs of the chair scraping against the hardwood floor.

"Callie?"

I'm tearing through my backpack, yanking out a pen.

Nothing to write on, nothing to write on. Nothing to write on!

Lindsey's class ring sparkles as she withdraws the plate before me and replaces it with a sheet of paper.

I hear my mother's voice, echoing from the confessional: *I'm remembering. Something in the breeze reminded me. I've forgotten where I came from. I don't know where I came from, don't know where I came from . . .*

My cell phone buzzes, jarring me from the memory.

I study the words I've just written:

Something in the breeze freed lakeshore memories inside me beside beside beside me abiding like the tide abiding like the tide abiding like the tide.

"Are you okay?" This is the first time I've graphed out in front of Mr. Hutch. He's leaning over me, a hand on my back. "Is she breathing?"

I draw in a sharp inhale. "Yes."

Lindsey's fingers are wrapped around my wrist.

Through my tears, I see her turquoise eyes. "I'm sorry," I say.

The corners of her lips threaten to turn upward. "Me, too."

A sigh escapes my foster father.

"I need to lie down," I say. "May I be excused?"

"We'll talk in the morning," Mr. Hutch suggests. "Get some rest. Lindsey, stay put. You're not going anywhere."

I shove the latest poetic splattering of my brain waves

into my bag and walk up the stairs.

Once I'm safe in my room, I pull out my phone to see a message from John: *harbor. midnight.*

Must sleep. I don't think I should be going out tonight. But I text back: *chaos here . . . confirm later.*

I dry my tears on the crocheted scarf my mother made for me when I was little, and I reach for my deck of Tarot.

Just feeling the cards in my hands brings me closer to my mother. I don't believe in the cards, but I do believe in her. I close my eyes and breathe in her essence. No matter what the doctors at the Meadows tell me she is, I know she's my mom beneath it all.

I lay the cards on my heart and pray for the answers to come.

THIRTY-THREE

Tattered sheets. I first hear the scream in the back of my mind, but it soon shrills in my ears, like a sharp whistle blown for two-second intervals, and stirs me from a deep sleep. My heart is beating like mad, and my head is pounding in time. I try to reach for the lamp switch, but my fingers are numb.

I'm in my bedroom at Lindsey's house, but I feel as if I'm on a boat, rocking in the moor.

I want to write the words etching into my brain, but I feel paralyzed, as if I have to concentrate on each individual muscle motion in order to move even a smidgen. I throw all my energy into getting another notebook from my nightstand drawer.

I'm panicked. What if I'm tied? What if I can't move, no matter what I do to try?

When my fingers touch the drawer of the nightstand, the screaming in my head stops. Tarot cards, abandoned on my mattress, bend beneath my elbow. I yank on the glass knob and open the drawer.

My hand, damp with sweat, meets first with the edge of a notebook, which I pull out before grabbing a felt-tip pen from my surplus supplies.

I bite off the cap and scrawl tattered sheets the ties that bind.

The light on my ceiling illuminates the space, although I thought I'd turned it off.

I'm hyperventilating, my head resting on my notebook, my eyes pinched shut to ward off the unwelcome, bright light. I hear footsteps in a distant hallway.

"Callie?"

Yeah.

"Callie?"

Lindsey?

I try to focus on my foster sister, but she's fuzzy, just an outline of a person.

She fades away, but the light doesn't. It blinds me. Everything turns white: the square of shag carpeting like a polar bear hide, the sheers billowing in from the white-framed windows, the caps on the waves in the distance.

And across the miles, a crew of men is digging up the

cobblestone walk. There's a body beneath the stones.

"Dude."

I hear Lindsey's voice in the periphery of my mind. Smell raspberry Tootsie Pops, which I assume she's eating. Feel the cold white gold of the rosary against my chest.

"Wake up," she says. "You're having crazy dreams."

I feel her pulling the notebook from my lap.

Without opening my eyes, I lift the covers, and into my bed she climbs.

She rests her head against mine; we're sharing a pillow.

I want to drift back to sleep, but when her feet begin to swish against the covers, I concentrate on the motion, on the sound, and commit it to memory.

"Are you up now?" she asks.

"Yeah."

"What do you dream about, when you start thrashing around like that?"

"Hannah, mostly. My mom. My father."

"Life's pretty fucked up sometimes, huh?"

"Lately, it's like someone took everything I knew as normal and put it in a confetti cannon."

"Your normal wasn't too normal to begin with," she says.

And now, I have all these little pieces, all these clues, and I don't know what to do with them. "I don't even know what's real anymore," I confess.

"I'm real," Lindsey offers.

I open my eyes, meet her gaze. "You hate me." I listen to the swishing of her feet against the linens. "And I don't blame you."

Swish, swish, swish, swish.

Finally, she responds: "Do you love him?"

My every muscle stills. "I don't know."

She slurps on her candy. "If you love him, I'll back off."

"We don't really talk about that sort of thing, you know?" I focus on the little green light on the smoke detector. It's blinking at me. Needs a new battery. "Lindsey, do you believe in serendipity?"

"I don't know what to believe anymore." I feel the shrug of her shoulders. "I can't rely on anyone. Not even you, and I used to think you were my rock."

"I didn't think someone like you needed a rock."

"Everyone needs a rock."

I digest this for a moment, think about what Ewing said: *Lindsey has her own share of problems.* "This thing with John . . . it isn't just a fling designed to get back at Elijah. It's sort of . . . he's helping me deal. I'm remembering things. I'm getting better."

"Seems like you're getting worse, no offense." *Swish, swish, swish.* "You think you'll ever stop writing like that?"

I think about this for a minute. "Yeah. Yeah, I do."

"And you think John's helping?"

"Look, this thing with John . . . It sort of just . . . happened, you know?"

"Oh, I know 'just happened,' all right."

"He met my mom, before she went away. On Fortune Night at the Vagabond. She knew about his watch . . . and it turns out this watch used to be his cousin's, but his cousin's been missing most of our lives."

Her feet stop moving for a few seconds, but then resume.

"He knows things. Has information I need. And I know this must sound cliché to you, but I tried not to do this. It just sort of . . ."

She finishes my sentence: "Happened."

"Yeah."

"So . . . you love him?"

"There's too much going on right now to think about it. But I think I could. Maybe. Someday."

"Why'd you take the heat for me tonight? After everything I said about you? I've been a royal bitch, and—"

"Yes. You have."

"—and you still tried to cover for me. Why?"

"You're my sister."

A few silent seconds pass before she replies: "Just like that. You're over it."

"No. It hurts. But"—I came here six months ago with nothing—"you're all I have."

She hesitates for a moment before saying, "You're all I have, too, now."

This isn't even remotely true, but it illustrates the vast differences between us. I don't expect everything is going to turn out okay, I don't think some guy is going to fall under my spell just because I've given him a glance, and I don't think I deserve the moon every time I bat my pretty lashes. "I'm just a girl, okay? Just trying to survive. I don't expect anyone to make it easy for me. But you . . . You have different expectations about this world, so you react differently. This thing with John . . . if I'd been with him solely so you couldn't have him, it'd be one thing, but it didn't happen that way."

"You still kept it from me."

"Do you think it would've made a difference, if I'd told you?"

"Do you think it would've made a difference, if I'd told you what happened at that party last spring? How Jon and I just sort of . . . ended up together? I mean, I didn't plan on hooking up with him that night, to tell you the truth. It just sort of . . ."

My turn: "Happened."

"Yeah."

"You know, just ending up with someone doesn't mean you're a bad person, even if you don't make anything of it. So you hooked up. You learned something, even if all you learned was that you didn't like hooking up with him. Doesn't make you a whore."

At the mention of the word, her feet still. "I'm sorry about calling you that."

I don't know what to say. It isn't okay.

"I can tell people what I said wasn't true." Lindsey tilts her head to touch mine.

After a few moments, she presses a kiss onto my cheek. Lays her head on my shoulder. Begins to move her feet again.

THIRTY-FOUR

_____

The water can be a cruel and unpredictable lover. Sedate on the surface, but with an undercurrent, raging when we least expect it. I've lived here my entire life, and I've always found serenity in the wandering waterways of northern Illinois. The water is passionate, and I'm fervent when I'm near it.

It's almost midnight.

John's watch is in my hand. I'm going to give it back to him tonight. Not because I don't love him, not because I don't want to try to make things work, but because I want to know I'm deciding to be with him not because of some crazy memories about a guitar, or because he dug up a rosary, or because my mom remembers his watch, but because I feel connected to him now. I want to make choices for a change, instead of taking chances.

I lean on the rickety rails of the pier and gaze again over the dark waves. With only a sliver of moon in the sky, I won't enjoy the view tonight, but I can conjure the image with my eyes closed. That's the way it is, when you belong somewhere.

Sounds of a gypsy guitar and whispered murmurs filter through the dirty windows of the Vagabond, and drift to my ears on misty fingers. This is home. This is where I want to stay.

From behind, a hand winds around me, rests on my belly. Johnny.

I smile and spin to face him, but halfway there, a musty glove covers my mouth.

My eyes widen when I meet the gaze of Reverend Palmer Prescott. I scream, but his hand muffles the sound. I struggle to get away, but lose my footing. I'm falling into an abyss of starry night and . . .

I hear the splash in distant hallways of my mind, as if this isn't happening to me, as if I'm watching it happen on television, despite the chill of cold, cold water seeping through my clothing, dripping down my face, drenching my hair and flesh. I grasp for the edge of the pier, but he's shoving down hard on my head.

Another attempt at a scream awards me only a mouthful of Lake Nippersink.

He's too strong. No sooner do I surface than he shoves me back under. I take in another mouthful of lake.

Everything fades to nothingness.

I can't move my feet, can't move my arms, but they ache and burn with fatigue. My eyes itch, sting, and render only a blurry halo of light, when I try to open them.

Must be another dream, another torment of my memory . . . another sleight of consciousness—or lack thereof. I wait for the words to bounce inside my brain. Wait.

Listen.

Listen.

Listen. To the buzz of proverbial crickets in my mind. Silence.

Feel the rise and fall of the waves.

I'm on a boat. I must be.

The words are gone.

Johnny?

My tongue forms his name, but I can't take breath enough to voice it. I know he isn't here. I don't feel him near me.

But I feel a presence hovering . . . like a demon.

When the scent of anointing oil registers in my nostrils, I beg myself to scream, but still no sound comes. My ears fill with the sound of my rapidly beating heart, and no matter how I try to wiggle life into my hands and feet, they prickle, as if they're still asleep.

Oil. That's why it's hard to see.

An image emerges before me, all bulk and few details. It's the scent of the oil on his fingers that identifies him, more than his shape:

Palmer.

I jolt, but still can't move, and something pinches my forehead at the temples.

I concentrate on minuscule muscles, twitch my toes.

"Father," I manage.

I feel the pad of his thumb on my forehead, marking me with the sign of the cross, the way he did when I was twelve and I'd chosen, before the entire congregation, Jesus Christ as my Savior.

No matter how I thrash, no matter how my limbs break out of their numbness, I'm immobile, bound on a bed, tied with strips of sheets. My legs are crossed, the right over the left, with one foot atop the other. However desperately I need to rub the oil from my eyes, my attempts are futile, as my wrists are tethered to the corners of the bed frame.

When I blink, and a few details come into focus, I wonder if it would've been better not to see anything at all:

I can tell by the way the room moves to the whims of the water, by the scent of the buoys and old wood, by the slush of waves against the hull that I'm definitely aboard a boat.

I'm freezing, and my clothes stick to my flesh like a wet blanket. My teeth chatter, but not only with the cold. I know what's about to happen.

Across the room, a match strikes. In the glow of the flame, I see the man with whom the state placed me, the man who—if my dreams and nightmares are real—kidnaps and rapes girls . . . and swears God tells him to do it. His hair, usually meticulously groomed, has grown wild and scraggly, and his beard, longer, like Jesus Christ's.

"It's time for you"—the flame ignites a pillar candle— "to honor thy father."

There's a rubbing noise on the right side of the hull where the vessel bumps against the buoy. I turn my head to see if I can tell which boats are docked near, but the stabbing sensation at my temples halts the movement. I feel a trickle. Smell blood. I'm dizzy. I think there's something surrounding the crown of my head, stopping me from moving.

Out of the corner of my eye, I see a staircase. At the foot of it is a box, and peeking from the corrugated cardboard is a leg of torn denim.

I listen harder, but can't hear the guitar usually emanating from within the Vagabond. I must be in a remote slip at the harbor.

"Are you a good girl?"

I'm trying to be.

"Or are you the work of the devil? Put on this earth to tempt me, and you're good at what you do. But there's still a chance for you. If you pay penance for all those before you, God will save you in the end. After all, we're all forgiven, thanks to Jesus Christ."

I recognize the symbolism of my position. I'm bound to the bed, much in the same way Jesus was bound to His cross.

I pinch my eyes shut and pretend I'm at home, in bed. I wiggle my feet to emulate the sound of Lindsey's swishing. Maybe it'll bring me back to reality. Maybe I'll be able to wake up from this horrible nightmare, if I concentrate, if I listen for the *swish, swish, swish* of my sister's feet down the hall.

"God gave the ultimate sacrifice for His people," Palmer says. "It's time I do the same."

The flame of the candle glints off the blur of an object in his hand—the knife my mother once used to stab him.

"Honor thy father?" he asks.

My tears mix with the blood dripping from my forehead, and wash a measure of chrism from my eyes. I wiggle my feet faster, but to no avail.

"Honor thy father?"

A sniffle escapes me.

"Honor thy father!"

"Yes! Yes, I do!"

The pain at my temples intensifies. The blade of the knife skates over my abdomen in a laceration.

The flame of the candle bursts into a white light, and warm, coppery blood trickles over my hip. The raw sting and burn of the wound threatens to overtake my consciousness, but I can't let go. I won't.

Distant whimpers dance in my ears. In my mind, I'm running through the labyrinth behind Holy Promise, searching for a lost girl.

Hannah? Are you here? Hannah, answer me!

Hannah?

"Help me."

My breath catches in my throat when a girl's voice reaches my ears. But is it my voice, a voice of the past, or is someone else on this boat?

"May the Lord accept the sacrifice at His hands," Palmer says.

"Reverend." The pain in my abdomen compromises my ability to speak, but I articulate to the best of my ability, all the while wiggling my feet and hands, praying my tethers will fall free.

Palmer's eyes widen, and his voice loses its conviction: "For our good and for all His church."

My father roughly presses his hand to my abdomen. The salt of his fingers burns, as he presses into the open wound.

I flinch with the pain, but muster strength enough to say the words I know he needs to hear: "I love you, father." One of my feet slips from its post. "I honor you."

The whimpering sounds again.

Palmer leans in closer. "You . . . you honor the devil." Putting all his weight into his hand, he shoves down on my abdomen. I feel my flesh tearing with his weight. More blood gushing from where he cut me. Hard.

I yelp with the pain and pressure, which is so great I have to fight to stay alert. The periphery is closing in on me like a dark halo.

"You consort with the devil"—he jabs at me again, as if I'm a ball of dough requiring kneading—"tempt good men to the dark side. Turn holy men into sinners."

Howling now, I writhe on the bed. He's crushing me, washing his hands with my blood. "Johnny! Help me!"

"Calliope!"

At the yelled interjection, which comes from outside, Palmer startles.

For only a split second, he turns away, but it's long enough for me to yank my feet free and tuck my legs.

I hear John outside: "Calliope! Ca-lie-uh-pee!"

With all my might, I channel my energy into my thighs and land a kick against Palmer's chest.

"Nymph! Servant of Satan!" Saliva sprays from my father's lips, as he comes at me again with the knife. "The Good Book is the key to salvation. Sift through it as the hours pass."

I gasp when I recognize his words. I'm kicking like mad for freedom, for my sister, for my mother, for Hannah, and in the chaos, he fumbles the weapon.

"Help!" I scream. "Someone, help!" My wrists ache, my abdomen sears, something continues to pinch and draw blood at my temples. But I kick and tear and gnash. I fight the way Hannah couldn't, the way my mother never did.

I yank free from the tie at my left wrist and swipe at the chrism in my eyes.

The boat rocks, the room spins. My fingers close around an ivory handle just in time.

He's coming at me again, and I know he won't stop, no matter how many times I kick him.

I slash at the linen binding my right wrist, and I tumble off the bed, as if through a kaleidoscopic tube. I'm numb. Everywhere. Cold. So cold.

"Calliope!" John screams from the maze of piers.

"I'm here!" I scream. "I'm here." But I'm fading away. Running through the labyrinth in my mind.

Palmer's so close that his breath rumples my hair.

"Calliope Knowles! Calliope!" The voice morphs to many and seems to be fading into the great beyond. I imagine the boat riding the waves out from the pier, but I know we're still docked, as the buoys still rub against the starboard side.

The grating sound becomes the swish of Lindsey's feet.

Dig. Chink. Sift.

Uncontrollable tears stream down my cheeks. I concentrate on the image of John's watch. I feel it in my hands, my fingers tracing the words on the back: Only you. Only you. Only you.

Imprisoned obsession, she can't escape. Amber ashes in her hourglass.

Dig. Chink. Sift.

THIRTY-FIVE

A gunshot deafens the harbor and rings madly in my ears, along with a scream I don't remember releasing.

I scramble to my numb feet.

At the foot of the stairs, next to the box, stands a man in navy blue, a police officer, with smoking weapon poised. Slowly, he lowers his gun.

Palmer slumps against the bed.

I can't catch my breath, face-to-face with Hannah Rynes, who's hanging nude on the wall as if on a crucifix. She's whimpering. Her fingers are blue from constriction. She's bleeding from a gash in her abdomen, and from her temples, where a crown of thorns encircles her head. I fling its twin from my head and fall to my knees in dizziness.

My blood is on my hands, and Palmer's is splattered on the wall next to Hannah.

"Do you know where you are?" an officer asks me.

I close my eyes and call to mind the details. I remember all the nights I spent in borrowed spaces with Elijah, and think of the rub of the buoys. I think of the words I've written:

Fluttershy
abiding like the tide
Stripped linens dried in the breeze

I concentrate, rubbing my temples until I see it in my mind. "I'm at the harbor." I remember everything I've written, everything I haven't understood until this very moment. Every word was a clue. "I'm on a boat."

He nods—"Do you know your name?"—while another officer cuts Hannah's tethers.

"Calliope Knowles."

I hear a radio call for backup: "We're on board a cruiser called *As the Hours Pass*. Slip sixty-two. North Point Marina. Suspect down. Two victims. Need two ambulances. Fast."

Hannah meets my gaze while officers carry us across piers to the ambulances waiting on the shore. She's wrapped in an LCPD-issued blanket similar to the one pulled around my shoulders, and I suspect she's still nude beneath it. A tiny patch of red is bleeding through the fibers of the fleece, and scratches mar her forehead. Crown of thorns. Cut in the abdomen. Tied in a cross formation, and anointed for last rights. I know what was about to happen next: *bleed her and feed, burn her in an urn, crucify, quarter, and stone her. Buried alive, she'll claw at the case. Smile, when you condone her . . .*

"Do you know your name?" an officer asks Hannah.

She replies: "Serena."

I flinch.

"He calls me Serena Noel."

"Do you know where you've been?"

"What he always says about the Good Book," she whispers. "Sift through it as the hours pass."

She'd recently been in the garden house. She's the one who wrote on the wall.

THIRTY-SIX

A week has passed since the authorities shot and killed my father, since LCPD rescued Hannah Rynes from her year-long ordeal, since I spent two days at Lake Forest Hospital. Now I'm sitting in a room at the station, ready to close the book on all of it. It's sort of surreal to think that Palmer's gone. Every now and then, I play what if.

If John hadn't been approaching the harbor when he did, he wouldn't have called the police to report that he'd seen—at a distance—Palmer knocking me into the water. If the police hadn't gotten there in time, what would've happened to Hannah and me?

"Want a stick?" Dr. Ewing extends a pack of gum in my direction.

"Thanks." I slide out a silver-sheathed stick and unwrap it, fold it into my mouth. Cinnamon. Elijah's favorite. Not as satisfying as a Tootsie Pop, but it'll do.

"How you doing?"

"Nervous."

He tilts his head. "Hmm."

"I can't imagine I'm going to like what I see today."

"Can it be any worse than what you've already seen?" He looks at me over his Buddy Hollys. "Worse than what you've already survived?"

"I guess not." The stitched-up laceration on my abdomen burns. It's going to leave a nasty scar. In time, Ewing says I'll view the marks Palmer left on my body—the freshest, as well as the ones embedded into my flesh years ago—as proof of my survival, but for now they're simply evidence of what I endured. I still flinch when I feel someone looking at me, still look over my shoulder because I feel someone following me. Maybe I always will.

My gaze wanders, and not for the first time, to the window in the door, through which I catch glimpses of the room across the hall, where a team of investigators questions my mother. "Why do you think they're fingerprinting her? I mean, what if something I've said implicates her?"

Ewing props his elbow on the metal arm of the chair and rests his chin in his hand. "Do you think you're responsible for anything your mother may or may not have done?"

"Well, no. But guilty or not, she's the only mother I have. Crazy or sane, I love her."

Ewing churns his gum between his teeth and, straightening in his chair, gives my arm a pat. "One step at a time, okay?"

"Yeah." But I can't stop looking at her. Her long merlot hair is swept up into a bun, the way she used to wear it when she was working on an art project. Her lashes, naturally thick and full, appear to be rimmed with mascara today, and a touch of lipstick fleshes out her lips. I can't remember the last time she wore makeup. She's gorgeous, and although I resemble her—I look nothing at all like Palmer—I can't help staring at her as if I'm seeing her for the first time.

"Hey, kid." Detective Guidry glides into the room, a cup of coffee in one hand, a thick file tucked into the other. "How are you feeling?"

I shrug. "You know."

"Gotta feel better than the last time I saw you."

I chuckle—"Yeah"—although the last time he saw me, I was in the trauma unit at Lake Forest Hospital, taking about forty stitches. "How's Hannah?"

He nods. "She's a survivor. Like you." Guidry takes a seat, spreads open his file.

"She remembers who she is? She knows what happened to her?" It feels sort of as if I'm intruding in asking about her, as if maybe it's none of my business how badly Palmer screwed her up. Maybe she deserves to heal in private. But I can't forget the way she said my mother's name, as if it were her own. She didn't know who she was.

"We showed her pictures for about eight, nine hours," Guidry says. "It started coming back to her."

I can imagine it might've been horrific to remember. I think that horror is the reason I chose to forget. When I glimpse a stack of photographs clipped to his file, I deduce I'm about to go through my own version of an eight- or nine-hour slide show. The top picture is a shot of the door embedded in the earth.

"No notebook today?" Guidry smiles.

I reach down to the floor to pat my backpack, if only to reassure myself it's still there. "I always have a notebook. Just not much in this one that concerns you."

"I love to hear that."

"No more than I love to say it."

He grins. "Ready to look at the items my evidence techs found?"

I don't know if I'll ever be ready enough, but I'm already looking at the boxes neatly lining the table against the far wall. They're the fold-up type without tops, and they're filled with manila envelopes, filed vertically, so one could easily flip through them like files in a drawer. My rosary is in one of those envelopes . . . along with things I have no desire to see.

My fingers gravitate to the tiny ring strung about my neck.

"If ever you feel like you can't go on," Ewing says, "like

you need a break, let me know. You're not on trial here."

"For once." I crack a smile, but the boxes of evidence taunt me from across the room. In many ways, it feels as if each of those envelopes contains a smidgen of Palmer Prescott. And I never want to see any part of him again.

"Anything you say, anything I say, is going to be recorded," Guidry says. "This is part of an ongoing investigation. If you have questions, go ahead and ask them, but don't be offended if I can't answer them."

"Okay." Tears rise. Nerves tickle my gut.

Despite how far we've come, there's still a journey ahead of us. We're only as far as the heart of the labyrinth, in a sense. We're here to contemplate, to reflect, to reconcile, but we still have to fight the battle awaiting us here. We still have to follow a path out into the rest of the world.

My heart pounds, and my fingers tremble, as Guidry retrieves box number one from the table behind him.

"You okay, Callie?" Ewing asks.

I nod and wipe away tears.

Guidry opens an envelope and empties out plastic-encased pieces of catalogued evidence—things found on the boat, at Holy Promise, in boxes at the Meadows, and in the annals of a history I didn't understand as I wrote it.

Guidry: "Object one."

"That looks like the spare key to the garden house." I study the cross emblem hanging from the key chain. Pewter. I turn it over in my hands. *Holy Promise* is etched onto the back, similarly to the *Lorraine Oh* on the back of my rosary pendant. "Where'd you find it?"

"In a box under the stairs on the boat."

A chill races up my spine. "So he had access to the garden house all along."

"Maybe."

I'd been in the labyrinth only a handful of times since Hannah disappeared. I wonder if Palmer had seen me there with Elijah, with John. I wonder if he'd been waiting for an opportune time to take me. "Did Andrew Drake know he'd been there?"

"We don't think so." Guidry hands me another plastic bag.

It's a heart-shaped, decoupage box, a tiny one. "Looks like something my mother made. A long time ago." I sift through memories until I land on one that warms me: Mom and me in the north dormer in the apartment above the Vagabond. Glue and paper cutouts scatter over the floor. Squares of tissue paper flutter around me when the breeze sweeps in off the lake. "You might want to ask her, but I think it's her work."

"And this." He hands over a tiny plastic bag.

At first I don't know what it is, but on closer scrutiny, I see that it's a lock of hair, baby-fine. Burgundy-brown. Like mine.

"Do you know whose it is?"

I shake my head. Not definitively. "Could be mine, I guess. Could also be Cleo's."

"Cleo." Guidry states the name, more than raises a question, but I offer explanation:

"My mother talks about Cleo. I have flashes of memories that suggest she was pregnant after she had me. I know we don't know for sure, but I see Cleo as my baby sister."

The next envelope sheathes only one item: a pair of jeans, the same pair, I suspect, that I saw in the box under the stairs on the boat.

"Next." Guidry produces pictures of a small duffel bag, navy blue, embedded in dirt.

Instantly, my eyes gloss with tears, my heart hurts.

"Callie?" Ewing presses a hand to my shoulder. "Do you recognize the items in this picture?"

I nod and wipe a tear from my cheek. "It's a vague memory. From when I was little. I remember seeing a duffel bag in the rowboat."

"Do you know what was in it?" Guidry asks.

I don't, but . . . "Given it's photographed where I think it is—under the door John and I found at Highland Point—and you found remains of a baby there, I'd guess you found the baby in the bag."

Guidry doesn't confirm or deny, but presents another piece of evidence: a dirty, yellow sundress with pearl buttons down the front of it. I recognize it as the one I was wearing in the rowboat glimpse, the one I deduced Hannah must've been wearing once we left the garden house. But it looks older than I thought it would, and smaller. It looks like it could fit a third grader. "Tiny."

"Mmm hmm."

"Do you think, maybe . . . maybe it was mine when I was little? Or maybe . . . did Palmer maybe kidnap someone before Hannah?"

"That's a possibility," the detective tells me.

"Who?" I think of John's endless research. I wonder if he could pinpoint a missing girl who might've been wearing a yellow dress.

Guidry sips his coffee. Gives me a shrug. He can't answer my question—maybe because he doesn't know the answer, or maybe because he does.

When he places before me an encased pair of yellow floral cotton briefs, I stifle a whale of a sob. It's hard to focus; everything blurs. I pinch my eyes shut, press my hands to my eyes, but the image is still there:

the labyrinth at Holy Promise. White gravel, the type that glimmers when the sun reflects off of it, digs into my back when I collapse at the base of the fountain. I can't move. My arms and legs are numb. Palmer's hands register on my cheeks, but I can't respond.

Everything turns white. It's a struggle to breathe.

The gravel bruises my skin as he pulls me up from the ground.

I'm floating past juniper, through the creaking gate, into the garden house.

I slump onto the hard floor.

"No. No, no, please, no!"

"God says it must be so."

I hear the springs on the cot groan and rasp.

I try to open my eyes.

Through a sliver—it's so bright in here—I see them: yellow floral panties. Discarded on the floor.

I can't keep my eyes open, can't stay alert. Can't move.

"Callie?"

Ewing's voice jars me.

It's like a bad dream, I tell myself. It's over. Over.

I take my hands from my eyes and dare to open them.

The pair of panties is the first thing I see, mangled, wrapped in plastic, memorializing horror: "Hannah's." I sniffle and wipe away tears. "They're Hannah's."

My gaze drifts across the hallway to where my mother is nodding, as if listening intently to the three investigators. As if magnetized, she redirects her stare to meet mine. A slow, close-lipped smile spreads onto her face.

I hold her attention, and she holds mine, until Guidry clears his throat—"Do you recognize this photograph?"— and then it's only for a split second that I look away from my mother.

"Callie?" Ewing hands me a tissue.

My mother gives me a nod.

After a moment, I manage to focus on the photograph before me. It's me as a toddler. Maybe two years old, not older than three. I'm wearing a pink nightgown; I'm sleeping on someone's lap. "It's me."

"Who else is in the picture?"

The someone isn't visible beyond his lap and a hand on my back. I don't know how anyone would identify him after all this time only from legs clad in denim and an arm feathered with dark blond hair. I turn the picture over, in search of a notation, but it's blank. "I don't know."

I extend the photograph toward Guidry, but at the last second, I draw it in for a closer look.

I glance up at Guidry, but the photograph quickly draws my attention back.

Only you, only you, only you.

"Callie?" Ewing probes.

"It's John's cousin."

John and I were right—his cousin hadn't simply run away. Mom knew what was inscribed on the back of John's watch because she'd seen it before. And she said she gave all young boys the same reading, in hopes one of them would take her seriously, in hopes one would find the rosary and return it to me. She said it would help me go home.

I swallow hard and address the detective. "John said his cousin wanted his family to have the watch before he ran away."

But he didn't run. Maybe he meant to steal the girl he loved and her two young daughters away from Reverend Palmer Prescott, but he never found the chance. Maybe

Palmer stopped him. Maybe Palmer made him disappear. It would make sense that his family didn't know about my mother, if they were planning to disappear together and start over in a place where no one knew them.

My mother's voice echoes in my mind: *He made me dig the hole.*

My shoulders begin to shake with intensifying tears. "He's the one she was talking about."

"Who?" Guidry asks.

"It's him." Tears blur my vision. When I wipe them away, streaks of mascara line my fingertips. "Palmer buried him under the cobblestones behind Holy Promise. Ask my mother. She'll tell you. She left Palmer for this guy. She met him at the Vagabond. He played guitar." I hear it in my head, the memory now as plain as day: *Let my love open the door.* "She had his baby. Palmer killed him and buried him."

"Behind Holy Promise?" Guidry asks. "What's his name?"

Ewing places a hand on my shoulder.

"I don't know his name." I can't believe I never asked. "I was just a little girl . . . two or three. I don't remember. But he's been missing for fourteen years. John's cousin. The watch. Look."

I hand the photograph to Ewing, who scrutinizes it, as if it contains the answer to all the world's mysteries.

"Could be the same watch you showed me in session," he concedes. Then to Guidry: "Do you still have the watch?

The one you found at the harbor that night?"

While Guidry and one of his men confer in a sidebar, I pick up the next piece of evidence. It's my mother's diary. I flip open to a random page and read her poetry:

> *Staring into mirrors*
> *At the image of myself.*
> *Not missing, not gone, not yet.*
> *I'm right here.*

I close the book, but my head starts spinning.

"Warren?"

His hand lands on my shoulder again.

"Hannah said Palmer called her Serena."

"Hmm."

"At first, I thought it was just because my mother was gone, and in some twisted way, he wanted to replace her. But maybe . . ."

Detective Guidry's listening now.

Palmer put my mother away. What better security for his crimes than to declare her insane? So her word couldn't be trusted? And maybe she's crazy. Maybe she is. But maybe he made her that way. After one year, Hannah had forgotten who she was. What if . . .

"Ask my mother if she knows who she is."

I'm met with furrowed brows.

"Ask her what her name is!" I push away from the table

and stand. "I want my phone. She's Lorraine Oh, the name on the back of the rosary."

"Callie," Dr. Ewing says.

"Where's my rosary?"

Guidry's thumbing through files. "It's here."

"I want to talk to John."

"I'll bring him in," Guidry says.

But he isn't moving fast enough.

"Warren, can I borrow your phone? I'm not trying anything funny. I'll put it on speaker. You'll hear everything."

Guidry slides an evidence envelope across the table and hands me a phone.

I snatch it up. Dial. Pray John will answer a number he doesn't recognize. I know he'll help me.

"Hello?"

"John, it's Callie."

"Callie. Hi. I'm sorry I can't be th—"

"Listen, Johnny, listen. I need you to look up a missing girl who'd now be thirty-two. Named Lorraine. Born November twentieth. Can you do that?"

"It'll take a minute, but . . . I've already—"

"Please!"

Guidry hails another officer, whispers into her ear.

I hear John clicking computer keys through the speaker on Guidry's phone.

Dr. Ewing slides a notebook in front of me.

As heady as I am, strangely, I don't feel the compulsion to write.

"Oh my God," John says.

An officer appears at the doorway, looking stunned.

"Oh my God," John says again. "I never looked this far back before, not in relation to the rosary, but . . ."

"Her prints match," the officer at the doorway says.

"Match what?" I ask. My head is spinning faster now.

"Callie." John's voice sounds urgent through the speaker.

Guidry's thumbing through a file.

John again: "Oh my God . . ."

The detective slides a sheet of paper across the table for my viewing.

I blink through the dizziness.

I can't believe what I'm seeing.

THIRTY-SEVEN

'm looking at a picture of a younger version of myself. Talia Jane Bliss.

I see a page of my notebook in my mind:

Bliss bliss bliss bliss bliss bliss bliss . . .

Talia Jane Bliss. Missing at age nine from Lorain, Ohio. Usually, when I look at images of my mother, I'm staring into what might as well be mirrors of the future, but this time, I'm looking into the past.

"I think we can place a call to Lorain PD now," Guidry says.

"Lorain's a place, not a person." I spill the rosary from the evidence envelope and flip over the crucifix: Lorraine Oh. I remember what she said about the rosary, that it would help me remember where I came from, even if she'd forgotten. "Look."

I read the details of Talia's abduction: She'd been rehearsing for a choir concert at church after school. She never returned home. Last seen wearing a yellow sundress with imitation pearl buttons, ruffle-cuffed socks, and black patent leather Mary Janes. In her possession: her family's heirloom rosary. Assumed to be with the choir director, Deacon Holden Rush, sketch provided, also missing.

My gaze travels to the inset at the bottom of the paper.

Eerily, the candid snapshot of the perpetrator resembles the sketch my mother was working on the last time I saw her at the Meadows: the sketch of Palmer, but without the beard.

Oh, Mom. I'm sorry. I'm sorry I didn't listen hard enough, sorry I didn't look long enough, sorry sorry sorry sorry for not noticing . . .

Sobs rack my body now. I press my knuckles to my lips, but nothing will silence my tears now. "Mom, mom, mom . . . Oh, God."

Dr. Ewing gathers me into his arms, where I dampen his shirt with my tears, but within moments, I hear the door open. I hear my mother's voice:

"I'm not trying to be difficult—I'm not—but I haven't said my name in over twenty years."

"I want my mom," I manage to say. "God, I want my mom."

"I don't even know if I can remember it," she says. "He made sure I forgot."

"Mom!"

Within moments, one of Guidry's men leads my mother into the room, and I catapult into her embrace.

She's raking through my hair, pressing kisses to the crown of my head.

THIRTY-EIGHT

Sounds of drums beat through the Vagabond Café, and the scent of the lake carries in on an autumn breeze. Calming, serene. Uncharacteristically warm for late October, but then, it's about that time of year, a last-minute reminder of summer before the cold snaps throughout the lakes region, and breathes frost into every wave that washes up on the shores.

"What color is the grass?" my mother asks me.

"Green." I don't know why she's asked, but I know she's trying to explain things to me in terms she can articulate, in terms she thinks I'll understand.

"It's green, it's green, it's green. But he would say it's orange. After a while, if you know what's good for you,

you say the grass is orange, but of course it isn't, and you know it isn't, but that's what he wants to hear, so you say it. And orange becomes green—he made it green—but there's hell to pay because you're wrong. The grass is green, and he'll prove it to you."

I take a sip of my iced cocoa.

Mom shrugs. "Believing in him was necessary."

"For survival?"

She flickers a glance up at me, but quickly looks back to the table. She fingers the words I wrote years ago, long before I'd seen reason to forget what they meant. They're the words of a child . . .

Travel on, yellow brick road . . . wind her past throughout her soul.

. . . but they suggest that I'd sensed, even when I was very young, that my mother had been trying to remember what she'd forgotten.

Everyone I know is here, at the event Mrs. Hutch organized both to honor Thomas Fogel and my half sister, Cleo, and to celebrate Palmer Prescott's surviving victims. She rushed home from her charity trip the moment she heard of my ordeal—because Lindsey convinced her we needed her.

I close a fist around my rosary and the baby ring beneath it. "Hey . . . you understand, right? About the Hutches?"

Her lips press together; she doesn't answer. It's sort of a rhetorical question, anyway, as I don't want to hear how I've hurt her by deciding to stay in Lake Nippersink with the Hutches, when she returns to Lorain with the aunt, two uncles, and grandparents I've just met—the people gathered around the largest table on the floor.

"I'll always be your daughter," I remind her. "I'll visit."

My mother picks up her cards, pulls off the sock, which I now know belonged to Thomas Fogel. It was all she had left of him.

The moment Thomas crosses my mind, my gaze trails to the other side of the café, where John shares a table with his family. He looks at me the moment I look at him. Smiles.

"Listen, Calliope."

I redirect my gaze to my mother.

She begins to shuffle the deck. She's going to offer me a reading because she doesn't know how else to say what she has to say. "Concentrate on a question."

"Can you tell me how it all happened?"

Her hands freeze for a few moments before she finishes the formation.

"I know he took you." I also know she's yet to make sense of everything she's remembered. Have to be careful. Can't push. "You were nine."

And Palmer was about twenty-four.

"Can you tell me about Thomas Fogel?"

She looks to the platform, where musicians and poets perform on open mic nights, as if she expects to see him there. "I killed him."

Just as I'm about to contradict her, she adds:

"He's dead because he loved me."

"Well, that's considerably different, isn't it?"

She strikes me with a stare, the type I've come to recognize as a borderline between illusion and reality— downward slanting brows, lower lip descending, vacant eyes, as if she's confused.

I shut up.

"They're taking me back," she says.

"I know."

"Callie?"

"Yeah."

"You're home, baby." She glances back at her family. I see in her pained expression that she's torn between the life she had before and the life she created with her perpetrator.

"I'll always be your daughter."

"I need to . . ." She slithers out of the booth, already gravitating toward the family she'd all but forgotten until Guidry's team reminded her with a slew of photographs.

I wonder how many times she'd tried to remember via her art, her music, her words. Already, we know she attempted to scratch the name of her hometown into her rosary, which she'd managed to keep hidden from Palmer for nearly two decades. She was right. She'd planted a clue, even if she couldn't remember where it was supposed to lead her.

"May I?"

I blink away from the scene across the Vagabond and

meet John's glance as he's sliding into the booth next to me.

"Heard you're staying."

I tuck a ringlet of hair behind my ear. "Yeah."

"That's good."

If I concentrate, I can feel my roots pushing into the earth here, I taste the soil that has nourished me, I hear my name in the gusts of breeze whipping inland from the lake. Besides, I can't imagine life without Lindsey—even when she's hopping mad at me. She'll always be my sister.

And my mother, whether she's Serena or Talia, will always be my mother.

John wraps an arm around my shoulders. His lips brush my temple when he says, "Talia—or rather Thalia, with an *h*—is the Greek muse of comedy."

"Dude." Lindsey's sliding into the booth, taking the place my mother recently abandoned. She's wearing a dark green, form-fitting tank dress, and ridiculous high-heeled pumps. Tied around her waist is a black hoodie, which I know reads *Free to Bleed, Free to Weed* in an emblem on the front pocket. "What is *with* this useless *h* in names? Less is more."

Elijah's sliding in after her. He flashes me a grin. "How you holding up?"

"Hanging in there." I feel a familiar synergy in my head. A phrase traipses through my mind. I pull my notebook and a pen from my backpack and write:

When funeral gongs tolled for millions young and grand . . .

"Still writing?" Elijah asks.

"Yeah, but it's different now."

Now that I don't need the words to remember, writing is a choice. Later, I just might read my work on stage, and delight in hearing the snapping praise of the patrons of this waterside gem of a café.

The strum of an acoustic guitar catches my attention.

We all turn to see John's father take the stage and sit on the bench centered on the platform, a spotlight filtering down over him. Silently, he begins to play.

At first, I don't recognize the song. But then the space fills with a beautiful soprano in perfect pitch:

"Let my love open the door."

It's my mother. She's singing.

I sink into the melody, allow it to consume me.

John embraces me with careful arms and joins my mother for the next line.

I breathe in the scent of the idyllic shoreline in the distance.

Measure by measure, the Vagabond rises in song.

My soon-to-be adopted parents take to the dance floor.

I meet John with the bridge, then belt out the chorus.

And Lindsey's stomping in time atop the table.

I silently bid adieu to the road behind me, and hand in hand, John and I meander toward my new family, to cross the next bridge, whenever we may find it.

ACKNOWLEDGMENTS

Calliope Knowles has been haunting me for well over a decade. I put her on many a canvas before she found a home on the pages of *Oblivion*. None of this would have happened without the support of many.

First, appreciation is due to author Jessica Warman, who introduced me to agent extraordinaire Andrea Somberg. In turn, immeasurable thanks go to Andrea, who is amazing and ambitious, tactful and straight. Without her faith in this concept, this novel would have remained forever on the hard drive of a pink laptop. Unbelievable gratitude to Greg Ferguson of Egmont USA, who latched on to Calliope's plight from the very first word he read. *Oblivion* wouldn't be the same without his input. The entire staff at Egmont receives kudos for a flawless production—especially copy editor Veronica Ambrose and The Black Rabbit cover design team. Thanks to writer friends Miles Watson and Patrick Picciarelli for so much more than their advisement regarding law enforcement procedures, for celebration and consolation, for making writing a not-so-solitary occupation. Warm hugs to Kelli Klinger, who shed much light on dark areas in psychoanalysis. Much appreciation, of course, to Joshua, whose general support both astounds and delights. And finally, I extend gratitude to my daughters, Samantha and Madelaine, who know when deadline is approaching because Cheez-Its suddenly become honorary sources of protein . . . and clocks are held in general disregard, making my tiny dancers nearly late to the studio. I am blessed to work with, around, and for all of you. XOXOX!